Seneca Falls Library
47 Cayuga Street
Seneca Falls, NY 13148

Tom Sawyer's Dark Plot

TOM SAWYER'S DARK PLOT

THE FURTHER ADVENTURES OF TOM SAWYER AND HUCKLEBERRY FINN

TIM CHAMPLIN

FIVE STAR

A part of Gale, a Cengage Company

GALE
A Cengage Company

Farmington Hills, Mich • San Francisco • New York • Waterville, Maine
Meriden, Conn • Mason, Ohio • Chicago

GALE
A Cengage Company

Copyright © 2018 by Tim Champlin
Five Star Publishing, a part of Gale, a Cengage Company

ALL RIGHTS RESERVED.
This novel is a work of fiction. Names, characters, places, and incidents are either the product of the author's imagination, or, if real, used fictitiously.

No part of this work covered by the copyright herein may be reproduced or distributed in any form or by any means, except as permitted by U.S. copyright law, without the prior written permission of the copyright owner.

The publisher bears no responsibility for the quality of information provided through author or third-party Web sites and does not have any control over, nor assume any responsibility for, information contained in these sites. Providing these sites should not be construed as an endorsement or approval by the publisher of these organizations or of the positions they may take on various issues.

LIBRARY OF CONGRESS CATALOGING-IN-PUBLICATION DATA

Names: Champlin, Tim, 1937– author.
Title: Tom Sawyer's dark plot / Tim Champlin.
Description: First edition. | Farmington Hills, Mich. : Five Star, a part of Gale, a Cengage Company, [2018] | Series: Adventures in time - 1849 ; book 2 | Identifiers: LCCN 2018014250 (print) | LCCN 2018021055 (ebook) | ISBN 9781432844714 (ebook) | ISBN 9781432844707 (ebook) | ISBN 9781432844752 (hardback)
Subjects: | CYAC: Adventure and adventurers—Fiction. | Characters in literature—Fiction. | Sasquatch—Fiction. | Time travel—Fiction. | Missouri—History—19th century—Fiction. | BISAC: FICTION / Action & Adventure. | FICTION / Historical.
Classification: LCC PZ7.1.C476 (ebook) | LCC PZ7.1.C476 Tot 2018 (print) | DDC [Fic]—dc23
LC record available at https://lccn.loc.gov/2018014250

First Edition. First Printing: October 2018
Find us on Facebook—https://www.facebook.com/FiveStarCengage
Visit our website—http://www.gale.cengage.com/fivestar/
Contact Five Star Publishing at FiveStar@cengage.com

Printed in Mexico
1 2 3 4 5 6 7 22 21 20 19 18

For son, Chris, and his wife, Jane,
two wonderful parents

PROLOGUE

Chignall "Chigger" Smealey tugged down the final loop of the diamond hitch and shoved the flank of the pack mule away from him, snorting at the dust kicked up into the lantern light from the floor of the stall. "We need t'get outa here and lay a plan t'get us some *real* money," he mumbled, wiping his nose with a sleeve. "This ain't hardly payin' for beans and a bunk."

His curly, reddish brown beard was beginning to itch. When could he shave again? His partner, Gussage "Gus" Weir, had urged him to grow it as a disguise since they were both still wanted for kidnapping and extortion. Gus Weir had shaved his own heavy black mustache for the same purpose. But he had a better reason, Smealey thought, since a Sioux war party had already singed off half of it for him.

"We'll be on our way soon as I see a good chance," Gus Weir assured him, reaching for another wooden packsaddle stacked with others in a back corner.

Smealey started to suggest how they might hurry along that chance, but Weir stiffened. "Sshhh!" He put a calloused hand on Smealey's forearm.

"What?"

With a finger to his lips, Weir turned down the wick of the coal oil lantern until the flame was snuffed out.

Smealey stood still in the velvety blackness, listening to his heart thumping in his ears and the animals munching hay in nearby stalls. He heard nothing unusual. But at four o'clock in the morning, he didn't really expect to. What had spooked Weir? His partner had been much more cautious and jumpy since they'd been captured by a dozen Sioux warriors three weeks earlier. Only by the luckiest chance were they even alive to be here at Fort Kearny in Indian Territory, packing mules and loading Argonauts' wagon trains.

Then he heard a low murmur of voices at the far end of the stable. Doubtful that it was a sentry making his rounds, or he wouldn't be talking to someone. Likely some early risers wanting to be two hours down the trail before daylight. Why was Weir so jumpy? The two of them weren't the only ones who had access to this civilian portion of the stable. The cavalry mounts were stabled in another wing of this L-shaped sod building.

Smealey's eyes adjusted to the darkness and he saw two figures pass a square window opening faintly illuminated by moonlight.

Maybe he should cough or move to keep from startling these two, Smealey thought as the pair approached.

Before he could react, the two men paused, two stalls away, and one of them struck a Lucifer and lit a coal oil lamp hanging on a gnarled cottonwood support post.

"You ain't riding outa here with all my money," a deep voice grated.

"It's not your money anymore," a higher-pitched voice answered. "Besides, you should have thought of that before you dealt yourself into that high stakes game." He looped his saddlebags over the wooden partition.

The top of the stall was even with Smealey's nose and he could barely make out the movements of the men some twenty feet away, beyond the shuffling horses in the two intervening stalls. In the dull yellow glow from the sooty glass chimney, Smealey saw the head of a tall man with black hair and beard who was bracing himself, rather unsteadily, with one arm against the side of the stall. The shorter man ducked out of sight for a moment and then rose. He wore a stylish gray hat. A white collar showed below gray muttonchop whiskers.

"A bit of advice from somebody older and more experienced," the cultured voice said. "A man should never drink when he's gambling—especially with strangers." He flung a green-striped saddle blanket over the back of a horse, fanning the odor of sour mash to Smealey's nose, overpowering the chronic reek of ammonia.

Silence followed for several seconds. The shorter man grunted as he hoisted the Grimsley saddle onto his mount and settled it into place. The trooper saddle looked new. The pommel and cantle swept up in graceful curves from the dark blue padding of the seat. A tiny brass shield on the cantle winked in the lamplight.

"You have no idea what I went through to get that gold," the taller man said, his voice sounding strained, desperate.

"I'm sure I'll find out when I reach the goldfields," the cultured man said, bending out of sight to fasten the straps.

"I was panning good color on one of the creeks," the tall one said. "But I took sick with the ague and was laid up for three weeks. When I was back on my feet, I discovered somebody had jumped my claim, pulled all my markers, and not a single person would admit to seeing them do it." In the face of indifference, he seemed compelled to tell this older man his story.

"Sounds like you should have hired a guard."

"I did, but he was in on it. When I confronted him, he and several of his friends grabbed my gun and beat me up. They threatened to kill me if I didn't leave."

"Should have taken them to miners' court," the cultured man snapped.

"Besides a lot of dust in the gravel, I struck a rich pocket on a rocky ridge uphill," he continued, unhearing. "My God, I was hacking out rotten quartz veined with gold." His eyes stared off at some distant vision while his voice grew more urgent with the telling. "I put off registering my claim because it was two days by foot in the rain and mud to the claims office."

"Ah, there's the crux of your problem," the older man sneered. "Didn't have your priorities in order. That's why there are mining laws. The early bird gets the worm—or, in your case, the first one to register gets the gold." He threw the saddlebags across and tied them with strips of rawhide beneath the curve of the cantle.

The man's face, even in the shadow of the hat brim, triggered a vague recognition in Smealey's recent memory. Where had he seen or heard this man?

"Several no-accounts were eyeing me," the tall man went on, "and I suspected they'd already sent someone downriver to the claims office to see if I'd filed. Then I took sick and lost my chance. They said they wouldn't kill me if I skedaddled. They let me keep most of the dust and nuggets I'd accumulated. They gave me a horse."

"Mighty white of them. Sounds like they beat you to the punch fair and square," the older man said. "Maybe you're simply not equipped to take care of yourself in the goldfields, or among real men. Perhaps you should never have gone out there," he added, no trace of sympathy in his voice. "I won't make the same mistake." He dropped the stirrup in place and prepared to back his horse out of the stall. "And with the gold I just won to add to my grubstake . . ."

"I'm givin' you a chance to return the gold you stole from me."

"Stole? I didn't any more steal from you than those men who beat you to the claims office." A pause. "I don't have to do this, but here's a couple of eagles to help you on your way."

"I know you were cheating, but I can't prove it," bearded man said.

"If you can't prove it, then I wasn't cheating," the older man retorted. "Move back. I need to be on my way."

A thudding and scraping as the horse was backed out of the stall.

"I'll give you one last chance to return my gold and we'll call it even," the tall man said in a deadly monotone. The whiny, pleading voice was gone.

"Even? I didn't play six hours of poker to turn around and give back all my winnings. I used all my skill to earn that gold from you and those other amateur Argonauts."

A violent scuffle exploded. Muffled blast of a gunshot close up. Smealey caught his breath. Then another, sharper crack, like someone stepping on a dry stick. Smothered voices, a groan and thud of someone falling. Garbled cursing.

Smealey ducked and grabbed his partner's arm. "We gotta do something!" he gasped.

"We got no guns!" Weir hissed in his ear.

They crouched in the darkness for several seconds, listening to the horse being led outside.

As the sound receded, Smealey raised his eyes above the wooden stall and saw only the low-burning oil lantern on the nail.

Weir grabbed a pitchfork and led the way out of the stall. The older man lay facedown in the dust, legs inside the stall, a stain reddening the back of his gray suit coat. The silk-lined hat had rolled three feet away. The victim's gray hair splayed out like a silver halo around his head.

Smealey heard the soft thudding of hoofbeats outside, fading rapidly.

Weir squatted, grabbed the man's shoulder, rolled him onto his back, and pressed two fingers to his throat. The smoldering white satin of the vest and the widening red on the shirt told its story. A .31 Colt pocket pistol was still clutched in the man's right hand, a wisp of gray smoke curling from its muzzle. Smealey's nose stung with the lingering smell of burnt gunpowder.

"Close up through the heart."

"They musta drawed on each other the same time," Smealey said. "Reckon the tall guy was hit?" He looked away from the sodden shirt.

"Dunno. He lit outa here pretty fast."

"What're we gonna do?" Even with a long history as a thief, he wasn't used to this kind of quick, deadly violence.

Weir took a deep breath. "You know who this is?"

"No."

"It's Senator Cyrus Shirten. He's a big-shot Whig. I heard a couple men from one o'them wagon trains talking earlier. Said he's under some kind of investigation for embezzlement of funds from the U.S. Treasury."

"Might be why he's lightin' out across Injun Territory," Smealey said. "You reckon anyone heard those shots?"

"Not likely," Weir said. "The immigrant trains are parked a half-mile from here. There ain't no walls at this fort for sentries to man. With luck, them guards were making rounds somewheres else and didn't hear the shots from inside this sod building. They were muffled—not even loud enough to spook the animals in here. From the looks of these burns, that drunk shoved the muzzle right into his chest and pulled the trigger."

"We have to report this to the sentries or the commandant, or somebody."

"You outa your head?" Weir sneered, looking up. "We'll be accused of this for sure."

"But we can testify to what we saw and heard."

"You keep forgettin' we're both wanted for kidnapping and extortion. Thanks to that bunch o'Sioux Indians, those kids got their gold back. But you and I still got a price on our heads. Once the officers at this fort start askin' questions, we'll be found out for sure and then it's the penitentiary for us."

"Anybody should ask, who's the tall guy who did this?" Smealey wondered. "Don't recollect his name." He was breathing deeply, trying to calm his wildly beating heart. Witnessing murders was not something he wanted to become accustomed to. Weir seemed to have recovered his composure in less than a minute.

"Um . . . called himself Bit Barjee," Weir said. "He was workin' odd jobs here at the fort helping out the sutler and the blacksmith and such when we come in two weeks ago with that wagon train what snatched us up offen the trail. Blacksmith said Barjee was lookin' to partner up with somebody to head back out west."

"Bit might be leakin' a bit if he stopped that slug from the senator's pocket pistol." Smealey grinned at his pun, starting to get his fear under control—mostly due to relief at not being one who was shot.

Weir turned up the wick on the lamp and began examining the dirt floor and the wooden gates of the stalls. "Don't see any signs of blood." He turned back to the dead man. "Don't touch nothin'," he said. "We have to get a plan together. If we warn't wanted, we could stick here and tell our story. But we can't or we'll go to prison sure."

"If we take off, they'll think we done the murder," Smealey said, glancing out the window hole in the nearby wall. The moon had set and deep darkness cloaked the fort. "We're damned either way."

"Don't matter. We can't hang around here. We can send a letter or something to the commandant later telling what we saw. We'll say we had to light out because we were skeered of being accused, since we were newly arrived strangers and all. But the main thing now is, we hafta stay free. They'll find Barjee gone and his horse still here somewhere and figure he done it. One thing working in our favor is this—all these rotten politicians are famous for dueling. Maybe the Army will put two and two together and cipher out that he and Barjee got into it over that card game, challenged each other to a duel, and Shirten lost."

"Maybe," Smealey said, dubiously. "But this don't look like no formal duel."

"Don't matter. That's still a possibility. C'mon—no time to discuss this. Let's git!"

"How?" Smealey asked, beginning to panic at the hopeless-ness of their situation. "We don't have any horses—*or* guns. And horse thievin' is a hangin' offense, just like murder."

Weir frowned. He crouched and felt the pockets of the deceased. He came up with a gold watch and chain and forty dollars' worth of gold eagles. "Reckon he won't miss these, and the killer will be blamed," he said. "The gold they were arguing about must've been in the senator's saddlebags."

"We can do without guns for now, but we gotta have transportation," Smealey repeated.

Weir looked thoughtful. "There are still four mules back there we haven't packed yet," he said, pointing. "They're rested up and fed since they been here at least three days. We'll take two of them. They belong to the seventy-wagon train that come in this past weekend. The owners will think they wandered off, or died on the trail and somebody miscounted." He stepped toward the tack room. "Find a couple bridles and bits laying around here. Don't take no good saddles—only worn-out ratty ones." He turned down the lantern until there was barely enough light to see what they were about. "Shake a leg, but be quiet about it. We'll slide outa here, easy like, and be down the trail at least ten miles toward St. Joe before the bugler blows reveille."

CHAPTER 1

"My best agate against a pound o'tobacco there's a big mudcat lying in deep along this drop-off." Tom Sawyer flipped his baited hook into the green water of a shady area near the bank. "Big enough t'provide supper for the four of us," he added.

Huck Finn glanced at Tom's bobber. "If you win, what're you gonna do with tobacco?" he asked. "You don't smoke or chew."

"Give it to Jim," Tom said.

"A whole pound o'tobacca be harder to come by den a big catfish," Jim said from the middle thwart.

"That's for sure," Huck agreed. "I generally don't have no trouble snaggin' catfish when I set a trotline. But this here float fishin' wears me out and don't seem to bring up much."

Jim lifted his line to see a bare hook. "Look like a turtle snatched him a snack," he said, reaching for the can containing the extra worms in wet coffee grounds.

Close inshore to Jackson's Island, the Mississippi River was rubbing off the force and speed of its current, allowing the double-ended white yawl to barely drift along.

A few seconds later, Tom's hook snagged on some underwater brush. After jerking the line this way and that, he had to use his Barlow knife to cut it loose as the boat continued moving. His set lips and red face showed his irritation. But nobody mentioned his losing the bet as they drifted past the spot where the big mudcat was supposedly lurking.

Zane Rasmussen, a thirteen-year-old visitor from the 21st

15

century, hadn't taken part in this conversation. He was feeling too lazy and relaxed this fresh summer morning, reflecting that this had to be the best of all possible worlds, including the one he'd come from two months ago. Although he still missed his family, he found himself thinking less and less frequently about the physical things he'd left behind—soccer, cars, bicycles, computers, air-conditioning, television, airplanes. He compared his reaction to the way Huck said he felt after being kidnapped from the Widow Douglas by his pap, then spirited off to a log cabin in the Illinois woods. After a time, Huck had fallen back into his old ways, wearing raggedly clothes, not washing or combing up, not having to say grace at meals; he could get up and go to bed when he pleased, could smoke and cuss and didn't have to go to school or church. In short, he forgot about all the civilizing ways the widow had imposed on him. It was only a matter of time and habit.

Zane still didn't know exactly how he'd been transported here across more than a century and three-quarters of time. He only recalled eating a candy bar containing peanuts and dark chocolate—two things he was violently allergic to. He'd thrown up before passing out near a creek in Delaware. Next thing he knew he was waking up on what turned out to be Jackson's Island and the year was 1849. Even stranger, he'd been found and befriended by Tom, Huck, and Jim, the embodiment of fictional characters he'd known from Mark Twain's novels. It didn't take long for him to accept them as real, even as they accepted him as a real traveler in time. Apparently, the universe was more mysterious and complicated than he'd ever realized. Many things had to be accepted that could not be explained.

He'd been in the Mississippi Valley of 1849 only since early summer, but it seemed much longer. What at first struck him as an alien environment was now familiar and comfortable. His dead cell phone lay gathering dust in his rented room in the village.

Zane sat at the tiller with little to do but nudge it slightly to starboard or larboard to avoid snagging the boat's short mast in the overhanging branches. The boys hadn't bothered to unstep the mast—just dropped and furled the gaff-rigged mainsail to keep it out of the way while they fished. The twenty-foot professionally built yawl had been purchased from the owners of the big side-wheel steamboat *Millicent* in June and had proved extremely valuable during their perilous summer adventure of snatching Tom and Huck from kidnappers.

"Mighty fine boat," Jim allowed, as if reading Zane's thoughts. He baited and dropped his hook overside again.

"That's for sure," Zane agreed. Though he had little boating experience in his former life, this steamboat yawl was far superior to the dugout canoes and flat-bottom punts and skiffs that were so common in the area. Tom was especially taken with the boat, mostly because he no longer had to "borrow" skiffs from inattentive villagers.

Jim and the boys had retrieved the boat when they came back down the Missouri River to the spot where Jim, Zane, and Becky Thatcher had left the yawl dragged up under the trees on the shore near St. Charles. Providence had apparently protected it from being stolen in their absence.

"Yassah, 'longside dis fine yawl, my ole dugout canoe be like driftwood," Jim continued, rubbing a calloused hand along one of the varnished oars. "When de wind git up, she slide 'cross de water like skippin' a flat rock."

"It sure beats clawing up agin' the current," Huck said. "Used to be it took all day to row a skiff or paddle a canoe twenty-five miles upstream in slack water, or five hours to go downstream the same distance. But once we struck the hang of *this* thing, we can move across the wind or nearly straight up agin' it. Who'd a figured that ole retired sailor, Jasper Larson, would be livin' right in our village at the exact same time we needed somebody to teach us to sail?" Huck added.

"Ain't no mystery," Tom said. "Can't you see the hand o'Providence in it?"

"When she be flyin' 'long, I kin scasely get m'breath," Jim continued. "Be like ridin' a blazin' fast horse or snatchin' de tail of a kite. You gots t'keep yo head down and a tight rein on'er."

Zane couldn't help but think that people fifty years from now would be equally astonished and grateful at the invention of the first outboard motors.

The sunshine flooded them again as they passed the foot of the island. Zane guided the boat away from an approaching sandbar.

"Uh!" Huck grunted as something heavy grabbed his bait and yanked the line, jerking the end of his cane pole down to the water.

"Hope it ain't a turtle," Tom said.

"Naw. They don't move that fast." He pointed at his line cutting through the water.

It took a minute or two, but Huck managed to guide a big catfish alongside and he and Jim lifted it by the gills into the boat.

"Dis be a fine fish," Jim grinned. "Make two meals fo' all of us."

"If we gonna fry him up for an early supper, we don't want to waste any of this fish," Tom said. "And the meat'll go bad afore we could get it home to Aunt Polly or Widow Douglas. Let's wait a bit and see if we catch a smaller one or two, and turn this'un loose for another day."

And that's just what they did.

An hour later they sat in the shade of some tall trees on Jackson's Island, with the boat tied up nearby. Jim and Zane gathered driftwood to kindle a fire while Huck skinned two medium-sized fish and Tom laid out the tin plates and forks and prepared to roll the fillets in cornmeal.

Good times always seemed to fly past, and to Zane it was no time at all until the meal was done. All four were lazying about on the grass, getting drowsy from the food and the quiet. Jim and Huck were smoking their pipes. Conversation lagged and the only sound was the sighing of wind in the treetops far overhead.

"Mighty considerate o'de widow to lemme slide out and take de day off," Jim remarked, leaning on one elbow and puffing contentedly.

"Maybe she ain't got as much work for you as before when you was plowin' the garden in the spring and then tendin' all the vegetables through the summer," Tom said.

"Yeah," Huck agreed. "I live at the widow's place, too, and I notice'er scratching around, looking for sumpin' to keep him busy half the time. Getting on toward August and the watermelons're full ripe and cucumbers about used up, 'ceptin' for the ones she's making into pickles . . ."

Zane thought Jim looked a bit startled, even hurt, at these remarks.

"Ah has considerable work 'round de place, cleanin' out de tool shed and tendin' her chickens and dat fine Morgan hoss dat pulls her carriage. And fixin' de roof o'de barn. I always be fetchin' stuff for her from de village and keepin' an eye on de others, includin' dat high yaller gal in de house . . ."

His voice trailed off as the three others looked at him. To Zane it sounded as if Jim was trying to justify his full-time employment. Maybe there were economic pressures he'd never known before he got his freedom.

Jim sat up on the grass and knocked the dottle out of his corncob pipe against the heel of his hand. Then he dropped his eyes and busied himself using a twig to dig out the rest of the ash. "Ah hopes she ain't fixin' t'get shut o'me. Ah needs de work," he said softly.

"Don't worry, Jim," Tom said, apparently sensing they'd made their old friend uneasy. "She ain't gonna let you go. If she was to catch the cholera that's ragin' around, or consumption or yaller fever, and die, me and Huck would hire you in a minute— and find you a nice place to live, too."

"Don't talk like dat, Mars Tom," Jim said, frowning. "De widow, she ain't gonna die—not fo' a long time yet."

"I didn't mean she was," Tom hastened to say. "But things happen, and Providence got its own ways. I don't reckon ole Missus Swanson knew she was fixin' to take sick with the pox and be carried off within three days. And Huck's pap dying and floating down the river in the flood in that old house . . ."

"Pap brought it on hisself," Huck put in. "If somebody hadn't done for him, whiskey woulda killed him for sure, anyways. I ain't blaming Providence, 'cause Pap was hurrying things along his own self, and the devil was likely waiting close by."

"Maybe we better quit talking about dying and losing jobs and unhappy things like that," Zane said, interrupting to change the direction of the conversation. "I'm a stranger here, but we been through a lot together since I came, and no telling when I might have to go back home. I want to have some more fun times and not think about sad things."

"You couldn't be more right," Tom said, brightening up. "I was thinkin' the same thing m'self." He reached over to where he'd set his plate on the ground. "It so happens I got sumpin' here I want to show everyone." He pulled up a wrinkled newspaper he had carefully folded. It had some water spots and grease stains where it'd been wrapped around the tomatoes and corn pone they'd brought from home. "You know," he said, "the last few weeks been mighty good for all of us—including

Becky, who ain't here just now. We been famous again and I'm about worn out with retelling our story from all the adventures we had. But things is about to die down and get dull again. And I, for one, ain't about to let us waste no more vacation time lazying around and fishing and flying kites and camping and such. I mean, all them things is fine, but I got a better idea."

Zane liked Tom, but he could outtalk a preacher or a pettifogging congressman. And there was no use trying to hurry him along to get to the point of his tale. Zane had learned that Tom thought things out before he opened his mouth and would take his time and work his story from the beginning, throwing in all the style and details he'd figured out. Huck and Jim must have known this, too, since they didn't interrupt.

"You know that Injun Joe's old partner, Chigger Smealey, and that Gus Weir, the slave catcher from New Orleans, got our $12,000 in gold as a ransom for Becky Thatcher's life. Well, then, me and Huck was captured and they let Becky go when we delivered the ransom . . ."

He was retelling all the episodes of their summer, Zane thought, as though all four of them hadn't lived through it themselves. But Zane let him continue. Tom would eventually get to something new. Besides, Zane was slowly breaking his old habit of impatience. Events—and stories—in this earlier world unfolded at their own pace.

". . . so we recovered 'most all the gold and them rascals was blown away in the storm, and we come home heroes again," he eventually finished. "But now, we can't wait for no kidnappers to show up and make things lively. If we don't want folks in the village to go to sleep again, we have to make our own excitement. And I got just the thing . . ." He unfolded the stained newspaper and opened it to an article and held it up. Zane didn't expect anyone could read it from several feet away. And Jim couldn't even read it close up.

"This here is a story in a St. Louis paper I smouched from Mister Rollins at the drugstore. It says the Injuns out in Oregon has been seeing a monster in the deep woods. It's a big, hairy cretur, about eight foot tall, that roars like an elephant and screeches like a cougar and smells like a civet cat. He don't get around much by daylight, but the Injuns seen him by the light o'the moon when they been out hunting."

Tom paused and the other three looked blankly at each other.

"Any of you hear tell of such a thing before?" Tom asked.

"Yeah, I have, and it's all hogwash," Zane said, falling into local slang. "They call that creature Bigfoot or Sasquatch or Yeti, or the Abominable Snowman, and sightings are still being reported in my time nearly two centuries from now."

"Has anyone in your day ever caught one?" Tom inquired. "What are they like? Do they eat all kinds of stuff like a bear or a boar hog or a catfish? Do they hibernate? Do they look like big men, or big apes?"

Zane took a swig of water from the canteen and tried to recall what he'd seen on several TV shows about this. "Most scientists and wildlife biologists don't believe there is such a thing. A lot of sightings have been reported in different parts of the world. Tracks have been found. But there has never been one captured or even the body of one found. It's probably a myth—like flying saucers."

"Dishes fly where you come from?" Huck marveled.

"Never mind," Zane said. "I'll tell you about that later." He didn't want to get sidetracked into another subject.

"This piece in the paper says the Injuns claim their ancestors knew about Sas . . . Sascotch a long time ago," Tom declared.

"Nearly every Indian tribe I've ever heard about has a different story of how the world was formed and where the ancient people came from," Zane said. "That don't mean there's any truth to it. Some of their ancestors just made up stories that seemed to make sense to them and passed 'em down to the next generation. And they just kept getting repeated. Same thing about this Sasquatch the Oregon Indians report they saw."

"But it ain't jest Injuns," Tom said. "Even a passel o'the new white settlers and trappers claim they saw a big hairy cretur, too."

Zane shrugged as the others looked to him like he possessed an extra hundred and seventy-five years of knowledge about this subject. Maybe it was his new glasses that made him look wiser, he thought. Before replying, he took off the spectacles and began polishing the glass lenses on his shirttail, removing the fingerprints. "Likely drinking too much of that homemade bust-head whiskey," he said at length, employing a term he'd heard his grandfather use. Then he replaced the glasses on his nose, noting with satisfaction how the thin wire bows curled around his ears to hold them on. That St. Louis optical place had done a really professional job checking his vision and making these new glasses to replace his old plastic ones stolen by a Sioux warrior.

"You ain't heard the rest of this," Tom continued, crinkling the newspaper to expose the bottom half of the page. "Says here some people—and a lot o'religious folk who don't drink no busthead whiskey—believe these huge creturs are the survivors of a giant race of men that lived on the earth before the time o'Moses and the big flood."

"It warn't Moses," Huck said.

"What?"

"It warn't Moses. A man name of Noah and his sons built a big, tubby boat with no steam engine and stuffed it with animals. *They* was the ones floated on the flood."

"I'll be a snowy day in the hot place when I take Bible lessons from the likes o'you, Huck Finn!" Tom looked more embarrassed than exasperated at being caught in a blunder.

"Blamed if you ain't missed the point altogether."

"Do it say sumpin' in de Bible about all dis?" Jim was solemn, keen on the subject as he leaned forward.

"Um . . . this reporter quotes the Book o'Genesis where it says '. . . *there was giants in the earth in those days* . . .' but he don't add nothing else."

"I'm almighty curious about them giants, too," Huck said. "Now that I can read pretty good, I'll borrow the widow's Bible and see can I find the rest of it. When ole Miss Watson was alive, she was 'most always peckin' at me to learn about Moses and the Bulrushers and them other folks that's been dead a good long time—like Noah. O'course, if I go to studyin' the widow's Bible now, she'll suspicion I'm up to sumpin'."

"Naw," Tom said. "She'll just be glad that her dead sister a'pushin' the scriptures on you has took at long last."

"I don't recall hearing anything about ancient giants," Zane said. "Just Bigfoot."

"Well there's more here that proves they musta lived some time in the past," Tom said. "See this here drawing?" He held up the paper to show a sketch of what looked like a skeleton in a rocky cave.

"Anybody can make a picture of a skeleton," Zane said. "You can't tell anything about the size of it from that drawing."

"What about *this* picture?" Tom said. "The artist drew this to show what folks been seein' in the woods." He pointed at a hairy upright figure looking like a giant ape.

"Any schoolkid could draw that," Zane said.

"Well, just you listen to this then," Tom said. "It says that bones o'men seven t'nine foot tall was found in a cave in White County, Tennessee, in 1821 and also in Williamson County." He lowered the paper. "Ya know, Tennessee ain't that far from here. Some o'my kinfolk about twenty-year back come from right over there. And it also says the biggest mounds they dug into was right down the river here in Illinois across from St. Louis. Place called Cahokia. But only a few o'them skeletons was giants." He found his place in the article again. "Um . . . the reporter writes there was giant skeletons found in California in 1833, and the skulls had two complete sets of teeth. But the men who dug'em up buried'em again 'cause the Injuns was all upset about it."

"Dat woulda scared de stuffin' outa me, too," Jim said.

"I don't reckon a skeleton has ever hurt anybody yet," Tom scoffed. "What's to be skeered of? They've found dinosaur bones in lotsa places, too, and they're a lot bigger—with long, sharp teeth, tails, and claws. But dinosaurs is long gone and nothin' to worry about. O'course," he added, "this is a different kettle o'fish. These here are *human* bones."

"Well if they was around the same time as the dinosaurs, I reckon the humans had to be giants if they was gonna fend off them scaly rapscallions whilst hunting for meat with nuthin' but stone-headed spears and arrows," Huck said.

"And dey likely needed two sets o'teeth to chew all dat bone and gristle," Jim allowed. "Dinosaur meat gots to be mighty tough."

"They probably didn't eat the dinosaurs," Zane said. "Those giants likely ate the same large animals the meat-eating dinosaurs were after—like mastodons for example."

"What's that?" Huck asked.

"A kind of big hairy elephant with long, curving tusks," Zane said. "They're extinct, too, but there's been a couple of them and some woolly mammoths found in my time, frozen in the ice up north, preserved just like they were when they died."

"Wow!" It was Tom's turn to be amazed.

"So, then," Huck added, continuing the thought, "when the dinosaurs and the mas . . . master dongs was wiped out, warn't no more need for giants. So, little by little, folks begun to shrink down some—jest the same's catfish and carp only grow to fit the pond they're in—or get a lot bigger if they's in the river with plenty o'room."

"That's so," Tom said. "Maybe that's why not all the skeletons dug up in those burial mounds was giants. A goodly number o'them was normal size because humans was just then commencing to get smaller. But it musta took thousands o'years." He looked back to the newspaper. "This writer winds up by saying there been lots of other giant human skeletons seven to ten foot tall found all over the place—Indiana, Ohio, New York, Minnesota, Wisconsin," Tom said.

"If dey found bones dat big in de groun', dat sho nuff means some fearsome giants was walkin' 'roun here some time or other," Jim said. "If dey was a whole passel of 'em, de good Lawd mighta missed a few when He sent de mighty flood. And de few He missed mighta gone t'breedin' and dere great-great grandchil'ren is still runnin' loose in de woods, scarin' folks."

"All that sounds like it coulda happened that way," Zane said. "But I'm no scientist. And if I go the rest of my days without seeing one, I'll be just as happy—either in 1849 or in my own time. But I'm not sure they really exist." His head was in a whirl. Traveling back in time was crazy enough, but then seeing some evidence that a race of giant men had lived on the earth long ago began to overwhelm his sense of reality. His eighth-grade class had begun to study Shakespeare a few months previously and a quote from Hamlet popped up from his memory: *There are more things in heaven and earth, Horatio, than are dreamt of in our philosophy.* The famous playwright had written that about three hundred years ago in faraway England, so Zane took consolation in the fact that he, himself, wasn't the only person who was constantly amazed by strange wonders.

"That brings me back to why I brought this up in the first place," Tom said, laying the paper down. "This here is a perfect chance to get the village all in a sweat, so we can waltz in and become heroes again."

"How so?" Huck asked.

Zane had a feeling Tom was about to propose some wild, harebrained scheme that could get them all killed instead of making them heroes.

"They's some big wooded islands down the river maybe a half day or so from here. I'm thinkin' if we was to somehow get the word out, and spread it around the village, quiet like, so nobody knows where the rumors started, that one or a dozen o'these here giants has been spotted on that island, and they're spreading north up the river, we could get folks riled up. Then we step forward and volunteer to go camp out there a few nights in the full moon and wait for these hairy creturs to show up. We come back and tell everyone we run'em off and saved the village from possible invasion at great risk to our own lives."

"Ain't nobody gonna believe that," Huck said. "Colonel Elder, he fought agin' the Mexicans and has been 'most everywhere, Judge Thatcher, who is uncommon bright, and Mister Dobbins, who has lots o'schoolin', is all smart enough to see right through that story."

"I ain't thinking they'll be took in by a story in a newspaper," Tom said. "We gotta show'em proof they'll believe. We'll make this a deep, dark conspiracy, and they won't never know we're behind it. Most o'the common villagers, as a general thing, are easy to fool. They cotton to any wild, superstitious tales they hear. They'll think it's all true if they see it writ up in print—especially in a big St. Louis newspaper." He held up the stained paper. "I'm gonna clip out this piece, along with the masthead, to show where it come from and post it on the big notice board by the post office where everybody will see it. I'll print a 'nonymous left-handed note with it that says these giants has been seen spreading up the river from the swamps of Loosiana from one island to the next, and will be invading St. Petersburg looking for blood come the next full moon, which ain't but a week or so off now." He paused to make sure he had their complete attention. "This article has stuff about the giant race of men that existed long ago. All we gotta do is convince everyone that some o'them giants is still close by and ain't to be messed with by any common folk."

"What about the paterollers?" Huck asked.

"They're called patrollers, you numskull," Tom said.

"Whatever they are, they're mostly young men with guns. And they been walkin' the streets nights 'cause o'rumors abolitionists was coming to raid. Them regulators . . ."

"Patrollers."

"Them patrollers will puff up their chests and get out their guns and brag they can protect the village from anything like big hairy creturs they ain't never seen. They'll say they can blow'em to kingdom come with their muskets and pistols."

"What a mud turtle you are, Huck Finn! We got to work on people's *fears*. Them patrollers are only there to keep the village safe from abolitionists sneaking into town, snatching slaves, and takin'em over the river t'freedom in Illinois. Patrollers ain't fixin' to go up against giant hairy creturs ten foot tall that could shrug off musket balls like hail and then wade in and tear'em limb from limb . . ."

"Can dey really do dat?" Jim asked, wide-eyed.

"I don't know," Tom said. "But they don't know, neither. What we have to do is make'em *believe* these giants're that powerful. That's part of the conspiracy."

"Besides that newspaper piece, what kind of proof kin we show'em?" Huck asked.

"Footprints," Tom said. "We'll show'em giant three-toed footprints. I'll smouch a couple fair-sized wood blocks from the Taylorville newspaper and print shop—they likely ain't had a poster print job order in a year or more and will never miss the blocks—then come over here to the island with a hammer and chisel and a file and carve out two big footprints. That'll be the hardest part, but if we take turns at it, we can save our hands from blisters and get it done in a day or two."

He paused as if gathering his thoughts for the next part of his plan. "Then, after everybody has seen that article on the notice board, and commences t'gossiping about it, we'll off-hand, and casual-like, say we're planning a camping and fishing trip for a day or three downriver. If anybody should warn us about these giant beasts, we'll act like it ain't nuthin'to be afeered of. But we'll promise to keep a sharp lookout." He glanced around at them.

In spite of himself, Zane was riveted by his every word—as were Jim and Huck.

"I looked on a map," Tom continued, "and about fifty miles from here as the river runs is Westport Island, which is perfect for what we want. It's three-miles long and a half-mile wide—nearly the size of Jackson's Island here. But Westport lies toward the Missouri side with only a narrow sliver—Kickapoo Island—in the chute 'twixt Westport and the Missouri shore. Nobody livin' anywhere about. Thick woods all over it, except for a little swampy ground on the upper end." He paused, dramatically, before continuing with the plot. "Then Jim will strap the wood blocks to his feet and run for a quarter mile in some soft mud. I'll out with a bucket of tallow and make molds of two of the tracks. Then we'll scuff ourselves up a bit with scratches and cuts from blackberry bushes, like we been in a desperate struggle. Maybe I could fall into our campfire and burn my arm a little. We'll kill a rat or a possum and smear some o'the blood on the boat like we wounded the giant beast as he made a final grab for us. But we was barely able to shove off with the oars at the last second and the beast fell into the river. Victorious, we'll sail back up to our village and show'em the molds of the prints and tell how we was trackin' the beast and he attacked us in the light o'the full moon, jest a'screeching for blood. He was ten foot tall and fast and come for us. We run for the boat whilst firing our pistols at him. He was wounded but still deadly and went t'ripping at us with his claws—oh, I got to remember to make claws on those blocks—tearing our clothes and skin. But at last he fell, mortally wounded, into the water and bled to death or drownded. That way his body won't never be found later for evidence." He paused, apparently devising a way to add more horror to their fictional tale. "Maybe a claw mark on an oar. I think we could make a horn that would give out some kinda awful roaring noise in case there's a steamboat passing by or some fishermen on the river to hear it. They'd swear later it warn't like no beast on earth."

"Why does I needs to be part o'dis, Mars Tom?" Jim asked.

"Why, to make the tracks more real, o'course," Tom said. "You're bigger and heavier and if you run, the tracks will be farther apart so it looks like a giant with a long stride is just walking along. We'll bust up a few branches and add some reeds and brush to fashion a nest where the beast coulda been sleeping. Seeing all that, there won't be nobody from this village who can say for sure there ain't some kind of mighty beast living on that deserted island. All that'll scare most folks outa their wits. I'll think of other things as we go along—throw in some details to make it more lively. After a time, when the giant bloodthirsty cretur don't show up, things will die down, but meantime, we'll be heroes again."

"The way you make it sound, I almost believe it myself," Huck said.

"We gots to be mighty careful," Jim said. "Ah ain't so sure ah wants t'be part o'dis conspiracy. Dey might throw ole Jim in jail if dey suspicion ah be part o'sumpin' shady."

"We got to have you, Jim," Tom said. "Don't you see—you're a big part of this conspiracy. We can't make it work without you."

"Creating your own excitement with a conspiracy seems to be a lot more work than letting it happen on its own," Zane observed.

"That's the thing about it," Tom said. "We can't wait around for Providence to decide it's time for another adventure, and then hand it to us, ready-made and boxed up."

CHAPTER 2

Bit Barjee dismounted in a muddy street of St. Joseph, Missouri. He tied the horse of the late Senator Cyrus Shirten to a sagging hitching rail in front of the first red and white striped barber pole he saw at a tonsorial parlor. A shave and haircut would not only refresh him after his long, hot ride, but mainly, by ridding his face of the heavy black beard, he could radically change his appearance if any lawman or soldier was on his trail. He'd already bought a square of canvas to drape over the Grimsley saddle so it and the saddlebags of gold couldn't possibly be seen and recognized. As yet, he'd done nothing about altering the brand on the flank of the sleek mare that had carried him here swiftly and easily from Fort Kearny in only three days and part of two nights.

Relieved that he was the only customer at the moment, he sat in the barber chair under a layer of hot lather and kept an eye on his horse out front while also watching a steady stream of people on horseback and in wagons passing by the front window. In spite of the fact that it was already July, apparently the rush to the goldfields had barely slowed. Desperate people would do desperate things, and many of these Argonauts would wind up on this side of the Rockies when winter shut down passage to Eldorado.

He, himself, had departed from Independence, Missouri, miles to the south of here early in the spring, having no idea at the time that he'd be back in Missouri so soon—or under what circumstances. He was still in full flight and concentrating on getting as far away as possible. Thus, the memory of his shooting had been pushed aside for now. He suspected it would return to haunt him later, but first he had to focus on surviving and escaping. He was determined not to be caught and punished for a spur-of-the-moment shooting at a time when his judgment had been clouded by whiskey. Of course he knew being drunk was no excuse before the law. But he justified his action by reasoning the senator had almost certainly cheated him. No man alive could possibly have had that long a string of good cards by chance. Secondly, he felt he had done the country a service by ridding the government of a man who apparently made a habit of thievery, if accusations of his stealing from the U.S. Treasury were even close to being correct. He smiled grimly to himself. Maybe he should apply for a reward from Congress.

While the haircut and shave soothed him, he remained tense under the big, striped drape, watching the front window between slitted eyelids, one hand resting on the butt of his holstered Colt. In spite of the fact that he had been severely hungover the first several hours of his ride and thirsty and tired after that, he dared not relax too soon.

Thankfully, there was no telegraph this far west so news could travel only as fast as the swiftest horse or steamboat. If someone from the fort was on his trail, they could find ample witnesses among men of the westbound wagon trains who'd likely seen him riding past to the east. Would his best chance of escape be in the wilderness of Missouri or some other state, or would he have a better chance of blending unseen into city crowds of a place the size of St. Louis or Chicago?

He resisted the urge to ask the barber if there was a good road from St. Joe to St. Louis. Someone might come along later, asking questions. He'd figure it out himself, or ask among the westbound Argonauts who had brought their wagons from the direction of the Mississippi River. Or, he might ride east a day or so, and then ask someone he met on the road. He'd considered selling the horse and saddle and taking a down-bound steamboat to St. Louis. Much easier, and more comfortable. But the moment he'd dropped the hammer on the senator, he'd given up any idea of comfort for the foreseeable future. And he didn't relish being hemmed in on a steamboat by other strangers. The river level was falling, and he could be hung up by sandbars that would delay him for days. He wanted to be constantly moving. But, worst of all, if he sold the fancy trooper saddle and the beautiful horse, they could be easily identified if the law was on the lookout for them, and would know the killer had come this way.

The barber finished with him, splashed on some aromatic bay rum, then snapped the big drape off with a flourish, flinging hair everywhere. He held up a mirror for Barjee to see himself. Not only did he look pale and gaunt, he felt that way. And when he clapped on his dirty, water-stained hat, it was a bit large on his shorn head. He paid the barber with a one-dollar gold coin and told him to keep the change. Enough of a tip, but not too much that would attract attention.

He walked his horse to the nearest livery a block away and left him with orders for a rubdown and a bait of oats. The hardy animal was too tired to keep going without a night's rest, and he was sagging badly himself. As fast a run as he'd made from the fort, he gambled he could risk one night's sleep and a hearty meal before starting on. Even if they'd known which way he'd gone, no one could possibly get here before he was long gone. The wealthy Senator Cyrus Shirten had obtained a fine horse, apparently one capable of making it all the way to California.

Shouldering the leather saddlebags, with the weight of several small sacks of nuggets and dust inside, made him nearly stagger with fatigue. He glanced at the westering sun and decided, before the banks closed, to convert all this into coin.

Was it the devil of a bad conscience sitting on his shoulder that made him constantly feel eyes were watching him? He stood at the teller's window, trying to appear relaxed and nonchalant, resisting the urge to look about with the furtive glance of a guilty man.

"Looks like you already been to the goldfields and made your strike," the teller remarked, sounding a bit envious as he adjusted the gold scales.

"Yeah. Pure luck. And I didn't want to press it by staying too long," Barjee said. "Too many crooks there can pick you clean if you get greedy and hang around for more."

"Well, this should last you a considerable time." The clerk continued to weigh and measure and jot down figures with a pencil. "How would you like this, sir?"

"Quarter and half eagles mostly. Easier to break. You can throw in a few one-dollar coins, and some ten-dollar pieces, too." In spite of his circumstances, he felt elated. He'd always dreamed of being able to walk into a bank and say that.

The experienced teller shoved the small rawhide pokes back across the counter. "Ought to turn those inside out and wash 'em. I'm sure there's some dust clinging to that rough hide."

"Thanks." For a man who'd gone west on the sale price of his widowed mother's small brick house in Cincinnati, he'd come back wealthier than most men he'd ever known—certainly many times richer than his late father, who'd been a Welsh coal miner before he migrated in his youth to mine bituminous coal in the New World. In fact, he'd named his oldest son Bit, for bituminous, the soft coal he dug from the black tunnels. His father had died at age fifty from breathing the dust of that mine. Barjee turned away feeling a small pang of regret that he could not share his fortune with his parents.

But, leaving the bank, the new burden of his crime began to bear down on him as heavily as the sagging saddlebags.

"Well, we made it this far and our luck's holding," Smealey said as the mooring lines of the stern-wheel packet, *Jezebel,* splashed into the water.

"We ain't off the griddle yet," Gus Weir muttered, standing beside him on the main deck. Two black roustabouts dragged the lines aboard and looped the dripping hawsers around the forward bitts. The wheel began to thrash, and the morning sun flashed off the boat's brightwork as she swung into the Missouri River current away from the St. Joseph landing and headed downstream.

"It's a good start," Smealey said, glancing about to make sure none of the deckhands were close enough to hear their low conversation.

"Keep your mouth shut and your head down," Weir said, tugging down the slouch hat he wore.

The two fugitives each had five ten-dollar gold pieces in their pockets from the sale of the two unbranded, stolen mules to westbound travelers.

Smealey had expected more trouble selling the animals with no paperwork or bills of sale, but St. Joe was still a boomtown and the two stout mules had been snatched up at an inflated price.

"I could use a drink to celebrate," Smealey said in a low voice.

Weir shot him a hard glance and Smealey cringed, looking away. "All right, all right, no drinking until we're far away and safe."

"That's right. And that won't be until we're in St. Louis, or better yet, New Orleans," Weir grated.

"I ain't goin' t'New Orleans," Smealey said. "Too hot and

swampy and feverish for me."

Weir shrugged, turning away to finish topping off the firebox with cordwood. A blast of withering heat issued from the open fire doors.

Smealey had never worked as a deckhand, but had ridden enough steamboats to blend in, watch the others, take orders from the mate, and act as if he knew what to do.

When they weren't on watch, many of the deckhands gambled with dice or cards. Mostly, the whites and blacks congregated into their own groups. But, even so, arguments and fistfights or knife fights were not unusual.

However, on the *Jezebel*, a bully mate ruled the main deck and nothing rowdy occurred. Though the hands were allowed to gamble during their short periods of free time, word had gotten around to the newcomers that any kind of arguments, scuffles, drinking, or actual deadly combat would immediately bring beating with a club, flogging, being thrown overboard, or dismissed without pay at the next woodyard or landing.

Conrad Winger, they were told, had been an overseer on a Louisiana plantation before going on the river a few years before and he ruled his deckhands and roustabouts, slave or free, white or black, with the same even-handed discipline he'd wielded from the back of a horse in a cotton field.

"He don't take no guff," a muscular black man told Weir and Smealey an hour after they came aboard as newly hired deckhands.

The stocky figure of the mate had appeared on the forward ladder.

"We's all in de same boat heah and Winger be de *man,*" he said out of the corner of his mouth as he and Weir were heaving chunks of cordwood into the suffocating heat blowing back from the open firebox.

The mate strolled aft along the deck. Smealey tried to appear busy sweeping up pieces of bark and dirt that had fallen off the woodpile when Winger paused to look him up and down and moved on. A few yards later the mate stopped again by a black sitting on a cotton bale and punched him with the butt of his short club. "Get up outa there, nigger. Nobody but deck passengers lies down during duty hours. If you ain't got sumpin' to do right now, you can get t'polishin' the brightwork. We'll be at our first woodyard in two hours, so make yourself useful until we get there." He strolled away with a rolling gait, smacking the club into his open hand.

"Don't make no difference if you's white or black or a freed man like me," the black man continued softly. "He treat us all de same. If you wants t'keep yo job and de skin on yo back and the lumps off yo head, better stay busy, and keep yo mouf shut."

Smealey made a mental resolution to do just that.

The young black man turned a white-toothed grin toward him and Weir. "Makes fo' a nice, peaceful trip, but we don't have no excitement 'less he take a notion to punish somebody."

"How many days to St. Charles or St. Louis?" Smealey asked. Might as well get as much information as he could from this congenial black man.

"Hard t'say. De big muddy, she got a mind of her own," he said, nodding toward the chocolate-colored water flowing past a few feet away. "If we's lucky, maybe a week. I been on dis boat awhile, and de water droppin' now since spring runoff. Don't know de two pilots on dis run. If dey good, I'd say maybe eight or nine days. If one'o'them's a mud turtle or jes learnin' de wheel, we'll be buttin' into sandbars all de way, and riggin' spars to grasshopper over every little while. Le's hope dat don't happen or we all be sweatin' down to a greasy spot."

Smealey nodded, silently making up his mind to use the time to work hard, stay out of sight, and figure out, privately, if he would continue to keep Weir as a partner when they reached St.

Louis, or let the slave chaser go his own way to New Orleans. Smealey was reasonably confident no one would take the trouble to chase them all this way for stealing two mules and saddles, even though wanted posters might be circulated and tacked up here and there in Missouri and the Territory. But being possible suspects in the murder of a U.S. Senator was a different matter. The authorities could be scouring every escape route from Fort Kearny to apprehend them for questioning. Maybe if they split up, there would be less likelihood of their being recognized by anyone hunting them. He'd tucked the fifty dollars gold in his boot for safekeeping, and was seriously considering drawing his pay and cutting loose from Weir when they docked at St. Charles.

CHAPTER 3

Tom Sawyer wasted no time putting his shoulder to the wheel of his conspiracy and shoving it into motion.

He bounced out of bed early next morning intent on traveling to the hamlet of Taylorville, some seven miles south of St. Petersburg. He knew the general plan but, typically, that plan was sorely lacking in details. Except for carrying a folded gunnysack with him, he hadn't the foggiest notion how he would smouch the wooden printing blocks once he reached the Taylorville Print Shop. As usual, he would trust to Providence to guide him when the time came. It never occurred to him that perhaps Divine Providence might not be on the side of a thief.

Up before the sun, he'd washed down his toast and jam with coffee before his Aunt Polly was stirring. This was by design since he wanted to be off ahead of the oppressively hot weather. But, mainly he intended to avoid fielding any questions from his aunt. He'd been through so many hair-raising escapes and near disasters in the past two years, she had stopped assuming he was merely bound for innocent play when he left the house. Thankfully, his half-brother, Sid, and his cousin, Mary, were both spending a fortnight at their uncle's farm, so he had no worries about avoiding the troublesome tattletale Sid.

Paper was scarce in this house so he rummaged in the sitting room until he found a piece of broken slate he'd scarfed up after the schoolmaster discarded it last spring. Taking a lump of chalk from his pocket, he inscribed the following note: *Aunt*

Polly—Gone swimming with Huck and Zane. Back for supper. Tom.
He admired his literate prose for a moment, and then, as an afterthought, added the word *love*, in front of his name. There. That would do it. Since his wild adventure earlier this summer, he had become more aware of her actual concern for his welfare, so was taking pains to be considerate of her feelings. Her hair seemed to be growing grayer with each passing month and he sensed maybe she wasn't indestructible after all.

He placed the slate on the kitchen table and, snatching up his gunnysack that smelled of garden vegetables, slipped out the front door, being careful to shut it quietly behind him.

He paused fifty yards up the street and tilted his straw hat against the early rays of the sun just topping the trees east of the river. Was there an easy way to travel to and from Taylorville? Becky Thatcher lived across the street. Maybe she would lend him her pony. That would certainly beat walking all the way. He bit his lip, eyeing her windows, which were still covered by drawn curtains. No. It was too early. She'd still be in bed. And he didn't want to disturb her father, the judge. Besides, her pony was stabled three blocks away. She would be full of questions about why he needed the animal, and he didn't want her guessing something was afoot that she might horn in on. The conspiracy had to remain a secret among the four of them— himself, Jim, Huck, and Zane. The note he'd left his aunt was at least partially true. Huck and Zane *were* going swimming in Bear Creek today. He wished he were going with them, but he had more important business.

After his day off, Jim would be back to work at the widow's.

He took a deep breath and started off at a brisk pace, headed for the river road at the edge of the village. In consideration for his feet, he had actually put his shoes in the gunnysack in case he had to walk all the way and his bare feet weren't up to the pounding on the ruts and rocks.

Tom fell into a swinging gait and made quick time, meeting no one on the road. He had to sit down and rest only once, and not because he was overly tired, but only to cool down a bit in the shade and wipe the sweat in the windless air. He'd forgotten to bring a canteen of water, but knew there was a town pump in Taylorville. Based on the experience of many such trips, he'd estimated two hours for the journey and hit his estimate almost exactly.

Pausing for breath, he sat down on the edge of the boardwalk midway along the main street. Taylorville was not as big as his own village, and only a few pedestrians were abroad this morning.

They paid him no heed twenty minutes later when he pumped himself a drink in the town square and sidled toward the print shop in the middle of the block. Being a kid had its advantages. Unless you were a hero, or in big trouble, grownups tended to give you all the notice they'd give a porch post. On the other hand, a grown man, and a stranger at that, would draw instant curiosity.

From the angle of the sun this long summer day, Tom guessed it was not yet past nine o'clock. He'd gotten here too early. The print shop would be open, but now he had to formulate a plan to get inside, distract the owner long enough to snatch the wooden blocks, and slip away. If he were caught in the act of stealing, he could be in serious trouble. Worst of all, it could wreck their conspiracy.

Many shop owners closed up for an hour or more around lunchtime when they went home to eat. Rarely did they bother to lock the doors of their businesses. On a slow day that was also fearsomely hot, the proprietor might knock off in early afternoon and take a nap.

He sat down again on the edge of the boardwalk to think it through. With the money he had left over from his previous adventure, he could have bought as many printing blocks as he wanted. But that presented several problems. First, he had no idea where these were even made or sold. Secondly, a boy his age would attract attention buying such a thing. With Tom's history of pranks and concocting troublesome schemes, any grownup who knew him would be immediately suspicious. And lastly, he wanted no adult to know he had these blocks in the event someone might later recall his purchase and deduce that the giant footprints could have been fashioned from them.

Sam Carver was the aging owner of the print shop. A fusty, musty man with curly gray hair and mustache, he went about his business with a distracted air. A steam engine he was not. But that didn't mean that he was unaware of what was happening around him. Tom would have to chance entering the shop to case the layout and assess his chances.

After resting a bit and catching his breath from the long walk, he tucked the gunnysack containing his shoes into an empty water barrel between buildings. A small bell jangled as he opened the door. He nodded to Mister Carver when the owner glanced up from helping a customer place an order.

Good. Tom could look around without giving a reason for even being in here.

But the customer concluded his business in a short minute and left.

"What can I do for you, young man?" the old owner asked pleasantly.

Tom had to come up with some plausible excuse. "Sir, I been wondering if you might have some old, broken type you're wanting to get rid of."

"Well, let me look. I throw it all into this bin, and sometimes turn it in for new every few months." He went to a wooden case against the wall and pawed around.

Tom glanced about the shop and saw, stacked in a corner,

four unused wooden printing blocks—exactly what he wanted. They were covered with dust.

"What're planning to do with it?

"Uh . . . I . . . my friends and I want to melt down the lead and make some toy soldiers."

"Ah . . . perfect thing for that," he agreed, scooping up a double handful and dumping the broken bits of type into a small cloth bag. "Will that be enough?"

"Thank you, sir. That's plenty," Tom said, thinking that not only would the lead make toy soldiers, it would also be ideal for molding bullets for the pistols they'd have to get.

"Anything else?"

"No, sir. Thank you, sir."

Tom smiled his thanks and departed. Retrieving his gunnysack and shoes, he trudged down the street to the edge of town and found a shady spot in the woods out of sight and stretched out for a nap. He had at least two hours to kill.

When the sun was nearly overhead, Tom slid out of the woods where he could watch the print shop a block away. As he'd surmised, Mister Carver went home for lunch. Scratching mosquito bites, Tom forced himself to wait until the owner had been gone about ten minutes before he returned to the shop. He slipped inside, cringing at the jingling of the bell on the door. It took only a few seconds to dump two of the dusty printing blocks into his gunnysack. When he turned to leave, his conscience smote him. Old Sam Carver was too nice a man to cheat. He dug into his side pocket and pulled out a tiny gold dollar and laid it on the counter. The old man would find it, figure a customer had come in during his absence, taken something, and left the money for it. It was a small-town custom. Nothing like that would ever work in a city.

On the hike home, he stopped and pulled on his shoes to

give his bare feet a rest from pounding the rough ground. The leather footwear was hot, even without socks, but his toes and soles thanked him for it.

He arrived home at midafternoon, dumped his gunnysack and shoes under his bed, didn't see his aunt in the house, and so tore off toward Bear Creek south of town. The only thing on his mind now was a desire to hit the water and cool off.

Huck and Zane were still there, but were lolling about in the shade, having spent all their energies swimming for several hours.

No one else was around so Tom stripped off his clothes to skinny-dip. Most of the sickening odor that still lingered from the deserted slaughterhouse nearby was blowing away from them across the river.

"The conspiracy is right on schedule," he told them as he bobbed in the cool water.

Zane and Huck were on the bank pulling on their clothes, spurred on by the sound of female voices from a picnic ground nearby.

"First thing in the morning I'll take the yawl over to Jackson's Island and start carving. If you two want to come and help, we could have a jolly old time fishing and swimming in between gouging and filing. You two might have some ideas about what a giant monster foot should look like."

"When do you plan to post that newspaper story on the bulletin board?" Zane asked. He wanted to be prepared for anything. There was little he could do to stop this conspiracy, but he was leery of tampering with adults' emotions like this. It was something he never would have thought to do in his former world. If something didn't go exactly as planned with this and they were exposed, they could be in serious trouble. In his 21st century world, they would likely receive a verbal parental reprimand or, at the worst, possibly a few months' probation by juvenile court for causing a riot, or endangering public safety.

His grandfather had told him about the Orson Welles radio program, *The War of the Worlds*, which was broadcast the day before Halloween in 1938, and how it had caused widespread panic when thousands of listeners thought the Martians were actually invading. As far as Zane knew, no one was ever punished for that, and the same kind of pseudo-documentaries had been done from time to time after that.

At least this conspiracy was not likely to get the three boys classed as incorrigibles by some court and sent off to reform school—*if* such a thing existed in this time and place.

In any event, he knew grownups often didn't have a finely honed sense of humor, especially when a practical joke was on them.

"I'll wait 'til I get done with the blocks. Probably only a day or two from now," Tom said. "Once that article goes up, things will start moving fast, so be ready."

CHAPTER 4

The Widow Douglas was nothing, if not generous. Her late husband, a steamboat pilot on the Mississippi River for a dozen years, had used his considerable salary to make investments that had proved profitable for both of them. Childless, the couple was able to afford a house on Cardiff Hill, overlooking the village, enough acreage that necessitated the working by four slaves, and status as one of the elite couples of St. Petersburg.

Unlike many wealthy people, the Douglases were down to earth, caring, and giving and were not envied or gossiped about by others. They were on a social par with Judge Thatcher, the minister, the schoolmaster, Doctor Weatherby, and the town's leading attorney.

His occupation kept Mister Douglas away from home for weeks at a time, but his wife managed their home and slaves quite nicely, directing the operation of their small hilltop farm.

But tragedy struck one bleak March day below Cairo, Illinois, when Douglas's boat was holed by a massive shard of river ice and went down in twenty feet of water, carrying the pilot and seven others to their deaths within minutes.

The bodies went under the ice in a swift current and were never recovered, but his widow was always consoled by Doctor Weatherby's assertion that all the victims had most certainly perished within minutes of shock and exposure with little pain. They did not drown, he assured her. "Your husband probably experienced a few seconds of cold," he said. "But, after that, he

47

would have been numb and comfortable. It would have been like drifting off to sleep."

She wore widow's black for a year, but her mourning was mostly personal and private. She was about town, bright and lively, contributing and helping with charitable causes, anonymously providing food to the needy, serving on the library committee, paying to have the church repainted.

Sometime later, although well along toward her middle years, she even volunteered to take in and rear Huckleberry Finn, the abandoned son of the town drunkard. A few weeks after her informal adoption, she was joined in the three-story hilltop home by her spinster sister, Miss Watson, who brought along her slave, Jim.

More than two years had now passed since then and her sister had succumbed to smallpox, freeing her slave, Jim, in her will. After Jim and Huck's unforeseen and hazardous summer escape downriver on a raft, things had returned to normal and the widow hired Jim to work for her as a handyman.

Since his father was now dead, Huckleberry Finn was back under the care of the widow, who was proudly turning him into a "responsible, literate, and courteous young man."

But early summer of 1849 had seen another near-tragedy with the kidnapping of Judge Thatcher's daughter, Becky, followed by a harrowing series of events involving Tom Sawyer, Huckleberry, and her faithful servant, Jim.

In thanksgiving to Divine Providence for everyone's safe return from this, the Widow Douglas, with the help of several St. Petersburg matrons, planned a village party and picnic. It was scheduled for the end of July to give everyone a chance to catch their collective breath, to allow for the grand 4th of July celebration to pass, and a traveling circus to come and go. It was timed to pick up everyone's spirits when the August doldrums were beginning to set in.

There was no shortage of volunteers, but she quietly insisted she be allowed to provide the main financial support for this community celebration, even to hiring a chef from St. Louis who would come and create several giant tubs of ice cream, a hot weather treat usually confined to those wealthy persons who could afford it.

Little did she know that Tom, Huck, and Jim, along with Zane—that rather unusual, articulate boy visiting from out of town—had plans of their own to keep the villagers on their mettle.

"Do you have ice cream where you come from?" Huck asked Zane as the three boys stood in the shade at the picnic scooping up the melting vanilla dessert.

"Oh, yeah, it's very common. I've had it all my life. And there are dozens of different flavors. The most common are strawberry, chocolate, and vanilla—like this."

"What are some of the others?" Tom asked.

"Um . . . chocolate chip, lemon, fudge, blackberry, Swiss mocha, banana, vanilla swirl and on and on . . . most any kind of fruit flavor and combination you can think of. I don't even know all of them."

"Do they stash it in the ice house during summer to keep it from melting?" Huck asked, gesturing toward the tubs of ice nearby that held the covered bowls of ice cream.

"We don't have ice houses," Zane said. "About fifty or sixty years from now, somebody invented refrigeration."

"What's that?" Tom asked.

Zane's spoon stopped halfway to his mouth. How to explain this without explaining electricity, which he didn't really understand himself? Then he thought of something they might be able to relate to. "Do you recollect learning in school about Benjamin Franklin, the statesman from the 1700s who signed the Declaration of Independence?"

"Sure do," Tom said.

"Well, he invented all kinds of practical stuff—the Franklin stove, the half-glasses for reading, the curved surface of cobblestone streets so water would run off into the gutters. But he's famous for his experiment where he tied a key to a kite string during a thunderstorm and lightning struck it. He was trying to figure out a way to capture lightning for people to use." He knew this was a great oversimplification, but had to cut it short. "Scientists later on managed to do it. It's called electricity and it runs through wires. Years later, they figured out ways to use it for all kinds of things, including lights, how to heat and cool houses, run machinery, and to make a box that's really cold inside to keep food from spoiling and ice cream from melting," he finished, licking the last of his ice cream from the porcelain cup. He started to tell the boys about edible cones to hold the ice cream that were first sold at a world's fair some fifty years hence. But he didn't feel up to the effort. It was amazing how many technical things had come along since 1849.

"I wish Jim was here," Zane said as the boys wandered over toward the makeshift bandstand where a six-piece brass band was warming up.

"I do, too," Huck said. "The widow put him in charge of the house whilst she and everyone else is down here."

"Jim's free, but that don't mean he can attend socials and stuff with white folks," Tom explained. "It's a shame, too. Jim's as good-hearted a man as ever I met."

"I reckon it's natural for whites and blacks to mix with their own kind," Huck said slowly, sounding as if he wasn't totally convinced of this observation. "They have their own weddings and hoedowns, and revivals," he said. "And I ain't never seen folks of any color sing and laugh and carry on with so much fun as they do."

Zane nodded. "There's still a good bit of segregation in my day, too, but society gradually changes in the years after the slaves are all freed and . . ."

"When will the slaves be free?" Huck interrupted.

Zane had to pause and count. "In about sixteen years—after the Civil War."

"What's a civil war?" Huck asked. "How can a war be 'civil'? That's foolish talk. They ain't so such thing."

"Uh . . ." Zane kept using terms he was familiar with, hardly aware of how they actually sounded or what his words literally meant. "It's only a name somebody gave it. It means Americans are fighting each other—the people who live in the northern states are fighting the people in the south. It will be a terrible thing," he added, "and happened long before my grandparents were even born."

Tom and Huck looked solemn.

Zane had purposely not told them about events that would happen during their lifetimes. Why throw a storm cloud over their carefree lives? But now the subject had come up, so he felt obliged to satisfy their curiosity and give a brief account of what was to come.

"It's gonna start twelve years from now and last four years. The southern states will pull out of the Union and form their own country called the Confederate States of America. They'll have their own government and their own money and everything. But after the war, they'll come back in."

"What about Missouri?"

"This was one of the border states," Zane said. "There's a big ruckus in the Missouri government—some want to stay in the Union and others want to pull out. I really don't remember which way it went, since I only read about it in history class."

"I'll be twenty-five years old then," Tom said, going a bit pale under his tan as if he'd just heard a prophecy for the end of the world. He didn't even ask who won the war.

"Will we have to fight?" Huck asked. "I don't have no grudges agin nobody."

Zane took a deep breath. "I'll likely be back in my own time by then, but if I'm still here, I think we should all head west to the Territory or California or somers and leave the fightin' to all those other fools."

"Good idea," Tom said. "Having adventures in Injun Territory or in the goldfields sounds a lot more fun than shooting people I ain't mad at jest because some general says to. Ain't no sense in that." He snorted disgustedly. "And why stop having adventures after you pass twenty? Some folks start to act all solemn and long-faced when they get growed up. Not me," he told Zane. "And I hope you *are* still here when we all get older," he added.

"Not sure I'll have any say about that," Zane said. "Providence will likely take a hand 'twixt now and then." The longer he was here, the more he tended to fall into the local idiom and way of thinking.

The Odd Fellows band struck up a lively air, and drowned all conversation. A crowd had migrated up around the bandstand that had been constructed of raw pine boards for the earlier July 4th festivities.

From under his straw hat brim, Zane noted there seemed to be a bigger crowd than he'd ever imagined lived in the little village of St. Petersburg. But then, seeing the wagons and teams parked under the trees on the outskirts of the big field, he realized it wasn't only the villagers—it was country folk from the outlying parts of the county who'd been invited to the celebration. He was surprised when he reflected that, apparently, he, himself, looked enough like one of these young people with his new wire-rimmed glasses, straw hat, collarless shirt, canvas pants, and hair curling over his ears to pass for a local boy.

On the far edge of the field, away from the bandstand, several younger boys were rolling their hoops; three were tossing a ball around; and two were wrestling, rolling in the dust.

Twenty minutes later, when the sweating band members took a break and made a dash for several mugs of foamy beer waiting on a nearby table, Zane, Tom, and Huck wandered off to get out of the hot sun, standing with large mugs of cold lemonade beneath some trees. Horses that had been unhitched from buckboards and carriages were hobbled and grazing in the luxuriant grass, muscles rippling and tails swishing at biting flies.

Midday heat waves rolled upward, turning the distant crowd and the tables of food under a tent into wavering images as if they were being seen underwater. Zane had an instinctive longing for the comfort of his air-conditioned house in the 21st century.

But then he shrugged off this moment of weakness and looked around to make sure they were alone. "Any reaction since you posted that article about Bigfoot?" he asked.

"Yeah, it ain't been up but three days, and the news was all over town by yesterday," Tom said, hunkering down next to the trunk of a big oak tree. "Aunt Polly's in a lather about it. Missus Harper come to the house and told her and they both walked down to the post office and took a look so Aunt Polly could see for herself. I hate that she's upset, but there ain't nothing I can do about that without I give away the whole scheme."

"The widow, she's been mighty busy with this picnic and all," Huck said, "but I heard her a'talkin' to Judge Thatcher about that notice this morning."

"What'd he say?" Zane asked.

"He kinder made light of it, saying he reckoned it was nothing but a prank. But he mighta been trying to put a cushion under her feelings and not give her no cause for worry. The judge, he's good about that."

"They'll think 'prank' once we come back with the proof," Tom snorted.

"But that ain't the general notion," Huck continued. "Word has spread like a brush fire in an uphill breeze and got to the widow's place. The slaves reckon it's witches done it."

"Really?"

"Yup."

"What do they think witches got to do with it?" Zane wondered.

"Some o'them argue that witches ain't all bad, that some are good and don't mean no harm. They's the ones—the good witches—that posted that note Tom wrote to warn everybody about hairy bloodthirsty giants spreadin' up the river."

"If you watch this crowd close," Tom said, "you'll see little clumps o'men putting their heads together and talking soft-like. And they ain't joking and laughing. You can bet it's sumpin' serious."

"I wisht I knowed what they was saying." Huck looked grim. "This kinda muttering around gives me all over shivers—like jumping spiders in the outhouse. Puts me in mind o'when the king and duke threw that royal nonesuch down in Arkansas. Them locals tried to let on warn't nothing amiss, but they went to whispering around, planning to come for us the third night o'the show. We scraped outa there jest ahead of a horsewhipping—or worse. You reckon all the big men in this town know what we're about and is jest laying low, waiting to pounce on us?"

Tom seemed to take this in and didn't reply for nearly half a minute. "I reckon not," he said slowly without much conviction. "Anyways, we can't quit now. We got to buck up and brave it through like we ain't noticed nothing unusual. If we was to go looking guilty, they'd suspicion sumpin' for sure."

Zane tipped up the mug and drained his lemonade.

"Now we know the word is out, and lots o'folks is in a sweat," Tom said. "So tomorrow, when all this celebrating is over, will be the right time for us to announce we're going downriver for a day or three a'camping and fishing. We got those printing blocks all carved and ready to go. Is Jim ready?"

"He still ain't much for the idea," Huck said. "But I reckon he'll do it 'cause we asked him to."

"What about the widow? Will she let him off work?"

"Yeah. He told her we was going on a fishing trip soon and wanted a grownup handy for protection jest in case. Well, the widow, she was all a'flutter about this picnic, and not paying much attention, but give him leave to go. Since he proved his-self when he was along on that adventure earlier this summer, she knows Jim can be trusted and ain't likely to do nothing foolish."

"Then that's about it, except for the guns," Tom said.

"What guns?" Huck asked.

Tom looked exasperated. "Huck Finn, you don't suppose anybody will believe we fought off a big, hairy, bloodthirsty giant if we didn't have no guns, do you?"

"I never thought o'that."

"You're a featherhead and no mistake," Tom said. "You don't think of much o'nothing."

Apparently Huck knew his friend, and didn't seem to mind being referred to as dim-witted and forgetful.

"We *got to* latch onto at least a couple o'guns, and right soon, too."

"Why do you need guns, Tom Sawyer?" a breezy, feminine voice inquired.

Startled, they all jumped when Becky Thatcher, sipping a lemonade, strolled into view from behind a parked carriage.

CHAPTER 5

A chill swept up Zane's back at the girl's appearance. Tom and Huck looked equally stunned.

"Wha . . . What're *you* doing here?" Tom stammered, seeming to recover from the shock.

"You said you needed guns. You going hunting or something?" She took a sip from the mug, which was wet with condensation.

How much had she overheard? Zane tried to read it in her face, but Becky's blue eyes were guileless and inquiring.

"Uh . . . yeah, that's it. We're planning a hunting and fishing trip downriver," Tom said, seizing on her guess.

"This time o'year isn't too good for duck hunting," she went on. "It's better in the fall when they fly south and there are flocks of them along the river."

"Well, we're going *now*," Tom said with finality.

"What in the world happened to your hands?" she frowned as Tom wiped his damp palms on his shirttail. "You put them in a meat grinder or something? They're swollen and all over blisters—the lot of you," she added, glancing at Zane's and Huck's as well.

Tom shoved his hands into his pockets. "We been chopping wood and wasn't wearing no gloves."

Only partially true, Zane thought. Carving the wooden blocks had been tougher than he expected.

She shrugged, continuing to nurse her lemonade. Zane noted she looked fresh and cool in a starched white, pleated frock that reached nearly to her shoe tops. He couldn't help but think how girls of his own time would be dressed at a July picnic—probably shorts and sandals and a light blouse or tank top.

There was an awkward silence for several seconds. Tom appeared to be searching for something to say. Huck seemed tongue-tied. She had interrupted their secret planning, but if she was aware of it, gave no indication. She flowed over to a parked buckboard and seated herself on the sloping wagon tongue.

"You boys going in a'swimming after a while?"

"We hadn't thought about it," Tom said, lamely.

"When is dinner?" Huck asked.

"Why, I reckon you can eat anytime you want to," Becky said. "There ain't no sit-down formal dinner. All the ham and vegetables and fixin's are laid out over yonder under the tent so folks can help themselves."

"Yeah, I guess we'll go eat then," Tom said, taking a step away from the tree. "And you know it ain't a good idea to go in a'swimming on a full stomach." Over his shoulder he said, "By the way, where's Amy Lawrence and Susie Bradford and your other girlfriends? Ain't none o'them here today?"

"You're not getting rid of me that easily, Tom Sawyer." She narrowed her eyes and looked at him. Then her gaze bored into Huck and Zane. "You boys ain't fooling me. You got something going, and I want to know what it is."

"It's just boy stuff—nothing you'd be interested in," Tom said.

"Tom Sawyer, you know that ain't true, or you wouldn't of been acting so guilty when I come up."

Silence.

"You recollect all the things Jim and Zane and I did last month to rescue you from those kidnappers, Smealey and Weir?" she reminded him. "If it hadn't been for me insisting we come after those no-accounts who had you in chains, you and Huck might be dead now. Zane and Jim were all for giving up and coming back home."

Zane realized she was telling the truth. She had nearly thrown a fit until they agreed to continue the pursuit—even when hope seemed lost.

Tom stopped and moved back into the shade. Becky had risen from her seat on the wagon tongue.

"I can't tell you, Becky," he said. "It's a secret, and it ain't only *my* secret. It involves lots of others."

"I can't wait to hear it," she enthused, as if she hadn't heard him correctly.

"I'm sorry, but you'll find out soon enough, I reckon."

The corners of her pretty mouth turned down. "How do you know I can't keep a secret, too?" she pouted.

"This don't concern you," Tom tried again. "Besides, girls can't keep secrets. They blab everything they hear."

"Cross my heart and hope to die if I ever tell," she said.

Tom shook his head.

"Then I guess I'll have to tell my father that you boys are up to some mischief and planning to stir up lots of trouble like you always do. Then he'll likely warn Sheriff Stiles to keep an eye on you."

Tom blanched at this threat. "We've gone to a lot of work to get this jest right, so we'll be heroes," he said. "Don't you want to see us become heroes again and be proud of me?"

"I don't want to see you get yourself hurt, and it must be pretty bad if you're talking about getting guns and you can't even give me a little hint of what you're up to."

Tom heaved a deep sigh, blowing out his breath as if he were a balloon deflating. He looked at Huck and Zane. "What about it?"

"Well, she *did* help save us from that torture," Huck admitted.

Zane nodded.

Tom said, "All right, Becky, we'll tell you. But you got to swear a blood oath not to mention this to a soul." He pulled out his Barlow knife and opened its single blade. "Gimme your hand."

"You ain't going to cut me with that dirty knife," she said, pulling back.

"How else you gonna sign a blood oath?" He licked the knife blade. "There, now; it's clean."

"You'll just have to take my word for it."

"Well, all right then. Repeat after me: 'I swear by all that's holy that I will keep mum about what Tom Sawyer is gonna tell me. If I should ever break this oath, may I drop down dead in my tracks and rot.' "

"That's the silliest thing I ever heard. You sound like a little kid playing games," she said. "I promise not to reveal to anyone what you are about to say. There. That should be good enough."

"Well, all right." He briefly told her the story of their conspiracy.

Her eyes went wide as he revealed their plans. "So it was *you* who posted that newspaper clipping by the post office, and wrote that note."

He nodded.

"I might've known," she said. "So that's why you need guns."

"Yeah."

"You talking about muskets or pistols?"

"We druther have pistols. Me and Huck have enough money to buy'em, but we don't want nobody to know."

"Hmm . . . Not likely Mister Phelps at the hardware would sell them to you, anyway," she said. "You might be able to buy some powder and caps, though, if he thought you were going duck hunting."

"Maybe we could get some grownup to buy that stuff for us," Tom said. "We'll need some bullets, too, or a bullet mold to make our own. I got some scrap lead a few days ago," he added, not mentioning the source of that.

"You know," Becky said, reflectively, "that's a mighty big lie you'll be telling the village. There's a commandment against lying."

"This ain't nuthin' but a stretcher for fun."

"Call it what you will, it's still a lie. Some poor old soul could get so scared and worked up he might die of fright or apoplexy. And all because of you boys."

"As I recollect my Sunday school lesson, Becky, the Bible don't say nuthin' about stretchers. It jest says you can't bear no false witness against your neighbor. And we won't be doing nuthin' like that. This is only a giant stretcher. Or, you might say a stretcher about giants." He grinned. "So, there!"

That seemed to settle her qualms. She turned away and put a hand to her mouth as if in deep thought. Directly, she turned back and said, "I got a proposition for you . . . If you let me come along on this adventure, I think I can find you two or maybe three pistols without any cost."

"Thanks, Becky. But you can see for yourself this is too dangersome."

"What are you talking about? I'd only be taking a boat ride down the river in that yawl, staying a night or two on an island, and coming back after we make it look like you had a big fight with a monster. How dangerous could that be?" she scoffed. "You forget that I was a prisoner of kidnappers for almost a week last month. And that was for real—not make-believe like this will be."

Zane thought she had a point, but then another problem occurred to him. "Your father, the judge, would never let you go with us," he said. "I'll bet he hasn't let you out of his sight since we got back from that adventure. It's a natural thing. He doesn't want to risk losing you again."

"Well, his being close by won't prevent something bad from happening," she said. "If you recollect, those kidnappers came up with guns and took me right from the buggy with him sitting next to me. So, I reckon if Providence isn't going to protect me, my father can't either."

"I mean he cares so much about you, he won't take any chances on you being hurt by coming along on this trip with us," Zane said. "Besides, a pretty girl like you spending two or three days with three boys and a black man? Even in my other world, a girl's father wouldn't let that happen. It's not proper, and would cause scandal and gossip even if you didn't do anything wrong."

She considered this for a moment. "Well, I don't care nothing about that. My reputation is not soiled. If folks are going to talk, there's nothing I can really do to prevent it. They would've already done their worst when I was the prisoner of those two kidnappers for a week. Some folks will always believe the worst about a person, no matter what, so that makes no difference to me. I can't let my life be ruled by old biddies who have nothing better to do than try to tear down a girl's good name."

Her face was flushing at the very idea.

"But I think I can persuade my father to come around to the idea," she continued. "He knows I'm more adventurous than most girls. And he knows from what's happened this summer that I'm tough and can take it without cracking. And it would be a bonus for your plan if my father *does* let me go. Because when we all come back and give this story about the giant hairy creature, there ain't as much likelihood folks would suspect you of a conspiracy if they see a girl was along on the trip."

"You got a mighty high opinion of yourself," Tom sniffed.

"I haven't been in as much trouble as you and Huck," she said.

Zane thought she was probably right, but ventured no comment.

"I still ain't sure it's a good idea for you to be part of this," Tom said. "If we was caught, we'd all be in trouble. And your father would blame us for mixing you up in it."

"Well, let me put it to you this way, mister Tom Sawyer—I was never much for playing with dolls or having pretend tea parties when I was a little girl. I have no intention of spending the rest of my growin'-up time being treated like a flowering potted plant that has to be watered and brought indoors when the sun is too hot."

Zane couldn't quite reconcile this tough talk as coming from a petite, blue-eyed blond girl who appeared delicate and charming in her starched white frock. But then he recalled the grit and determination he'd seen from her last month, and realized looks could be deceiving.

"Okay, Becky, then that's the way it'll be. If you can get permission to come along, you're welcome," Tom agreed. "All right with you two?" He glanced at Zane and Huck.

"Fine with me," Zane said.

Huck nodded. "But Jim ain't here to vote. I hope he don't mind."

"He won't."

"You just swore an oath to keep this secret," Tom said. "How you gonna talk your father into letting you come along if you don't tell him where you're going?"

"Silly, I won't mention the conspiracy—just that I'm going on a fishing trip with the three of you, with Jim along for protection from any hazards we might run into." She smiled. "How would I ever know that we could run into a giant monster on that island?"

"You said you could find us some guns," Tom reminded her.

"Oh, yes. Well, my father, being a judge and all, has confiscated weapons from criminals over the years. He probably has half a dozen stashed in a box collecting dust up in the garret. He'll never miss them if I borrow two or three."

"Good. See if you can find three in decent shape—not rusty or locked up, or nothing. Same size, if possible, but that's asking a lot," Tom said. "I'll see about buying some balls and caps. Easier than trying to melt the lead and mold the bullets. Won't take so much time, neither." He thought a moment, then turned to Huck. "Can Jim lay his hands on that little pocket pistol of the widow's he brought with him last month?"

Huck nodded. "If he don't have a chance to slip it outa the sideboard with that servant gal a'watching, then I will. It was all oiled up and in working order when he put it back there a few weeks ago."

"Does Jim still have that powder, shot, and caps me and Becky bought in St. Charles?" Zane asked.

Huck nodded. "He stuck it in a canvas sack and buried it in the barn loft hay to keep the powder dry. I don't reckon any mice been gnawing on it, or they'd have a real bellyache by now."

Zane had been reviewing the details of their mission in his mind, and thought of something that was critical. "Do you know the river well enough to be able to pick out this particular island fifty miles downstream?"

Tom hesitated before he answered, and Zane felt a quiver in his stomach. Tom wouldn't be above bluffing some answer and brag that he knew the exact location of Westport Island.

"Yeah, I can find it," Tom said.

Tom was the natural leader of this group. The conspiracy was his idea and he had planned it out. But he was bad about overlooking details.

"That ain't good enough for me," Zane said. "I mean do you have a chart with markings on it and labels of islands and towns and plantations, and so forth? We can't be foolin' around and guessing. As you know, most of those islands look pretty much alike, especially from a small boat. We need to be sure. It's not going to have a sign posted on the upstream side that says, in big letters, WESTPORT ISLAND."

Tom's face reddened, but Zane didn't care. This was one detail that had to be correct.

"I guess in a pinch we could use some other island if we was to miss it," Tom said lamely.

"No," Huck said. "I'll go along with 'most any plans you make. But when we come back here to the village and say we fought off a Bigfoot giant hairy monster, we gotta be able to tell the grownups *exactly* which island it is, 'cause they're sure to send somebody down there to look. And we want'em to be able to find the footprints and our old campfire and maybe some blood to make our story seem real."

"Ain't no river charts that're just right with all the markings," Tom said in his own defense. "The river's a'changing all the time when the level goes up or down a few feet. Nobody can get a handle on it for very long. That river is mostly in the heads of the pilots."

"Maybe so," Huck said, "but the big islands don't change shape much, 'less'an it's over a lot o'years."

"All right, then, here's how we'll do it," Tom said. "The map I got from the general store has the distances marked on it, and the main islands. We know about how fast the current's runnin', and we can estimate how fast we're rowing or sailing. When we figure to be close, we'll pull in to one o'them little one-horse towns and ask. They kin point us right. We'll poke around and find that little sliver of Kickapoo Island in the chute and we'll know it's the right place. And once we find it, we can go right to it again if we've a need to."

That seemed agreeable to everyone.

"Becky, if you'll slide those pistols outa your garret, we'll ask Jim to bring the powder and caps for 'em. In the next day or two, we'll collect the rest of our gear and lay in some supplies for cooking and fishing and bring the carved blocks and stow everything in our yawl. Probably need at least a couple o' three days to let our hands heal."

Becky nodded. "I think my father will let me go. He knows I'd be in good hands."

"We'll leave that to you to manage," Tom said.

"What I'll do first is this," she said, apparently enthused about some new plan. "Since we were on our way to visit my cousins down at Marsville when those kidnappers snagged me, I'll ask him if I can take my pony and ride down there now for a visit. He don't much like me riding astride 'cause he says it's not ladylike. And he sure doesn't want me to go nearly thirty miles down that river road alone. So he'll either have to escort me—and he was saying the other day how busy he was in court—or I'll tell him I have an offer to go exploring and fishing with the bunch of you. I think, if that's his choice, he'll either make me stay home, or let me go with you." She smiled. "There's safety in numbers."

Zane silently marveled at this blond bundle of deviousness. He wondered how many great events in human history had been determined by just such manipulative measures.

CHAPTER 6

"Oowww! That hurts!"

"Quit being such a baby and gimme your other hand," Tom said, grabbing Huck's arm.

"What is that stuff, anyway?"

"Says here on the label, *Tincture of Benzoin*," Zane said, reading off the brown quart bottle. "Hey! I know this stuff. We still use it in my day, but we call it 'tough skin.' We paint it on our feet to prevent blisters when we're playing soccer."

"Really?"

"Yeah. It leaves a brown layer on the skin that won't wash off. Sticks our cotton socks to our feet so they don't slide around when we get sweaty and rub the skin. Have to wear a pair of old socks, though, 'cause it won't wash out. We generally wear two pair o'socks."

"It's good for healing blistered hands and for toughening up the skin," Tom said. He had purloined the bottle from his Aunt Polly's store of patent medicines and cure-alls she kept in a special place in her kitchen cabinet. The boys had retreated behind the back garden to administer the treatment.

"Good for other stuff, too," Tom said. "Doctor Weatherby left it at the house when he come last winter to dose me for the croup. Had Aunt Polly mix it with water and boil it up to make steam and I breathed it to break up that crud in my chest."

"Yeah, it wears off after a few days, but it makes the skin dark brown," Zane said, sniffing its pungent, but pleasant aroma.

66

"Maybe I should take a bath in it," Tom said, using a small paintbrush to dab Huck's other hand. "Then I could look like an Injun the rest o'the summer."

"Probably not the best idea," Zane said. "Might clog your pores and you couldn't sweat."

"Why would you want to look like an Injun, anyways?" Huck asked.

"Well, if we ever get back out to Injun Territory, I could wear me some buckskins and moccasins and blend right in with them Sioux."

"If you paint this stuff on the bottoms of your feet, you wouldn't even need no moccasins," Huck said.

"I reckon not. My feet're tough already from going barefoot so much."

"Jim sure wouldn't need none of this, either," Huck said. "His feet has some mighty thick skin. If it warn't for the cold, he wouldn't even need shoes in the wintertime."

"I'll slather a couple layers o'this on my own feet," Zane said. "They're pretty tender. Can you pour some o'that in another little bottle to take along with us?"

"Sure. Aunt Polly never uses this. She'll never miss it."

Zane grimaced at the stinging when Tom treated his sore hands.

After the boys had liberally dosed their hands and feet, Tom poured a portion into a smaller bottle, stoppered it with a cork, and added it to their supplies. They went off feeling much better for their self-medication.

Sheriff Rueben Stiles was in a quandary. But he had an idea that might provide a way out.

He had held the office of Marion County sheriff for twelve years, and was greatly hoping he could hold it for at least one more four-year term before he retired to his house to putter about on his tiny farm and fish with his grandchildren for the remainder of his days. He was fifty-six years old and reasonably hearty, eager for another term in office.

But he had become aware of the rumblings and mutterings of a not-entirely-satisfied public. The kidnapping episode in June and subsequent events had played out mostly beyond his control. The kidnappers, based on the testimony of an experienced frontiersman and guide, and several local young people from St. Petersburg, had apparently perished in a tornado on the plains in Indian Territory. But nobody was sure, since the two men had vanished.

Most of the events surrounding the kidnapping had happened outside his county jurisdiction. But nevertheless, the public blamed him for being ineffective in even identifying the culprits, though one of them, Chigger Smealey, was a local man who'd been in trouble of one kind or another for years and was known to law enforcement along the river.

He got up from his desk and walked to the window to get better light on the two wanted posters. One had a crude drawing of both Smealey and Weir, the kidnappers, and was a new broadside. The other one depicted a heavily bearded man who was identified as Bit Barjee. Both posters had arrived in the morning mail at his office in Palmyra, delivered on a boat yesterday from St. Louis.

It wasn't unusual for Stiles to receive numerous fresh wanted notices each week. What caught his attention this time was the fact that apparently Smealey and Weir had survived their brush with the Sioux and the storm in Indian Territory, and were now wanted, along with this Barjee, as suspects in the killing of a United States Senator, Cyrus Shirten, at Fort Kearny in Indian Territory.

And, further, all three men had fled the fort, going east toward Missouri. Were they in cahoots? Stiles couldn't imagine the two kidnappers resorting to murder in any situation. He had them pegged only as thieves, robbers, and extortionists. And who was this Barjee?

But whatever their connection, it provided Stiles with an opportunity to put himself back into the public eye as a favorite in the upcoming sheriff's race. Even though it was out of his jurisdiction, the rewards were open to anyone, even freelancing bounty hunters. Stiles decided he'd take a steamboat downriver, start at St. Louis, and do a little snooping around. Barjee had been spotted riding the senator's horse near Jefferson City, in the middle of the state, so, apparently, was headed east. And a man who looked like Smealey had been seen, now wearing a full beard, on a southbound Missouri River packet. But, by now, these men could be anywhere. If Stiles could get a lead on any of these three fugitives it would be a feather in his hat. An arrest would mean reward money along with a big boost in his reputation as an effective, tough lawman, and would likely ensure his re-election.

Mind made up, he set about planning his trip. A week or ten days should be enough. If he'd come across no clues in that length of time, he'd come back.

He considered taking along his deputy, Jarvis McKee, but decided against it. He had to leave one man behind to look after things at the office and deal with any problems that might arise in his absence.

The poster on Barjee said that a reward of $800 would be paid by the federal government for his capture so the government officials were pretty sure the man had been in on the murder. Weir and Smealey were already wanted as kidnappers in addition to being suspects in this more serious crime, so the state of Missouri was offering a reward of $600 for the apprehension of either man. Stiles knew what Smealey looked like, and had a fair idea about Weir, and now Barjee.

He would confide in his close friend, Judge Thatcher, about his lone mission. Perhaps he would have a few helpful suggestions.

He carefully folded both posters and tucked them into his hip pocket. It was nearly noon of a bright, cloudless day. He got up, took his broad hat from a hook near his desk, put it on, and went outside. He'd walk home for lunch, tell his wife where he was going, and pack a small grip. The next boat south would leave at ten the next morning.

CHAPTER 7

Like many river cities of its size, St. Louis harbored an active black market for moving stolen goods. An unusually large amount of purloined merchandise, much of it from the cargoes of steamboats, found its way into the underground trade—casks of whiskey, boxes of tools, cases of leather boots, dishes, livestock, boxes of dried and pickled foodstuffs, kegs of beer, barrels of flour, molasses, and nearly anything portable. About the only thing left alone were the huge, heavy bales of cotton.

Roustabouts and deckhands were constantly lightening the cargoes of docked vessels to enrich themselves, their kin, and various thieves in the inner city. Some of it included the jewelry of passengers stolen by the cabin maids. Much of the thievery was accomplished with the connivance of mates and night watchmen.

Knowing such a trade existed and putting a stop to it were two different things—especially when many of the policemen were taking payoffs. The only ones who ultimately suffered were the companies who had insured the cargoes, and the boats' captains who were responsible.

It was into this underworld of illegal commerce that Bit Barjee managed to insert himself after several days of hiding out at a cheap waterfront hotel, spending hours sipping beer in various saloons near the river, dropping oblique hints to strangers and bartenders. It was a closed society at first, and he found no admittance.

But, given an opening, he let it be known, that he had a beautiful blooded horse for sale. This casual comment brought a flicker of interest from a bewhiskered drunk with tattoos on both forearms of corded muscle—a fouled anchor on one and a bloody dirk on the other. Possibly a former deepwater sailor?

"Aye, I've run aground here," the man said to Barjee's query, pouring the last of an amber liquid into his glass. The two-week growth of beard, the veined nose, and the weathered lines etched into his cheeks and forehead gave him the look of a sixty-year-old—all contrasted with the bright blue eyes, the whites of which were now bloodshot and bleary. The look of a sixty-year-old impressed on the face of a man probably not over forty-five.

After a short discussion, the man who didn't give his name said, "Bring your animal into the alley behind this saloon at midnight." He glanced about to be sure no one was within earshot. "If he's half as good as you say, I might know a man who'll take him off your hands for a fair price."

Barjee nodded.

"There's always a market for good horseflesh. But keep your head about you and your gun loose in the holster. This waterfront is worse than most seaports—crawlin' with scum who'll stave in your skull with a marlinspike for your watch fob."

"No saddle. It's just the horse," Barjee said, thinking how that the Grimsley saddle with the senator's initials could be recognized.

"Agreed."

"I'll see you at midnight, sharp."

"I'll need a little something to grease the deal." He held up the empty bottle.

Barjee signaled the bartender and indicated a full replacement, placing a coin on the table in payment as he got up. A bottle of decent whiskey would be little enough if it could close the deal for a stolen horse he'd had stabled at a nearby livery for several days. He'd be relieved to have the horse off his hands and be on his way.

While crossing the dense Missouri backwoods, and long before reaching St. Louis, Barjee had taken the precaution of altering the brand on the late senator's horse. It took only a campfire, and one of the spare iron horseshoes from the saddlebags to burn a couple of extra curves into the CS (Cyrus Shirten) brand, forming an O8—a fictitious, unregistered mark that nobody could trace. The horse itself, a bay mare, had no distinctive markings or colorations that would distinguish it at a glance.

The old seaman was apparently the intermediary on the sale. Barjee never saw the buyer. That night, as instructed, he brought the horse to an alley behind a row of waterfront saloons and turned it over to the bewhiskered sailor, receiving a small bag of gold coins. Barjee had no opportunity to negotiate a price. But, having considerable experience estimating the weight of gold from his mining days, he glanced inside the drawstring bag, hefted it, and felt more than satisfied with the amount.

As the sailor was leading the horse away, Barjee had a thought. "You know where a man could find himself a big, sturdy canoe?"

The bewhiskered one paused. "Got just the vessel for you."

"Where is it? Can I buy it and get it now?"

"In a rush are ye?"

"Time is money."

"Stay right here and I'll be back in thirty minutes." Then the nameless one led the horse down between two buildings and vanished.

Barjee nervously faded into the blackest shadows and stood quietly, all senses alert. He drew his pistol and held it by his side. This would be a perfect setup for murder and robbery—a strange city, a dark alley, an illegal sale for a bag of gold. Someone could weight his body with rocks and dump it into the river. No one would ever know what happened to him. Not that anyone cared or would go looking.

Yes, he *was* in a hurry. He'd been scanning the newspapers in the ten days he'd been here, and the murder of the senator had been front page news at least twice. The article said three people were being sought in connection with the shooting at Fort Kearny. He didn't really understand that, but the other two named were men he didn't know. He vaguely recalled hearing the names of Smealey and Weir. Were they at the fort at the same time he was? He tried to place them, but the drawings in the paper didn't look like anyone he'd seen before.

But his urge to vanish was really spurred when a drawing of himself in a full beard appeared in that morning's newspaper. It didn't resemble him, except in his own imagination. Was it conscience or the fear of being caught, tried, and hanged that had killed his appetite and set his nerves on edge? The newspapers said that authorities speculated the killer would try to leave the country by way of New Orleans. The thought of hiding out on a Caribbean island *had* actually been one of the places Barjee was considering, but the law had anticipated that move. Now what? He couldn't return to Cincinnati where he'd come from. That was the first place they'd look.

As he stood in the dark alley, eyes and ears alert, he went over past events again. He'd left his own dun and worn saddle behind. Maybe he should have taken the animal as a spare. But then he would not have made such good time. He had really only been protecting himself while he tried to get his own gold back, he reasoned. When the senator saw Barjee blocking his way, Shirten had yanked a pocket pistol and both of them had fired at nearly the same time. The senator's shot went wild.

If Barjee gave himself up and went to trial, could he testify that he was only defending himself? There were no witnesses and the senator was dead. So the jury would have to take his word for what happened. No. It was too risky. Senator Shirten was an important man. Barjee was nobody, and had run, stealing the senator's horse. If any of the other four men in that card game could be found to testify, they'd say that Barjee was drinking and was a heavy loser, and left the table angry. All those things would work against him as a motive for murder. He'd be convicted for certain. Even if he got off with manslaughter, he'd be guilty of horse stealing, a hanging offense in itself.

The minutes dragged, but he didn't step out into the moonlight to look at his watch. The old sailor would either return, or he wouldn't.

It seemed nearly an hour had dragged by when he heard an unsteady gait scuffing along the cobblestones. It was the old man.

Barjee stepped into view from the shadows, holding his cocked revolver beside his leg.

"This way," the bearded man said, not slacking his pace.

Barjee followed him. Three blocks later, they came in sight of the waterfront and the dimmed lanterns of a long row of docked steamboats, crowded guard to guard, bows tied off to cleats and posts near the sloping landing.

The old man walked another half-mile north, past Barjee's hotel, until the number of vessels began to thin out.

The old man stopped. "There ya go, m'lad."

Barjee could barely make out the outline of a canoe, painter secured to a jutting post.

A low growl followed by two sharp barks sounded from the nearby dark. Barjee jumped back, hair rising on his neck.

"What's this? A guard dog?"

"Yeah. He belonged to the former owner who met with an unfortunate accident. He goes with the canoe—as fine a vessel as ye could ask for. Even has an extra paddle."

The double-ended canoe looked to be about eighteen feet long.

"Does it leak?"

"Absolutely not. Cedar planked, caulked tight, and all varnished, inside and out. Not over a year old, and seaworthy as can be."

"How much?"

"I'll be askin' eighty dollars for her."

"And I'd be sayin' that's robbery."

"Then I guess you'll be finding your own canoe."

Barjee knew he was stuck. He hesitated.

"That dog'll cotton to ya after a bit," the old sailor said. "Fine animal but no place for him on this levee. He needs to be out in the wild where he can chase squirrels and ducks and such."

"What kind is he?" Barjee could barely see a vague figure crouching by the bow of the canoe.

"Not sure. Looks to be a mix. Maybe border collie and some kinda spaniel? Don't know."

Barjee said nothing.

"Well, is it a deal? I ain't got all night."

"Yeah." He fished in the bag of coins and brought out three double eagles and two eagles and handed them over.

"Obliged," the old man said. *"Bon voyage."* Drifting away, he began to softly sing some rhythmic ditty. Barjee thought it sounded like one of the sea chanties his long-dead grandfather used to roar out when he was in his cups. It was a long drag sea chantey, and had something to do with whiskey. He couldn't recall the name of it. The singsong chantey slowly faded into the night along the waterfront. Barjee gave an involuntary shudder. He hadn't heard that chantey since he was a small child. It brought up a spectral image of his grandfather, an old Britisher, drunk on rum, sitting in a chimney corner on winter evenings, pounding the arm of his chair to the beat of the sea chanties of his youth.

Would strong drink eventually send him on the long slide to ruin as it had this sailor and his own grandfather? It had already made him lose control and kill the senator.

He shook off these morbid thoughts as he walked back to his hotel and retrieved his saddlebags containing sacks of gold coins and a few personal items. The decorated Grimsley saddle he'd have to dispose of somewhere later.

He'd already paid in advance through tonight, so ignored the night clerk asleep in a chair at the front desk. For the confusion of anyone on his trail, Barjee had registered under the name Sidney Holdstrom.

Striding back to the canoe with his heavy saddlebags over one shoulder, and the saddle over the other, he hoped when daylight came no one recognized the boat and the dog as belonging to some recently murdered owner. He had enough problems already.

He squatted by the canoe. "C'mere, boy." He wished he'd asked if the old man knew the dog's name. "C'mon. I won't hurt ya." There was no growling now. But with a strange dog, he was taking his chances. Most dogs barked to give warning. Generally, a growl preceded an attack. But he'd always had a good rapport with animals and continued squatting and talking in a soothing voice. After a couple of minutes, the black and white dog came out of the deep shadow and sniffed his hand, his tail wagging tentatively. He looked to be about thirty pounds with medium length fur and the ears of a spaniel. Barjee sensed he'd gained the animal's confidence and, if he proceeded cautiously, everything would be all right.

He set his duffle in the canoe slowly so as not to startle the wary animal, then reached into the saddlebags for a piece of beef jerky as an enticement.

"C'mon, boy," he said, putting a foot over the gunwale. "Looks like we're in this together. Jump in. We have to make a few miles upstream before daylight."

CHAPTER 8

"I'm jumping ship here," Chigger Smealey said, ripping down the wanted poster from the outside wall of a chandlery shop near the St. Charles waterfront.

He and his partner, Gus Weir, stepped into the shade of a covered boardwalk. "It's time we split up. It 'pears the law is still looking for two men traveling together. And we're about the right age and size, even though I have a beard now and your mustache is shaved off."

Weir stared at the poster that displayed their likenesses. "Ain't too flattering, is it? They got my nose all wrong. It's too big."

"This ain't no laughing matter," Smealey said, glancing back toward the waterfront where their steamer, *Jezebel,* lay docked for the next hour. "This here is the poster from that kidnapping. They ain't had time to print and distribute a broadside about the murder we saw at the fort. Since we stole two mules and disappeared at the same time, you know they'll be looking for us for that, too."

"Yeah . . . I guess it's time to untangle our trails. I ain't used to being a fugitive, and it's hard to think like one. You plan to collect your pay, I guess."

"No. I'm sure that young purser recognized me," Smealey said.

"Really?"

"Yeah. Can't think of his name. He's the same one who was working the boat on our way out and has probably reported me to the captain by now. The two of them would love to split the reward for my capture—and yours."

"You sure it's the same purser? It ain't the same boat."

"Positive, 'cause he was making eyes at Judge Thatcher's daughter."

"Oh."

"If I was to draw my time from the mate, he and the cap'n would likely have the law on me like a cat on a June bug," Smealey said. "There's a police station only a few blocks from here. As it is, if the mate don't miss me for a couple hours, he's bound to think I'm still aboard on down to St. Louis. When we dock there tomorrow, the mate and the captain can snatch me unawares and get the reward. If I slip away now, maybe I kin get me a few hours head start upriver, or somers before I'm missed."

"Well, considering how far we've fallen in the world of commerce, I don't reckon it really matters whether you draw your pay or not, 'cause it won't amount to much," Weir said. "You and I are on the low end of the scale—bottom-feeders you might say."

"Yeah," Smealey replied, folding up the wanted poster and stuffing it into the back pocket of his pants. "And to think we each had six thousand dollars in gold hardly more than a month ago."

They were silent with their thoughts for a minute.

"Guess I'll go get me a drink afore I light out."

"If you want to get a jump on a clean getaway, I wouldn't advise that," Weir said. "Likely you'd wind up drunk and broke and be here all night. Of course, you're a grown man so I can't tell you what to do."

More silence.

"Just dumb luck we got caught by that Sioux war party," Smealey lamented. "Otherwise we'd be long gone with all that gold in our saddlebags." He paused. "But I don't seem to have no luck a'tall. First I lose the whole shebang to a couple o'kids, and then we pull off a really slick scheme to get it back. Then those Injuns nail us, and the kids get it back again."

"Regrets ain't profitable," Weir said, with a dismissive shrug. "Besides, you gotta look at both sides o'that."

"Both sides o'what?"

"Religious folk who believe in the workings of Providence wouldn't call it dumb luck. They might say those kids cut us loose to keep the Sioux from roasting us alive, so they saved our lives and deserved to get the gold back."

"You siding with them, now?" Smealey was irritated. He was feeling relieved to be rid of this man who'd been his partner for several weeks.

"No. Just trying to see things from all angles." He paused and appeared to be squinting at something across the street. "Speaking of seeing things . . ." he said, stepping down off the boardwalk. He strode away, boots kicking up dust from the unpaved street. He stopped in front of a warped board fence festooned with nearly a dozen printed and handwritten notices and broadsides. Two loose ones were fluttering in the hot breeze. He ripped a poster down and Smealey joined him in the shade of a large cottonwood tree. "What's that?"

"That is my immediate future," he said, tilting the wanted poster in Smealey's direction. "I've made a decision to leave the boat, too. If that purser recognized you, he likely recognized me as well. And I ain't taking no chances on it by going back aboard that steamboat. Besides, I've nearly had my fill of being a deckhand under that mate."

At a glance Smealey saw it was only another reward poster for a runaway slave.

"You going back to your old job of chasing down runaways for reward?"

"Yeah," Weir said. "When a man gets in a bind it's always a safe bet he can fall back on the job he knows best." He paused to reread the print. "This will require a man with all my experience and skill," he said.

Smealey, looking over his shoulder, saw only the amount of the reward in large figures. "That's a mighty high dollar for snagging and returning one slave—$1500," he said.

"This ain't no runaway field hand," Weir said. "Hmmm . . . So Bull Brady has had the gumption to take to his heels. Wonder how he got away?"

"Who's Bull Brady?"

"Only the terror of the boxing ring—champion of Louisiana and all the bayou country, rough and tumble, or fists. He's worth a fortune to his owner as a prizefighter. Saw him fight by torchlight one night down in the stubble of a cane field. He demolished a big buck in about two minutes. Ain't nobody can stand up to him—white or black. He's a wonder. Mountain of a man. See here . . ." he pointed at the text of the poster. "He stands six-foot-eight, and weighs three-hundred twenty. And there ain't a pinch o'fat on him anywhere. Somewhere along the way, he was taught to box, which makes him a lot more dangerous. They shouldn't call him 'Bull.' He has the finesse and grace of a big cat. His owner earns piles o'money on him traveling around booking fights with other slaves—or white men or mixed bloods. He'll fight anyone. Generally, one o'them backwoods, fellas who thinks he's stronger than Paul Bunyan figures he'll get rich with one fight, but he usually winds up with broken bones and missing teeth—if he survives." He pointed at the poster. "This drawing doesn't do him justice. Wonder how he got away? Or why? His owner treated him like the meal ticket he was. I don't know of a prize racehorse that got any better care and treatment."

"Maybe that was the problem," Smealey said. "He was treated

like a prize animal, not a man."

"Never knew you was a nigger-lover."

"I ain't. I'm just trying to think like he might be thinking. He wasn't getting none of that money he won, even if he had fine quarters and plenty to eat and anything else he wanted. Even a slave don't run away if he's happy."

"That's a fact. I catch slaves for money. Now and then one o'them would be fearful of being whipped and worked 'most to death in the fields of a Deep South plantation. But, generally, they were depressed to be losing their freedom. Why do you think criminals are confined to prison as punishment? It's because freedom's the most precious thing a man can have. If you take that away, you take away his spirit, his soul, his future ambition."

"I thought you were wanting to get back to New Orleans."

"When we had all that gold, I did," Weir replied. "That way, down on the gulf, if the law should get back on my tail, I could always ship out of the country in jig time and be gone. But now that I'm close to being broke, I have to grab whatever opportunity presents itself. And this here is my opportunity."

Smealey looked again at the poster. He was glad he wasn't the one going after Bull Brady. "How do you plan on catching him? Looks like a pretty tall order."

"I'll figure it out. Right away I got a lead on where he might be. See here, it says he escaped off a steamboat when he and his owner and handlers were headed north toward a big fight in Davenport. Hmm . . . got away one dark night maybe forty miles north of here. Jumped overboard and swam for it."

"Are they sure he even got away? Has he been seen since? That stretch of river is pretty treacherous, especially at night," Smealey said, picturing in his mind's eye the tangle of islands, the chutes, and the current. "Lots o'times, big, muscle-bound men like that ain't the best swimmers."

"Well, if he didn't make it and drowned, I won't be losing anything but time," Weir said. "And I'll also be away from our steamboat, *Jezebel,* and that purser with the sharp eyes. I'll be making my own getaway. We won't be traveling together, but we'll both be headed in the same general direction. Where you going?"

"On up to Iowa or Minnesota for now 'til things cool down," Smealey said. "Could be on into the winter months before the hunt for us gets overrid by later cases. Then I might drift back down thisaway when the snow flies to see what chance might offer. I still ain't entirely giving up on laying m'hands on that gold those kids took. It was rightfully mine and Injun Joe's b'fore Joe died. Then it shoulda been mine. Then you and I slickered 'em out of it. But Fate took a hand and done us out of it again. There ain't no justice in this world that I can see."

"I'm of the opinion that a man makes his own Fate," Weir said.

"You know the law ain't gonna be hunting us too strong, anyways," Smealey went on, "because those kids got the gold back, and we didn't hurt 'em none. Everybody but us came out on top."

"Don't matter about the facts o'the case. Until that reward money is withdrawn, some bounty hunters will see those posters and commence t'turning over rocks looking for us so they can collect."

"Well, I ain't worried so much about the kidnapping part of it. What I don't want to happen is to get pulled in and questioned about that murder we saw, and if we get clear of that, *then* they nail us when they find out we're still wanted for kidnapping and extortion—besides stealing two mules and saddles."

"We better move outa sight until that boat pulls out," Weir said, carefully folding the wanted poster and sliding it inside his shirt. "Then I'll see can I buy me some shackles and a pistol before I start up the river hunting Bull Brady." He thrust out his hand. "I reckon this is where we split the way. Best to ya. Maybe if we partner up again, we'll have better luck."

They shook hands.

"Right you are. About time things start looking up again," Smealey said, rubbing his chin. "Reckon I'll find me a barbershop and have this beard shaved. It's itching worse than a dose o'chiggers in this muggy weather."

"It's your best disguise," Weir warned.

"Don't matter. I'll take my chances."

Smealey went off down the street, without a backward glance at the steamboat. Once he looked back and saw Weir headed for a general mercantile. Smealey shuddered at the thought of going up against the escaped slave, Bull Brady. The giant brawler would be desperate to remain free. He had to admit it—Weir liked to live dangerously. He, himself, would be taking a lesser risk of recognition after his face was once again exposed from beneath the reddish whiskers.

CHAPTER 9

"Tom, surely you boys ain't a'going fishing and camping down-river this week, are you?" Aunt Polly looked over her glasses at Tom and Zane at the breakfast table three days after the village picnic. "You could run afoul of that giant beast they say is coming this way." She licked the end of her forefinger and tapped a stove lid. It sizzled. She set a flat griddle on it, added a dab of lard, then stirred the pancake batter in a bowl as she turned back to the boys.

Tom had to think fast. "If we wait too long, summer will be over and school will be clomping down on us," he said. "We'd best do it now whilst the weather's fair and Zane is still here. Jim's coming with us, jest in case of trouble. But there ain't gonna be any," he added. "Ain't no such thing as giants. That's only a fairy tale to scare little kids."

"But it was in the paper," she said, "And you know those big city papers don't print anything that's not true."

A loud sizzle as she poured a cup of batter on the griddle. "Land sakes, this summer has been a caution. I don't know what to make of all the troubles we been having. It's like Providence is bringing down afflictions on the village as punishment for our sins. But at least *somebody* is trying to warn us by writing that note and posting it with the newspaper story."

"Auntie, that note could've been put there by anybody, even Muff Potter—*if* he could write."

"Don't disparage that good ole soul thataway. It's not his

86

fault he didn't get any schooling."

"I didn't mean nuthin' by it, Auntie. All the boys like Muff . . . uh, Mister Potter. He fixes our kites and shows us the best fishing holes and such. I'm saying, nobody knows who wrote that note. It might be a joke."

"Well, we'd best not treat it as a joke," the old lady said solemnly, flipping the pancake with a spatula. "We could be mighty sorry if that thing shows up to murder us all in our beds."

Tom took a deep breath. He wanted this conversation to end and was on edge to have breakfast over and leave. "We'll be careful, I promise. But we can't stop living because of this." He started to add they would be carrying guns. But then decided to let that bit of information lie fallow. She wouldn't approve and would grill them about the source and reason for the weapons, demanding explanations he wasn't up to at the moment—or ever. He certainly didn't want her to know the pistols had come from Judge Thatcher's house.

Tom got up to pour coffee for the three of them. He gave thanks that Providence had delayed Sid and Mary's return from their uncle's farm in the country. Either of them would be leery of the story about the giant and would be perceptive enough to suspect that Tom, with his history of pranks, was likely behind it. But Aunt Polly was a trusting soul, especially when it came to believing the printed word or broadsides for patent medicines.

"How long will you boys be away?" she asked.

"Not sure, Auntie. Maybe two or three days at most. We plan to drift along or sail downriver to some o'those islands about forty or fifty miles from here. With the sails on that yawl we can come back home a lot faster if there's a decent breeze—from any direction."

She set a small stack of flapjacks on the table, along with a pitcher of molasses. "Well, Tom, you're getting older so I suppose you should have a bit more freedom. You'll be fourteen next birthday, and I think your friend, Zane, here, is about the same age. So, I reckon I got to trust you, though, Lord knows, I've had cause to regret that enough times."

Tom didn't bring up Huck's name because Aunt Polly had never really put away her suspicions of his morals and motives, even though he'd been in the Widow Douglas's care for a few months now. She still thought of him as the homeless waif who smoked and cussed, didn't go to church or school, did whatever took his fancy, and was generally a bad influence on all the other decent boys of the village. "You can't make a silk purse out of a sow's ear," was the way she put it, neglecting to credit Jonathan Swift for the adage.

The conversation lagged as all three sat down to smother their hotcakes with butter and molasses. Tom was grateful for the pause. He was eager to be off. The sun was up and the earlier they were on the river, the cooler it would be. They'd planned to meet Huck and Jim and Becky at the levee above the steamboat landing. Since not one of them had a watch, they usually estimated the time of day by the chiming of the clock in the brick tower of the Odd Fellows Hall—that along with the position of the sun, which rose early this time of year.

Tom and Zane wolfed down the flapjacks with a speed that would have given the old lady a bellyache for a week.

"Time to be off, Auntie," Tom said, slurping the last of his coffee and giving his aunt a peck on the cheek. When he was younger, he would have filched a handful of sugar on the way out, but he'd had plenty of sweets this day, so Aunt Polly didn't have to guard this precious commodity from his fingers.

"You sure you have everything you need?" she asked.

"Yes'am."

"You be careful on that river, now. It can be treacherous, even without any giant wild men . . ." her voice trailed off as they clattered through the sitting room and burst outside, banging the door behind them.

Any casual onlooker would never have known Jim and Becky were waiting together. Jim was thirty yards away, ignoring her and gazing at the river as if looking for something. It wouldn't do for him to be seen talking to a young white girl in public. The yawl was tied up nearby with all their gear covered with a piece of canvas tent and the furled sails.

Becky had provided the three pistols, as promised. Tom had spent the day before making sure they had adequate powder, balls of the right caliber, and caps. "That's enough ammunition to start a revolution," Zane had commented when he saw what Tom had collected.

"Can't never have too much," Tom had replied. "Powder might get wet, one of the cap boxes could fall overboard. Anything could happen."

They had laid in a supply of food—a small ham, several tomatoes, salt, sweet potatoes, a side of bacon, cornmeal, fresh garden greens, frying pan, utensils, fishing lines and hooks, a seine, and several jugs of fresh water. Each of them had a blanket to sit on and to ward off the damps at night. Most importantly, he'd absconded with one of two buckets of tallow Aunt Polly had purchased from the community hog rendering last winter. She kept the buckets sealed and handy in the pantry for cooking or candle making.

Tom had let Becky bring whatever she wanted. She'd brought a change of clothing, and wore a freshly laundered shirtwaist along with the riding skirt and sandals she'd purchased the previous month at the general mercantile in St. Charles. To protect her face from the sun, she wore her stylish wide-brimmed straw hat. It framed her face and blond hair and enhanced her good looks, Tom noted.

"Did you have any trouble convincing your father?" Tom asked.

"Not at all. I think he realizes I'll be in good hands." She smiled with a look that made his stomach feel like he'd swallowed a live minnow.

"Of course, if he'd known I slipped those pistols from his trunk in the garret it might have been a different story," she added.

Tom had met the other boys and Jim in the woods behind the widow's house two days earlier and they'd cleaned and oiled the weapons and noted the two different calibers so they could get balls and patches the right size. The pistols—one Colt, one Smith & Wesson, and one old-style pepperbox—a notoriously inaccurate weapon—were in reasonably good condition other than being dirty. Huck had also smouched the widow's .31 pocket pistol that Jim had carried on their previous adventure.

They'd taken the guns to Jackson's Island and tried them out to make sure all worked properly. Tom was assuming no one in the village would have been curious about the popping of gunshots. In any case, the sounds would have been essentially muffled by the west wind and the thick timber.

Tom and Huck and Jim looked to make sure they had everything aboard before Becky climbed in and Zane untied the painter.

"What's it like downriver?" Huck asked a gaunt fisherman who rowed his skiff up and grounded nearby.

"Hain't been downriver," the old man replied without looking up as he stepped out to tie off the boat. "Won't catch me down thataway so long as that giant hairy thing is roaming around the sloughs."

"Won't bother *us*. We're sailing down yonder forty, fifty miles and will spend the night on one o'them islands," Tom boasted. "With this clear water and hot weather, the catfish're likely down deep," he added as a reason for the trip.

The old man unbent his bony frame and looked at them. "Well, my heart ain't what it once was," he said. "Was I to see one o'them giants, my ticker might just give out afore that hairy beast had a chance to squash me like a June bug." He grinned, showing tobacco-stained teeth.

The old man sauntered away, carrying a cane pole and two fish on a stringer. Zane chuckled, then turned to shove off the bow of the yawl and hopped in.

"Ain't nobody here to see us off," Tom said, with a sinking feeling.

"You expecting the Odd Fellows brass band?" Huck asked.

"Wal, no . . . But I thought *somebody* might of cared that we're off risking our lives for the village."

"Maybe they ain't as scared o'this giant as we thought."

Tom didn't answer as he was too busy acting the role of ship captain. "Hoist the main!"

Jim and Huck complied, tying off the halyard when the boom swung above their heads.

"Tighten down the mainsheet. Stow the jib in the sail locker!" Tom ordered. The sail locker was in his imagination.

"Aye, cap'n."

"Three points south by east!" This was directed toward Zane at the tiller.

"South by east three points she is, sir!" Zane replied smartly.

And their voyage was underway.

St. Petersburg rapidly slid away and in a few minutes the village was only a distant white blob in the shoreline greenery.

Tom sat in the bow, facing forward, Jim and Huck on the midship thwarts near the oars, and Becky forward of Zane, who was at the tiller in the stern.

Tom wished he had a watch because he guessed it would take them about five or six hours to reach the vicinity of Westport

Island. He would have to estimate the time by the sun.

Because of the constant curves of the river, Huck and Jim were frequently jibing the boat to keep it on a port or starboard reach or directly downwind.

Tom knew they were making very good time and consulted his map to see if he could identify the islands they were passing. The boat seemed to be flying along, but it was only his inexperience with sailing that made it feel that way compared to the speed of current and oars. When a side-wheel steamer passed them churning downstream, he was elated at how long it took the big boat to pass them. The little yawl was slicing the sparkling wavelets and a small wave was curling away from the bow as they made seven or eight knots in open areas where the wind wasn't deflected by the tall trees. And the best thing, Tom thought, was the fact that they were not expending any effort at the oars.

Near midday when the wind dropped to a light breeze, they hoisted the jib and lounged in the shade of the sails, sipping water from their jugs while still making decent time.

Tom took his job as captain and navigator seriously, and estimated that by early afternoon they should be nearing their goal. They slid past island after island, some of which could have been only towheads. The riverscape appeared very different from boat level than it did when studying the map, where everything was clearly defined.

When he was almost sure he saw Hamburg on the Illinois side he instructed Zane to aim the bow close inshore so he could ask directions.

"Hamburg is the next village down, about six more miles," a raftsman told him when he hailed the man from a few yards away. "You can't miss it. There's a ferry landing there."

"Thanks!" Tom used an oar to stroke the boat back out into the current.

Less than an hour later, the boat passed the steam ferry that was pulling away from the Illinois shore.

"There she be," Tom said. "That means the last big island we passed was Mosier. The ferry landing is at this spot 'cause this place is the narrowest part of the river hereabouts for miles." He took a deep breath and blew it out, relieved. He'd done it—successfully navigated a long stretch of river without a mistake. He had reeled off the names of islands as they'd passed earlier—Coon Island, McCoy Island. Mosier Island was very similar to Westport, with a skinny sliver of land in the chute on the Missouri side.

"Next big island to starboard is Westport. Look sharp," he said to Zane. "We don't want to miss it, or we'll wind up in a tangle of shoals and little islands just south of it." He felt like the pilot of a big steamer. No one questioned his word.

They saw the big island looming up less than a mile ahead and Zane steered the yawl closer to the upper end as they approached. The boat slid in toward shore, sails flapping as the tall trees stole their wind.

"Strike the mainsail and jib!" Tom cried over his shoulder as he knelt in the bow. He tried to make his voice deeper and more authoritative.

Huck and Jim jumped to obey, the canvas collapsing in a rush. They tucked the sails around the boom and gaff to one side across the thwarts. Without being told, Huck and Jim unshipped two of the oars and took seats where they wouldn't interfere with each other. They stroked just enough to keep the yawl off the mud bank and out of the tangle of brush and driftwood that was piled there from past floods. The boat ghosted silently along while Tom scanned the shoreline. He pointed at the low, swampy area they were passing. "We'll look for a landing place down toward the foot of the island."

About twenty minutes later Tom pointed at a level spot about four feet above the surface of the river. "There! That's it. Bring'er ashore."

Zane ran the bow up onto the dirt bank and Tom hopped out, holding the painter. "No brush. Sandy soil, trees for shade—right for a campsite."

The others piled out, unloaded their gear, and dumped it on a blanket.

"Let's go exploring while there's still plenty o'daylight," Tom said, shoving one of the pistols under his belt, picking up a canteen, and marching off at the head of the column into the thick woods.

CHAPTER 10

Zane selected the .44 Colt Dragoon from their pile of gear on the blanket. "Hold on a minute," he called to Tom. "I want to load this thing before we go."

"Surely we won't be in any danger here," Becky said.

"Well—in case of snakes or something," Zane said, knowing all the time his chances of hitting a moving serpent with a handgun were nil. "You never know."

Tom came back and helped him so the loading of the unfamiliar weapon went faster.

"That's got it." Zane said, thumbing the last copper cap onto a nipple. "Thanks." He let down the hammer carefully and slipped the gun into his side pocket. It was heavy and he wished he had a holster for it. But as his grandmother would have said, "If wishes were horses, beggars would ride." He smiled at the recollection.

Huck didn't seem interested in arming himself, but then Zane realized Huck had experienced some dire predicaments in his life and survived them all—without being armed with anything but his guile.

Jim always kept the widow's pocket pistol loaded and ready to hand in his jacket.

They tramped through the increasing undergrowth and among the one-hundred-foot trees, the sun's rays only breaking through the overhead foliage in scattered freckles of light. It was as if they'd walked into a vast green twilight, still and solemn, protected from the wind and all other sounds except the mourning dove, which always sounded sad and far off.

Zane estimated Westport Island was about three miles long and probably a half-mile wide at its widest point, and tapered toward a point at each end.

They'd gone about a mile when the ground began to grow soft and small ponds appeared here and there. Apparently, this end of the island was inundated during high water.

"Dey's some otter tracks. Raccoon and ducks been nosin' 'round dis pond, too," Jim said, pointing. "But mostly deer comes here to drink."

"Be careful and don't go stomping around, making lots o'tracks until Jim makes the big ones," Tom told them.

"This looks like a good place," Zane said. "A mix of big trees and some brush near a pond."

Stepping on layers of pine needles and dead leaves with their toughened bare feet, the boys proceeded another thirty yards.

"Soft ground all around, and a good bit of the right kind of firm mud to make good casts of impressions," Tom agreed. "Jest so's not to track up this whole area, we'll walk back along the shoreline, then bring the boat back up near this spot. I'll fix Jim up so he can walk ashore from the boat. Might as well do this while there's plenty of daylight afore we make camp and cook supper."

They heard a noise, but it was only a big side-wheeler plowing upstream against the current in the channel.

"Ain't hunting slack water," Tom observed. "That Kickapoo chute must be silting up if it's too shallow for that boat."

After the steamer passed, they all worked their way back through heavier underbrush to the foot of the island. They saw no other boats or humans or any sign of life except a few birds, including a long-legged egret in the shallows.

A half-hour later, they had camp set up and a pile of dry

driftwood burning.

No one could be found who wanted to stay behind and watch their belongings, so they all piled into the yawl and Huck and Zane rowed back upstream along the shoreline to the muddy area.

By the time they pulled up and tied off to a snag, Tom had strapped the wooden blocks to Jim's bare feet, wrapping his ankles with rags to pad the cord that he knotted securely to hold the carved footprints in place.

Jim climbed over the side and clumsily made his way with help through the tangled driftwood and inside the treeline. He took a few tentative steps on his own.

"Mars Tom, ah ain't sho ah kin run wid dese hunks o'wood on m'feet."

"Walk a bit first, and don't step on the soft ground," Tom said.

They watched as Jim took a few awkward strides. With the blocks on his feet, he towered more than six and a half feet tall.

"We shoulda had him practice with those things on Jackson's Island this week," Zane said.

"Yeah," Tom agreed. "Didn't think of it."

"Ah gots it now," Jim said, moving with a little more assurance, and he waded through some thick bushes, brushing them aside.

"Go ahead and take off when you're ready," Tom said. "Run over past that swampy area and then run back here to the boat."

Jim slogged away through the woods, placing his feet wide apart as if on snowshoes. Soon he was just a hulking figure appearing and disappearing among the big trees as he broke into a jog.

"If I didn't know who that was, I'd be terrified," Becky said. "Looks just like some kind of giant creature in the woods."

"Perfect!" Tom said, rubbing his hands together. "Think how

he'd look at night."

"Couldn't see *nuthin'* of him at night," the practical Huck commented. "And ain't nobody here but us to see him now."

"Iffen the moon was full and you didn't know no better, you'd swear on your pap's grave you was seeing one o'them hairy giants," Tom continued, undaunted. "Then, look out! Them teeth and claws'd be on you like stink on a privy."

"Toommm!" Becky rolled her eyes. *"Please!"*

"Sorry," he muttered. But Tom was obviously enjoying himself. "And speaking of odor, that piece in the newspaper said everybody who come anywheres near one o'them creturs, told o'sniffing sumpin' that woulda made a pig farm smell sweet as honeysuckle by comparison."

Zane laughed out loud. By the time they got back to St. Petersburg, Tom's story would have taken on the dimensions of St. George slaying the dragon.

Tom was already down on his knees, breaking up sticks and pieces of driftwood to kindle a small fire. By the time it was blazing, Jim was slogging back through the woods to the shoreline.

He came up, panting, and leaned against a tree.

"What happened to you?" Becky asked.

Jim's pants and shirt and arms were smeared with gobs of black mud.

"Ah slipped and fell on de edge o'de pond," he replied, raking the clinging black goo and dead leaves from his pants and shirtsleeves.

"Wade into this shallow spot and wash off," Huck said, testing the depth of the river a few feet off the bank. Jim took hold of the gunwale of the boat and followed him into the river to the depth of two feet and then sat down on the bottom, splashing water on himself.

Tom retrieved a cotton sack of slippery tallow and dumped it into a deep pan he placed over the fire. "This won't take but a minute to melt," he said.

"Huck, stay here and help Jim get cleaned up and take those blocks off his feet," Tom said. "Me and Zane and Becky're gonna get some impressions of the footprints." Tom took the long-handled pan and carefully carried the liquid tallow into the woods.

Zane pulled the heavy pistol and handed it, butt first, to Huck. "This thing is weighting me down," he explained. "Hang onto it in case you need it before we get back."

Huck placed the gun on a thwart inside the boat, and turned back to Jim.

Tom, Zane, and Becky followed Jim's tracks into the muddy area toward one of the ponds.

"This mud feels cold and creepy," Becky said, squishing it between her toes. "But I want to keep my sandals clean."

They saw a torn-up area several feet wide where Jim had fallen and then two handprints where he'd pushed himself back up. "Those ain't the marks of a hairy giant," Tom said, scuffing out the handprints with his foot.

"Ah, here's two good clear tracks." He stooped by the sharp, deep impressions in the firmer mud and carefully poured the tallow into the footprints, filling them to the top. "That mud is cold and it won't take but a minute or two for the tallow to harden." He looked around. "Be good to leave our tracks alongside Jim's," he said. "That way it looks like we was tracking the giant."

"Wouldn't it be better to let those tracks dry first?" Zane asked.

"Don't have time for that," Tom said, studying the deep impressions several feet apart left by the blocks. "This mud is on the low, swampy end of the island. If we was to wait for it to dry, we'd be here 'til doomsday I reckon."

Zane noticed the remaining tallow had already begun to harden in the pan.

The line of tracks vanished off into the woods. They were very realistic looking. If Zane hadn't helped carve them, the sight would have sent a chill up his spine. Their mute testimony proclaimed the presence of some woodland creature of enormous size. He began to think this conspiracy might actually work, after all.

They waited impatiently for about five minutes, and Tom tested the surface of the tallow with a finger. "About two more minutes oughta do it."

"Becky, I'm glad you came along," Zane said. "This is mighty like the adventure we had earlier this summer."

"Not exactly. This one sure isn't dangerous," she said. "A lot more relaxing."

Tom took his Barlow knife blade and gently worked it around the tallow and lifted it out. An excellent, detailed impression. Except for a small chunk that broke off the edge, the second cast was equally as good. He set both of them in the cooled pan.

"Great job!" Zane said.

"Back to camp." Tom led the way to the boat where Huck and Jim were both wet, but clean. Huck had cut the cords that bound the fake tracks to Jim's feet and placed the rinsed wooden blocks in a sack in the bottom of the boat.

"Whew! Ah's rid o'dem big feet," Jim said, rubbing his ankles where the cord had burned his skin.

"Time for an early supper," Tom said, obviously elated with the impressions he'd obtained.

"Why don't I walk back to camp and leave some tracks in the soft spots," Zane suggested. "That way any men from the village will see where we were going and coming to track the monster."

"No need," Tom said. "We've already walked up to this area once. What we'll all do is this—before we leave in the morning, we'll hike up to this part of the island again and then run back to our camp where the boat is, and Jim will have to follow us with the blocks on like he was chasing us."

"Oh, my! Does ah hafta wear dose big feet again?" Jim moaned.

"We gotta do this right so even the best tracker from the village will see what happened," Tom said, " 'cause you know somebody will come nosing around to check our story."

They rowed back to the foot of the island and busied themselves cooking an early supper.

Huck dug a few worms in the soft soil with the axe, baited three hooks, and set out a trotline. "They's a narrow channel between here and that next little island yonder," he pointed out to Zane. "Shallow water over a bar. We should have a couple fish afore long."

Zane, who was seldom able to catch fish in his former life, was always amazed at how rapidly and confidently Tom and Huck and Jim could catch fish on demand. Like picking up fish at a fast food drive-thru. Maybe fish were more plentiful in this day and time. Or else the boys had been doing it all their lives and were more skilled and knowledgeable about how and where to fish.

Huck was as good as his word. In ten minutes, he was scraping the scales from two bass and skinning a decent-sized catfish.

Twenty minutes later the meal was ready. Becky had pitched in and helped slice the bacon and fry the sweet potatoes, and had set the plates, cups, and utensils out. There was no complaining, no shirking. Zane's admiration for her increased. Maybe it was only in civilized society that she acted differently. But even around other people, she was no more devious than Tom and Huck—maybe even less so. He noticed mosquito bites on her arms and neck and her riding skirt was streaked with mud and water and snagged by thorns.

Zane had never eaten a meal as tasty as this one. With an appetite sharpened by nothing but canteen water all day, he sat cross-legged on the blanket and ate the hot food with relish. The sun was sliding down the western sky, lighting up towering white cumulus clouds overhead. It was pleasant and relaxing to be with a few friends and away from crowds and traffic and noise. He was appreciating this 19th century world more and more with each passing week.

Huck and Jim filled and lighted their pipes and a general feeling of goodwill and a job well done seemed to fall over the group. The aromatic pipe smoke blended with the woodsmoke to form a sweet incense.

Zane dug out the Benzoin and the boys treated their palms and the soles of their feet to another dose, while explaining to Becky what it was. "Smells nice," was her only comment, when declining an offer to toughen up her skin. "Girls don't want tough skin," she said. "We use lotion to soften our skin."

"Well, we ain't done yet," Tom said. "Jim made a convincing set o'tracks and we got some decent molds," he said, examining the hard tallow he'd set to one side. "Looks a lot like those pictures in the newspaper."

"What's next?" Zane asked, knowing Tom had a plan worked out.

"We'll scuff ourselves up a bit more—scratches and small cuts and such, and tear our clothes with thorns like they been clawed. Becky looks fine like she is with all that mud and clothes torn." He looked at Huck. "You already saved the guts from those fish and smeared blood on the gunwale o'the boat to make it appear we fought off that monster." He paused, apparently thinking. "Don't look like no rain on the way to wash out our tracks. A three-quarter moon tonight. Come daylight we'll make those last tracks like the monster chased us to the boat. Then we'll hie for home."

"What about the guns?" Huck asked.

"Yeah. Almost forgot. As the last thing, we'll fire off a bunch o'shots into the woods. If anybody's out fishin' or a steamboat passing, somebody will testify they heard shots and that will make our story stronger."

"We can act scared when we tell our tale," Zane added, getting into the spirit of the ruse. "But we have to do this right and not act hysterical or anything, like we're in a panic. We need to show we have some backbone. Remember, we were attacked while tracking this Bigfoot and he came after us. We ran for the boat, shooting back at him. He caught us as we shoved off and he fell wounded into the water and the current took him." All this had been said before, but Zane thought it could bear repeating so they could all have their story straight. "Maybe we could leave a few things behind like some pans or a blanket or something, so it looks like we had to take off before we were ready. We could leave the fire burning."

"Yeah, that's all good, but we don't want to add too much detail. Remember, we was all scared and it was dark and we don't recollect too much o'what happened—only the main story," Tom said.

"That's right," Huck agreed. "But if we's fixin' t'be heroes, we'll act like we have lotsa grit. We can say Jim whacked the big hairy cretur with an oar blade and that was the final blow that put him down—along with two more bullets."

While they continued discussing their plans, twilight crept over the conspirators; the mosquitoes and lightning bugs emerged, while crickets and bullfrogs raised their raucous clatter.

Before the partial moon became visible through the trees, the red coals of their dying campfire and the blinking fireflies were the only light in the velvety blackness. Zane lay on his back on a blanket, hands clasped behind his head, and stared at the vast spangle of stars stretching across heavenly blackness. They looked brighter than he remembered. But, in his 21st century world, complete absence of light was a rare thing, and the atmosphere was usually polluted by exhaust from millions of cars and factories, dimming the view of the constellations. It was a joy now to experience the world as it had been.

But complete darkness was a scary thing. He took comfort in the fact that he was not alone on this island and that there was no such thing as Bigfoot.

CHAPTER 11

Gus Weir drew a long smooth stroke on the canoe paddle and glided silently into the shade of a tree that overhung a narrow chute between an island and the Missouri shore. He glanced up at the huge cottonwood whose roots still clung precariously to a clay bank six feet above his head. The next high water would claim another giant, he thought. If trees had brains and choices they would seed themselves in places away from the gnawing river, he reflected. But cottonwoods needed water and were almost always found where their roots could reach that life-giving substance.

Weir was feeling free, rested, and in a reflective mood. He was his own man and unencumbered for the first time in at least two months—freer than he'd been since giving up his pursuit of a runaway slave who'd fled to Minnesota. The bounty had not been worth the chase. It was when he was turning back toward New Orleans and had stopped overnight in Keokuk, Iowa, in early June that he'd met Chigger Smealey in a waterfront tavern. A man in his life sometimes blundered into blind alleys, and his whole association with Smealey, the kidnapping, the flight with hostages and gold, had turned out to be a disaster. It felt good to be back doing what he did best—tracking down runaway slaves for the reward offered by wealthy plantation owners. It was legal, and not nearly as dangerous as kidnapping and extortion.

After parting from Smealey at St. Charles, he'd equipped

himself with a Colt Baby Dragoon with powder and shot, and a pair of adjustable shackles that could be used on either ankles or wrists. Then he'd found a canoe near the waterfront that he'd purchased cheaply as its owner was eager to start for the goldfields. Fishing lines, matches, and a blanket, along with salt, cornmeal, dried beef, bacon, a frying pan, tin cup, and fork and spoon in a cotton sack, completed his outfit. And it left him with only a few dollars in his pocket. But he was paddling up the river, away from civilization, except for the small villages on the high banks above the river, so had no need for cash. He was not above pilfering some fresh corn from a field, or a handy muskmelon or watermelon to vary his diet. But he'd always been a man who could live off the land and required little in the way of luxuries. That was one reason he was successful as a manhunter—he concentrated on the job at hand, leaving personal comforts aside.

For the first four days, he'd stroked his canoe steadily from St. Charles, down the Missouri, and then turned upstream into the Mississippi. He had purchased a map that showed the general outlines of the river and the major islands, but took the river as he found it, working his way along in slack water under the bluff banks, through chutes that were silting up and choked with reeds and driftwood, patiently scanning the shoreline, the dozens of tiny islands, and bars. He never ceased to marvel at how wild and deserted this river was. The scattered villages and the occasional steamboats, rafts, and flatboats only served to emphasize the long stretches of loneliness in between where nothing was seen but hawks, long-legged wading birds, fish jumping, and shorelines of solid green or thick with cane.

As his canoe slid along, he landed at various spots and briefly scanned the canebrakes and towheads and heavily wooded islands, on the lookout for old campfires or any sign of human activity.

At first, he made only a cursory search, but didn't linger. He was headed for a spot some thirty miles above the confluence of the rivers. On his map, he'd penciled a small circle to indicate where, according to the wanted poster, Bull Brady had jumped overboard from a steamboat after midnight a couple weeks before. Only one deckhand had reported seeing him go and, since it was a very dark night, the spot was only an approximation. If the brawler had been lucky and was still alive, he could be many miles from the river by now, maybe even headed west, far from the slave states. Weir had to put himself in the mindset of this big man. What would he do? Where would he go? One thing was sure—a man that size would have to have a goodly amount of food and drink to fuel a body that was six-foot-eight and three-hundred-twenty pounds.

When Weir reached the area where the slave had last been seen, he began to move more patiently and surreptitiously, examining everything carefully—the shorelines, the woods, the swampy areas, keeping undercover during daylight hours. Even if Bull Brady was no longer in the area, he might have left some sign of his passing.

This particular stretch of river was not close to any villages or cultivated farmlands, so there were no crops to steal. Without fishing lines, it was very unlikely Bull would be able to catch fish with his hands by cornering them in the shallows, or spearing them with sharpened sticks. No, he'd have to live by stealing. As a boxer, he was fast and coordinated, if not cunning. With luck, he might be able to corner and kill some small animal or a snake to eat. But a slave used to being treated well and given all he wanted to eat would surely have a hard time out here.

By late afternoon, he had searched eight small islands that had barely enough vegetation on them to hide a large man. They were mostly sandbars that would be scoured and reshaped after every flood.

He came to Eagles Nest Island where he and Smealey had taken delivery of the $12,000 gold ransom from Huckleberry Finn and Tom Sawyer, had turned loose the girl, and captured the two boys. All that seemed like years ago, but it had been less than a couple of months. He grounded his canoe on the bar at the head of the island and stepped out to stretch his legs. In the vain hope that one or two of the coins from those two sacks of gold might have been dropped, he searched the sand of the bar. Nothing.

The abandoned house beyond the swamp where he and Smealey had hidden out for several days with the hostages was only a couple of miles beyond those sloughs to the west. He thought of going back in there to see it—not for nostalgic purposes, but only to find out if it was still empty. Bull Brady might have found the place and was using it as shelter. Then he decided it was a waste of time and effort. Bull had not abandoned the steamboat anywhere near here. And, without a boat, he would have had to wade or swim through the swamps to reach a house he didn't even know existed.

No. He would push on and make a few more miles before he camped.

He made brief work of Portage Island and Turner Island, and paddled as far as Bolter Island where he camped for the night. He didn't sleep well due to the mosquitoes and gnats and his anticipation of the next day's search. The area where Bull had escaped was coming up. Weir rose before the sun, snatched a sparse breakfast of beef jerky, and was underway. By early afternoon he had put Dardenne and Two Branch islands in his wake. He didn't bother searching any islands to starboard of the main channel. A white deckhand had stated that Bull had gone over the side in the dark and made for the Missouri shore.

Now came a long straight eight-mile stretch of river with no islands. Weir hugged the Missouri shoreline and made progress in slack water. Even so, by the time he was approaching Stag Island, it was midafternoon and he was beginning to tire. But the days were long and he hated to waste daylight. On the map, there was nothing west of Stag Island but miles of sloughs and swamps. No one could survive in there without a boat and food.

He paused on a towhead to rest for several minutes, and then took up his paddle again and shoved off, his stroke slower, more deliberate. Only two more miles to Sterling Island where Bull had vanished.

Since Bull Brady was well known, his escape had made the news. According to a newspaper account that Weir had managed to find in the St. Charles newspaper morgue, the steamboat had put in at Sterling Island and armed men had searched the island in the half-light of early dawn. But no one was found. They assumed he'd either drowned, or had somehow swum to another island.

The slave's owner had returned to Sterling Island with dogs two days later and made a thorough search, but found nothing. The dogs had picked up a scent, but it had ended at the water's edge on the western side.

So the owner had put out a broadside on Bull with a large $1500 reward posted.

All that had happened eighteen days earlier, so Weir felt the trail was getting colder every day he let slide past. There was no need to land on Sterling Island, he thought, as he paddled slowly along. If tracking dogs had found only the scent of Bull within two days, then he was no longer there. If he'd escaped alive, he might have swum on west to an unnamed tiny spit of land, and then to the nearby Missouri shore. Weir thought it unlikely the fugitive could have managed to swim another hundred and fifty yards north against the current to a small place the map identified as Four Acre Island. But he could have used the help of a driftwood log to drift diagonally downstream and land on the Missouri side.

Then a thought occurred to him. Why would Bull try to land in Missouri, a slave state? If he were going to escape, why not go for freedom in Illinois? According to the map, there were swamps and sloughs on the Illinois side, but Bull would not likely have known that. Perhaps he'd been picked up by a local fisherman, or had enough money in his pocket to bribe someone at a woodyard to hide him. Perhaps he'd bolted for the Missouri shore because he had kinfolk somewhere in the region. The possibilities were endless.

Weir took a deep breath. He also had to admit there was a likelihood the big boxer was dead. The impersonal river cared not how weak or strong or cunning a man was. It had a habit of carrying off the best and the worst.

He passed the upper end of Sterling Island and decided to land on the next one up, Osprey Island, about two hundred yards farther.

When the bow of the canoe grated on the sand at the foot of the island, he was fatigued and sat still for ten minutes while he recovered his breath and let the ache in his arms and shoulders subside. Then he climbed out and dragged the vessel up onto the beach. He walked another fifty yards into the treeline where the ground was level and covered with a solid layer of sandy soil. With only scattered underbrush, it was the best spot to camp. Since the sun was well down the western sky, that's what he decided to do.

After spreading his blanket and kindling a driftwood fire, he baited a fishing line with a small hunk of raw bacon and walked to the shoreline nearby to try his luck. It took about ten minutes, but then he saw the cork bobber go under and gave a yank on the line. A steady, heavy pull. He retrieved the braided line hand over hand, and dragged up about a five-pound channel cat.

The fish, skinned, filleted, and fried in cornmeal, proved a very satisfying meal. The last of his bread was going moldy in the muggy heat. Tomorrow he'd stop at the next village— Hamburg—and buy more. He'd wear a putty nose and his straw hat to further disguise his appearance, and would casually ask a few oblique questions in case anyone recalled seeing a really big black stranger in the area. Two or three times during his slave-hunting years, the most casual comment or question had been like turning over a shovelful of dirt to yield a gold nugget of information.

For some reason, he was more fatigued than usual this evening, he reflected as he lounged back on the blanket after supper, watching the sun disappear and twilight begin to shade the river. Maybe he was too old for this kind of work. If he could make this one big capture, perhaps he'd retire from slave catching. It was starting to seem more strenuous than it used to. Perhaps the runaways were more elusive now since the abolitionists and the Underground Railroad were ever more aggressive. If a bill being debated in Congress were to pass, it would make it illegal for anyone to harbor a fugitive slave. If the Fugitive Slave Act did not pass, he wondered what kind of work he might take up.

But then he shook his head and banished such thinking. He was still hale and hearty, had plenty of physical stamina, and was still one of the best in his line of work. He knew from experience that negative thinking like this was due only to the weakness of physical fatigue brought on by many hours in the hot sun, paddling a canoe upstream, fighting gnats and mosquitoes and the sun's glare off the water. A restorative night's sleep would set him right again.

Hours later something woke Weir. A mosquito was biting his neck. Cursing softly, he slapped it, still only half awake. Probably all kinds of sand fleas, ants, and beetles on this ground, he thought wearily. Maybe he'd have to rig some kind of hammock. He cracked his eyelids. Was it time to get up? Was that daylight filtering into his camp?

He rolled over on his blanket and opened his eyes. Through a break in the trees he saw a nearly full moon riding benignly in the night sky. He hadn't been sleeping soundly, and a combination of biting insects and the unusually bright moon had probably awakened him.

With a groan, he sat up and reached for his holstered pistol he kept close at hand. Slipping it in and out of the leather, he made sure it was still dry from the dew, then cocked it and eased the hammer down, working the action. No sand had gotten into the well-oiled moving parts. He slipped the holster onto his belt and yawned, still very tired. Sleeping alone in strange, isolated places never allowed him to completely relax, and even less so now when he had the instinctive feeling he was closer to a desperate fugitive. Logic and probability told him Bull Brady had already escaped away from this river or was dead. But a subliminal message whispered otherwise.

He stood up and stretched his stiff muscles. The idea of a more settled job came to him again. No, he merely needed sleep. Maybe he should find a village with a hotel and stay a day or two to rest up.

A slight movement caught his eye. He rubbed his face with his hands and looked again toward the deep darkness of the woods. Bright moonlight was spotty through the overhead canopy of leafy branches. Hunkering down on the blanket to stretch his back muscles, he squinted to help his eyes focus better. Maybe it was the wind moving some bushes or lower tree branches. But even as he squatted there, hardly breathing, with every sense alert, he realized there was no wind stirring. Except for the splash of a fish now and then somewhere far off, the night was deathly quiet. Could be a fox or a raccoon—some small animal was on the move. Maybe even an early-rising deer browsing. Somehow animals made it to these islands.

The slight movement came again, and a chill went up his sweaty back. It was a large animal of some kind. It had to be a deer because it was several feet above the ground in the thick forest.

He slid the Colt from its holster and stood up. The form began to move slowly. It was the size of a big man. *Bull Brady!*

Weir slipped on his shoes over his cotton socks, then paced softly toward the heavier batch of trees. He moved slowly and carefully, gun cocked, watching for the man—he was certain it was the shape of a man—to move again and separate his outline from the jumble of thick trunks.

The tall shape moved again, going sideways, but not away from him.

Weir decided to take the initiative and break the tension. "All right, Bull, I know it's you in there. Come on out into the moonlight and show yourself!" he yelled. "I ain't gonna hurt you, but I've got a gun, so don't do anything foolish." He took several long strides toward the figure.

The figure turned and strode away, passing through a patch of moonlight. *Damn! He's big,* Weir thought.

"Don't run. There ain't nowhere to go!" he yelled as the figure receded faster into the dense woods.

"Stop!" Weir yelled. He didn't want to shoot, but he had to capture this slave.

BOOM! He blasted a high warning shot. A streak of flame flashed from the muzzle.

The figure ran faster, and Weir chased, tripping over rocks

and roots in the dark. He wanted to capture the big slave intact.
He couldn't ruin his chances of collecting the $1500 reward.
He fired again in the general direction, hoping to scare him.

A piercing shriek of anger or pain froze Weir in his tracks. It
sounded like a mountain lion. Had his bullet found Bull? Where
was he?

Something crashed in the brush to his left and a figure lunged
out of the undergrowth and came for him.

In spite of the fact that he had a gun, Weir turned and dashed
toward his camp. Bull was a brawler and probably thought he
could manhandle his attacker. Weir longed for a rifle so he could
have used it as a club to keep from inflicting lethal damage.

The pair burst out into the moonlight on a sandbar at the
lower end of the island. Weir looked desperately for a club of
driftwood, but saw nothing. He'd have to shoot Bull to protect
himself. He whirled when Bull was only a few yards away. The
towering black man was almost on him.

It wasn't Bull!

Weir screamed in panic and fired. A bear? Something huge
and dark standing upright. The creature swung its arm and
knocked Weir sideways. He rolled over and sprang up, left arm
numb under the torn shirt. Gasping, he was conscious of the
suffocating stench of a privy. Fear gripping his chest, he dodged
to one side of the hairy figure and fired point blank into the
body once . . . twice. He was thumbing back the hammer for
the third time when the beast lunged forward with a screech.
Weir couldn't duck the lightning blow. His vision exploded with
stars and everything went black.

CHAPTER 12

So far things couldn't be going any better, Zane thought, as he stepped back to give himself some breathing space from the villagers crowding them up against the front of the post office. The intrepid voyagers had not even made it all the way home, once word spread that the party had vanquished the monster on Westport Island.

A young boy had seen them coming and scampered down to the levee to grab the line and help pull the yawl up to the landing.

"We got him!" Tom cried.

"Got who?" the boy asked.

"We killed the giant monster!" Tom said, feigning excitement.

"Really?" The boy was wide-eyed.

"Yeah, see the blood here?" Tom pointed at the fish blood still staining the wooden gunwale.

"I don't reckon any more o'them hairy rapscallions will fool with *us*!" Huck bragged.

"He like t'have got me, though!" Becky gasped breathlessly, pointing at her torn blouse and scratches on her arm from blackberry bushes.

"Tarnation!" The boy's mouth fell open and he turned and heeled it toward the village's main street, high-pitched voice screaming like a town crier.

It was as if a match had been touched to dry grass. Within two minutes, the town was ablaze and villagers were erupting from stores and houses, jumping over back fences, dropping trowels and ledgers, running in shirtsleeves and aprons to meet the party and get the news.

Zane had to admit it—Tom Sawyer was a genius.

On the way back upriver, all five of them had practiced asking each other questions to make sure their answers would coincide. It was critical they not be tripped up by any of the sharper adults in St. Petersburg.

The wind had faltered the next day after they'd laid the trap of their conspiracy, so they'd decided to spend another night ashore, camped on Cottonwood Island. This morning they'd set sail and covered the last few miles to St. Petersburg, tacking a zigzag course upriver and arriving at the levee about noon.

Tom had made sure no one accidentally rubbed off any of the fish blood Huck had smeared on the gunwale of the boat so the evidence would remain intact. He'd also stowed the carved wooden blocks in a gunnysack, to be hidden in the cave at the first opportunity.

The crowd that surrounded and pressed in on the small party near the waterfront surged over the lip of the levee and spilled down into the main street of town like some huge, slippery amoeba. Everyone was talking at once, and the shouted questions were drowned in the general uproar. Youngsters were trying to squeeze between their elders to get near enough to see and touch these mighty warriors who'd departed in anonymity, but returned to celebrity.

Zane found himself fervently wishing he could get free of the crush, find a cold glass of buttermilk, and go lie down in his boarding house for a nap.

But that was out of the question now. He'd anticipated a few probing questions by adults, including a grilling from Judge Thatcher who would be worried about Becky—and then maybe a general, reluctant belief in their tale. But this adulation and fame was far beyond anything Zane had imagined. People in this day and time had no computers, no television, no social media. They were hungry for news of any kind—instead of being overwhelmed by a flood of news and commercials *ad nauseam* like those living in his own day.

"Everybody back! Stand back and let's have some order here!" Colonel Elder, the grizzled Mexican War veteran, pushed his way through the crowd until he stood in front of Tom and Huck and Becky. "Quiet down! Quiet!" he bellowed in a deep voice, shouting down the tumult. "We're not getting anywhere like this. Let's hear what they have to say."

The voices gradually subsided.

"Now move back and give them some breathing room," the colonel said, in a normal voice.

The crowd shuffled back a few paces.

"That's better," he said when order was restored. "Judge Thatcher's standing in the back there." He pointed over the heads of the crowd. "Judge, would you mind coming up here? If you can ask these young folks a few questions, maybe we can get the straight of all this."

The judge, hatless, and wearing his black suit, edged forward until he stood to one side of the five voyagers. He turned to the crowd and raised his voice to be heard by everyone.

"I've adjourned court for the day," he announced. "Why don't we all get out of this hot sun and go over to the courtroom where we can sit down and hear their story?"

There was murmured assent, and the crowd began to break up and flow toward the white courthouse a block away.

Judge Thatcher took this chance to hug his daughter. "Are you all right?" he asked, looking at her torn blouse and the scratches on her arms and the mud on her skirt.

"Yes, Daddy, I'm fine," she answered with downcast eyes.

Zane had a feeling her subdued demeanor was due to embarrassment for the lies she was about to tell to her loving parent in front of the whole town. "We'll go home shortly and tend those cuts and bruises and you can rest," he said, taking her by the arm and guiding her away with the crowd. Zane wondered how solicitous he would be if he ever found out the truth.

As the crowd surged along, their feet thundering on the boardwalk, it seemed to Zane the entire village was here. He stole a glance at Jim, who was walking beside him. The big man's face was like carved mahogany. As a slave, he'd had years of practice hiding his feelings from whites.

"Don't worry," Zane muttered quietly. "We'll just tell our story. Then we can go."

Jim bowed his head slightly. "Dis be bad biznus fo' ole Jim," he said in a whisper.

Huck had been caught up in an even more dangerous grilling in Arkansas last year when a crowd of villagers tried to sort out the real relatives of the deceased Peter Wilks. If the king and duke and Huck had been exposed as frauds, they would have been lynched. Huck's deliverance in the storm at the graveyard could only be attributed to a benign Providence.

Zane's heart was pounding. Every step he took into this fakery brought him deeper into a tangle of deceit, one lie smoothing the way for two more. At that moment, he wished he could instantly disappear back into his own 21st century world. If he somehow escaped this without winding up in jail or receiving a public whipping, he was through with conspiracies and practical jokes forever. What had seemed like an exciting adventure when Tom proposed it, now appeared shabby and lowdown. Most respectable adults did not take kindly to being duped and embarrassed, especially by youngsters. Zane hoped an overworked Providence still had the energy to provide one more escape.

★ ★ ★ ★ ★

"All right, young man, have a seat there in the witness chair where everyone can see and hear you," Judge Thatcher instructed Tom Sawyer.

The judge, himself, slid into a high-backed swivel chair behind a sturdy oak desk on a dais that served as the judge's bench.

Zane was glad the black, leather-covered Bible and the gavel lay to one side, untouched, so this would not be like a legal proceeding. But speaking from the witness chair still made it seem that way. Zane had no experience with courts of law, but had seen many TV dramas featuring trials. He and Jim, Huck and Becky, all sat in the front row of chairs to be called in their turns. Without having to testify under oath, they could not later be charged with perjury.

"Okay, Tom, tell us in your own words what happened," Judge Thatcher said in a kindly voice. "Don't be nervous. Speak right up."

Tom haltingly began his story. Zane didn't know if Tom's voice was quavering because he was afraid of lying to the whole village, or was just a good actor when it came to pretending to relate a terrible experience with a monster.

"We was setting around the campfire jest before dark," Tom said. "And I noticed something moving off there in the woods. I jest figured it was a deer 'cause you know there's lots o'deer on them islands. And they come out to graze early in the morning and late in the day . . ."

"Yes, yes, go on," the judge said, as if he was familiar with the habits of deer. "How far away was it?"

"Oh, I think maybe fifty yards or more. Wouldn't you say?" he asked his co-conspirators in the front row.

Huck nodded.

"Never mind. They'll have their chance to talk in a few

minutes," the judge said. "Where was your camp, exactly?"

"We'd set up on some flat, sandy ground maybe twenty paces from the foot of the island . . ."

"And this was Westport Island?"

"Yessir."

"Are you familiar with Westport Island? You ever been there before?" the judge asked.

"Nosir. Never been there. I was able to find it from a map I had. It jest seemed like a good place to land and camp and do some fishing . . . maybe bag us a wild duck to roast."

"You had a gun along, then?" the judge asked.

"Yessir. We'd discovered some old ratty pistols in the cave and polished'em up some."

A tolerant ripple of laughter from the crowd.

Zane wished he dared lean forward and look at the faces of the other three to see how they were reacting to this recitation, but thought it better to sit quietly and pay attention. He had to be sure, when his turn came, not to contradict anything Tom was saying.

"We still had an hour or two of daylight since the days're pretty long now, so I suggested we go take a look," Tom continued.

"Did all of you go?"

"Yessir." He paused as if thinking.

"And . . . ?"

"We saw a big, hairy cretur—bigger than a gorilla—walk off into the woods, really fast, about thirty paces ahead—like he'd been spying on us and wanted to get away fast. Chills went up my back, I can tell you," Tom said, warming to his story. "We all saw'im, plain as day, didn't we?" He looked to the front row for confirmation, and Zane and the others nodded.

"He was walking upright on two legs?" the judge asked.

"Yessir."

120

The crowd was deathly silent, as if they were all holding their collective breath.

"How tall would you say this beast—or this man—was?"

"Hmmm . . . I reckon most of seven or eight feet."

A gasp and murmuring from the crowd.

"We was all pretty scared, and didn't try to go after him," Tom said. "Fact is, we thought o'pulling outa there and leaving the island whilst it was still daylight. We scouted around close and found a place like a nest made o'brush and grass where he coulda been sleeping. Where he'd been lurking we saw he'd left some tracks in the soft mud. I says, 'nobody ain't gonna believe this, so I'm gonna make some molds o'these here footprints to take home.' " He paused and fumbled in the gunnysack under his chair, producing the molds, and set them on the judge's table. "And here they are."

The crowd erupted, surging forward out of their seats to get a look.

"Sit down, sit down," the judge ordered, waving them back. "You'll all get a turn." He picked up the molds and turned them over, one at a time, then held one aloft for those in back to see.

"The tracks was about six feet apart," Tom said.

"I can tell he must have been heavy, from the depth of these tracks," the judge said. "What happened next?"

"Well, sir, we was all pretty fidgety and didn't figure on sleeping much that night 'cause we didn't know if he was through watching us. The moon was might near full, and we decided to stay in camp and take turns posting a sentry during the night."

The windows were wide open, and a slight midday breeze filtered in, but it wasn't near enough to stir the air in the crowded room. Paper fans of all kinds were rustling in the silence. Tom wiped his brow with a shirtsleeve. "Kin I have a drink o'water, Judge?"

"Fetch it," Judge Thatcher ordered no one in particular.

Someone in the back of the room jumped up and hurried out.

"Go on with your story."

"Well, we didn't sleep atall that night. We jest threw more wood on the fire and huddled up close as we could, and kept a'looking over our shoulders toward those dark woods." He was getting into it now. Gone were any signs of nervousness.

"We kept our guns primed and ready 'cause we didn't know what it was or what it might do."

"I heard you was warned about that thing before you left," somebody in the crowd called out. "You might've expected to see one if they's comin' thisaway."

"Quiet!" the judge ordered.

There was silence for a few seconds while Tom appeared to collect himself. Before he could start again, a man returned with a gourd full of water from the town pump and Tom gulped down a drink.

"Well, that giant appearing like that was mighty worrisome. We heard him twict in the night."

"Heard him?" the judge asked.

"Yessir. Or anyways, we figured it was him, but it sounded more like a screech—or howl, I guess you might say. Jest like they say a mountain lion sounds. Sent m'hair t'standing on end, I can tell you!" He seemed to shiver at the memory. "Then, 'long about first light we was all tired from no sleep, so we started busting up camp, putting things in the boat and getting ready to leave. We'd heard and seen all we wanted of that thing. But he warn't done with us yet, I reckon, 'cause jest at daylight here he come again, sliding through the trees toward the camp." He paused and there was a hush in the audience and even the fans stopped rustling, as if all the spectators were holding their breath, getting ready to run.

"We seen he warn't gonna stop at the edge o'the woods like before, so we dropped what we was doing and lit out for the boat. It warn't but about thirty paces away, but this thing was so tall that one o'his strides made two of ourn. Jest then I come to myself and saw I was gripping a pistol and took a shot over my shoulder. I think the others did the same, but I was so busy about then, I don't recollect much o'nothing. It's all kind of mixed up in my head. Becky tripped and fell. I yanked her up by the hand and she kinda staggered for the boat. But that cretur was right on us by then, a slashing with those big claws, and ripped Becky's blouse as she tumbled into the boat." His face was reddening and sweating as he gasped out the story.

The crowd was on the edges of their chairs.

"Huck fired and I did, too, and I know we hit him, 'cause Huck's old pepperbox let go with all six cylinders at oncet, but none o'that shower o'lead slowed him up much. Me and Huck give the boat a shove. And, Jim, he upped with an oar and took a mighty cut with it. The edge of the oar blade caught that giant right in the throat and he went down, a'clawing at us. But that retarded him jest enough for Zane to push us clear with another oar. I reckon two or three more of our bullets done for him, 'cause he fell agin the gunwale and then kinda slid sideways into the water as the boat drifted out. In a second or two, he went under and we ain't seen so much as a hair of him since."

He paused to have another drink from the gourd. "The current's right swift along there, and it must've took him, 'cause we come back there a bit later after we'd loaded our boat, and probed around with the oars but didn't find nothing. He's likely been drug a few miles downstream by now." Tom paused, and wiped his face with his sleeve. "And that's about it, Judge. We started for home. But we couldn't sail or row all the way in one day, so we anchored in the lee of Cottonwood Island and slept in the boat jest in case and ate some cold rations. We come on in the rest o'the way this morning."

The crowd broke into a buzz of conversation with heads nodding, and Judge Thatcher not shushing them. He sat there looking straight ahead as if stunned by what he'd heard. After a minute, he took the gavel and rapped for quiet, then cleared his throat as the hubbub died down. "Thank you, Tom. You can step down. Now we'll hear from Huckleberry Finn."

Huck looked as if he would rather have been in the presence of the hairy giant at that moment than in front of the whole village. But he moved to the witness chair and slouched into it. With a little probing from the judge, Huck gave basically the same story but with a little less flair than Tom's narrative.

He was excused and Becky called. She gave the best performance of a fear-struck girl that Zane had ever seen. At the judge's request, she held up her arm to show the slashed sleeve of the blouse, but related that she had only a few minor scratches from the ordeal, and that the others were basically unhurt, "other than being 'most scared out of our wits by this attack."

"That's enough, young lady, you can step down," her father said, and then called Zane. In order not to be repetitious, he gave the briefest account, and was dismissed.

Jim was not called and no one expected him to be. Blacks could not testify in court, so he was ignored in this situation as well until Judge Thatcher, apparently as an afterthought, said. "Jim, you were the only adult there. Do you have anything to add to this story? Anything different you saw or heard?"

Jim seemed to think for a moment and then replied, "No, suh, Judge. Ah reckon de youngsters 'bout told it all."

The judge sat back in his chair, then rapped for quiet again when the rumble began to build. "Let me ask each of you one more question. You can answer separately with your own opinion about what you saw." He paused, apparently to get the wording exact. "Do you think this creature was human or some sort of animal?" He leaned his elbows on the table. "Tom?"

"Human, sir," Tom Sawyer answered with no hesitation.

"Huckleberry?"

"I reckon it was human, sir. But he was more like a wild man from Borneo I seen in a circus oncet."

"Becky?"

"Daddy . . . Judge, I'm not sure. But I think he was more human than animal."

"Zane?"

"I'd have to say human, sir, even though the tracks were more like those of a beast."

"Did any of you hear him utter anything that sounded like it could have been human speech—any kind of language at all?"

They all shook their heads.

"Then we'll have to assume it is some sort of beast that walks upright. Since there are no gorillas, apes, or known animals of that kind in this part of the world, and you certainly would have recognized a bear on its hind legs, we'll have to classify it as an 'unknown' creature of some kind for now."

"It warn't no bear, Judge!" Huck affirmed.

"Judge!" A woman in the back raised her hand.

"Yes, Missus Carney."

"That newspaper piece that was tacked up at the post office said these could be descendants of giant humans that lived thousands of years ago."

"I'm not a scientist, Bridget," the judge replied. "I suppose anything is possible. Until we can find the body and study it, we'll have to say it's an unknown creature."

At mention of the corpse, Zane got a chill, although he knew it would never turn up because it didn't exist. But the lack of evidence could cast doubt on their story. Zane wanted to mention the blood on the boat again as proof, but dared not speak now. Many of the villagers and the judge himself had already seen it. In the 21st century, the blood samples could have been analyzed and shown to be fish blood. But in 1849? Was such analysis possible?

Zane glanced around to see if he could spot Tom's Aunt Polly or the Widow Douglas in the throng. He suspected they were here someplace.

As soon as this meeting broke up, he and Huck and Tom had to somehow smuggle that gunnysack of carved wooden footprints to the cave, or bury them or sink them with a sack of rocks in the river. They must not be found. They were still in a sack under the sails and a pile of gear in the boat.

As Zane's eyes swept the rapt, sweating crowd, he spotted a tall man with a drooping white mustache standing in back by the door. He looked familiar. As Zane turned back to the front, the recognition dawned. It was Rueben Stiles, the county sheriff he'd met earlier in the summer when Becky was kidnapped.

Before Zane could ponder this, he heard Stiles's voice raised. "Judge, if I might have a moment?"

"Yes, Sheriff, what is it?"

Stiles's boots clumped on the wooden floor as he strode toward the front of the room. "I have some news that could add mightily to these proceedings."

CHAPTER 13

Stiles stood to one side of the judge's table and faced the crowd. "Ladies and gentlemen, I arrived on the upbound steamer twenty minutes ago and got here in time to hear most of what was said." He paused, holding his wide-brimmed hat in front of him.

"I've been down south hunting three wanted criminals," he announced. "And I found one of them—Gus Weir, one of the kidnappers who held these youngsters hostage earlier this summer. He didn't die in that tornado in Indian Territory as we were led to believe. The storm and the Indians didn't kill him, but there's a better than even chance he might die now."

"Was he wanted dead or alive, Sheriff?" a man in the second row asked.

"I don't know, but I didn't shoot him, if that's what you're thinking. I found him severely wounded lying on a sandbar at the foot of Osprey Island. That lies off the lower edge of Westport Island where these young people had the run-in with the giant beast," he added, glancing toward Zane and his friends in the first row. "Weir had been horribly mauled by something or someone. He had several broken bones and serious gashes as if he'd been slashed by a sword and pummeled by a club of some kind."

There were gasps and the crowd erupted into turmoil, people springing from their chairs and clustering in groups. "By Gawd, another one!" somebody cried. "We gotta do something."

"It's a full moon. They'll be on us afore the week is out, you can bet," a shrill voice lamented.

The judge rapped the gavel. "That's enough . . . Quiet! . . . Sit down! Hear him out."

The noise subsided and the room settled into tense expectation.

"I didn't recognize Weir at first," Stiles continued. "In fact, I thought he was dead. There was a lot of blood on him and his clothes were torn and ripped to rags. But then I saw he was breathing, so I slid him onto a blanket and eased him into the bottom of my skiff. The nearest help was at the village of Hamburg about five miles upstream. I found some slack water on the Illinois side and rowed like the devil was after me, hoping I wasn't too late. That village has a doctor and a nurse. They're working on him now, trying to stop the bleeding and reverse the shock. The physician said the next day or so would tell the tale. I had no idea who this injured man was until we found some identification in the pockets of his clothes we cut off him. Even when I discovered it was Gus Weir, I wouldn't have recognized him. He'd shaved his mustache and his face was battered and swollen. Didn't look nothin' like his picture on the wanted posters. If he survives—which I ain't too sure of—I'll arrest him for kidnapping and extortion. He'll likely get a stiff jail sentence."

Stiles paused again and then said, "But what makes my tale relevant to this hearing is the fact that I saw some huge barefooted footprints in the sand near Weir. These tracks led off into the woods. I didn't follow them because I was rushing to try to save a man's life if I could."

"Did the tracks look like these?" the judge asked, handing him one of Tom's tallow molds.

Stiles turned it over carefully. "Not exactly. I recollect the ones I saw had another toe or two. If there were any claws they musta been retracted and didn't make a mark in the sand. I ain't no expert, but I'd guess those impressions were the approximate size and shape of grizzly bear tracks."

"Ain't never been no griz around here," someone said aloud. "Maybe it was a black bear."

Stiles shrugged. "Possible, I guess, though they don't attack unless aggravated or protecting cubs. I hope Weir comes around so he can talk and tell us what got him. I'm going back to Hamburg in a day or two to check on him. The doctor and his nurse seemed like capable people. They stopped the bleeding and were cleaning the deep cuts. Said the next day or two would be critical. His wounds could fester since they were full of dirt and sand. Flies had been all over him. I ain't a doctor but Weir looked bad off. Be surprised if he pulls through. But this man is mighty tough to have so far cheated the buzzards that were settling in when I found him. Fact is, their circling was what drew my attention to that sandbar to begin with." He paused to take a deep breath. "Nothing more I could do there, so I hailed the noon steamboat to come on home."

"Did you have a lead on this man, Sheriff?" somebody called out.

"I had paper on three wanted criminals last reported to be in the vicinity of St. Louis. Weir was one of them. I took a steamboat to the city to scout around, and was working my way back north in a skiff, poking along some o'those uninhabited islands when I spotted something on that sandbar and rowed over to investigate."

Zane knew this story of an actual attack by some savage beast would coincidentally reinforce their own phony story. It was a mighty relief to have their bamboozling confirmed by the sheriff. Maybe now, even the skeptics in St. Petersburg would believe their "stretcher" as Tom had called it. But Zane shivered at their being that close to some kind of real threat. What could this have been, ever so near to their own camp? He glanced at Tom, Huck, Becky, and Jim. They all looked as startled and mystified as he felt.

The crowd fell silent for several seconds, then Judge Thatcher ventured the obvious question Zane had been waiting to hear. "Sheriff, do you think it's likely this outlaw could have been attacked by the same creature that the youngsters killed? Or possibly, its mate?"

"Honestly, Judge, I'd be afraid to guess. But two such similar attacks on adjacent islands within a day or two seems unlikely to be coincidental. As a longtime lawman, I've come to distrust anything that smacks of coincidence. In my opinion, I'd say there is a very strong chance the attacks are somehow connected."

"Thank you, Sheriff. Anything else you want to add?"

"That's it for now." Stiles flicked both halves of the big mustache back from his mouth with the back of a forefinger, then edged away and started toward the back of the room.

"All right, then," the judge said. "You folks take a deep breath and relax, now. You know as much about this as I do. Go on back to your homes or your businesses. If anything new or important develops, we'll ring the ferry bell to assemble again. Meanwhile, we owe these young folks and Jim a debt of gratitude for dispatching one of those dangerous creatures." He began to clap his hands and the applause spread to the crowd and lasted for half a minute, while some even rose to their feet in tribute.

Tom's face was beaming with pleasure at once again being a hero. Becky's face was also glowing, but more with the heat and embarrassment, Zane guessed. Huck appeared uneasy and was glancing about as if looking for the fastest way out.

As the huzzahs and clapping died down, Judge Thatcher rapped his gavel once. "This hearing is adjourned!"

The crowd again erupted into a general rumble of conversation, followed by the scraping of chairs on the wooden floor as everyone stood and began shuffling toward the door.

Zane and his friends accepted congratulations from one and all as they joined the villagers filing out the one rear door, everyone talking at once.

"Huckleberry!" Widow Douglas rushed up and gave Huck a hug, squeezing the embarrassed lad to her ample bosom. "I was so worried when I heard what had happened." She turned to Jim. "And I'm so glad you went along to help. No telling what might have happened otherwise."

"Yes'um," Jim mumbled, ducking his head.

"Were either of you hurt in any way?"

"No'um," Huck said. "Just a few scratches. Collected a good bit o'mud and mosquito bites is all."

She laughed with obvious relief. "Go along with you! Mud and mosquitoes, indeed. I reckon we can deal with that."

"Tom, I told you and Zane you should not have gone on that fishing trip. I had a bad feeling about it," Aunt Polly's voice scolded as the good lady pushed her way to their side. She gripped Tom in a convulsive hug and offered her hand to Zane and also to Becky. "But I reckon all's well now. Praise the Lord for your safe deliverance. I reckon your guardian angels will need a long vacation after this summer is over."

Zane smiled at this. Little did she know . . . He was eager to gather the other four away by themselves so they could assess the situation. But he didn't want to appear too eager. Tom, for one, seemed to be reveling in his new celebrity he'd worked so hard to create. He'd turned to chat with his friend Joe Harper, who'd come up to ask him about the adventure.

Without arousing suspicion, Zane and the others couldn't take off to Jackson's Island by themselves for a private meeting at the moment.

Becky said goodbye and went with her father to eat lunch, and to rest and refresh herself away from the afternoon heat.

"Ah 'spect ah best get back to work," Jim said, giving them a knowing look, then turning to follow the widow toward Cardiff Hill. "Mebbe ah sees you dis evenin'."

"After supper when it cools down a bit," Huck added as he joined Jim.

Zane was not beholden to anybody, and, following this relief from pressure at the hearing, started toward their yawl at the waterfront. He wanted to take a cool swim and relax. It might be up to him to ditch the carved blocks of wood.

But then Tom saw him heading toward the river and called, "Wait up, Zane." He turned to his aunt. "Aunt Polly, I'll be along directly. Have to help Zane clean up the boat and drag it ashore."

"I'm going to make something special for supper, so don't be late," the old lady called after him. "Zane, you're invited, too. Mary and Sid will be home tomorrow. Thank the Lord, I'll have my whole family around me again." She started away toward their two-story frame house a block away, a spring in her step as if her energy and good spirits had returned.

Tom and Zane reached the boat, shoved off, and rowed upstream another hundred yards above the commercial landing; then beached the boat on the grassy bank, tying its painter to a small tree.

"Let's leave that bit o'blood on the gunwale in case somebody else wants to see it," Tom said, all business again.

"What about the blocks?"

"Hmmm . . . we can either carry'em to the cave and bury them, or take'em over to Jackson's Island and bury'em."

"I vote for the cave. No chance of them being dug up by some fox or washed outa the ground by high water," Zane said.

"You're right. And I know a couple secret places in there where nobody could find'em."

"What about tonight?"

"Well, I'd like to have Huck along to see where I'll hide'em, but we can't take a chance on leaving them footprint blocks in the boat the rest of the day," Tom said. "Tell you what—grab some of our traps, *and* the gunnysack, and we'll carry it all home and then traipse off to the cave with the sack, and avoid seeing anyone along the way. I'll tell Aunt Polly we're going there jest to cool off for an hour or two."

Zane dumped their blankets, fishing gear, and utensils in two sacks and added Becky's neatly folded but never-used change of clothing. He wrapped the pepperbox, the Colt, and the Smith & Wesson securely in a piece of canvas tent and tied a cord around the package. Tom tied up the gunnysack with the wooden blocks.

"Is Judge Thatcher going to keep those molds you made?" Zane asked.

"I reckon he will. I ain't gonna ask for them back. I expect he'll take'em to the veterinarian, Doc Peters, in Keokuk first chance he gets, to see if they match any known animal."

"Not likely they will," Zane said. "What worries me is that story the sheriff told. He don't look like the type o'fella who's much into making up wild tales just for fun."

"Yeah," Tom said, looking sober. "Guess it coulda been a black bear that was mad about sumpin'. Knowing Weir, he might have been shooting the bear for food, but only wounded it. Got him riled up enough to attack."

Zane and Tom trudged along several paces in silence. Then they looked at each other for a second without speaking.

"You thinking what I'm thinking?" Zane asked.

"Yeah," Tom nodded. "What if it ain't a bear atall, or even a gorilla or ape that escaped from some zoo? If it ain't none o'them things, what could it be?" He answered his own question. "Likely one o'them hairy giant men that's left over from the flood!"

After Tom and Zane dumped their gear in the woodshed behind Tom's house, they followed the back alleys and made it out of town without seeing anyone they knew on their hike to the cave a mile south of the village. Zane was nervous they'd encounter some of Tom's friends or schoolmates, or even worse—some knowledgeable adult—who would be curious as to what they had in the gunnysack. Carrying these wooden blocks carved into the shape of giant footprints was akin to carrying a sack of explosives. If anyone saw this damning evidence of their monumental lie, the word would be all over town in five minutes and the conspirators could never show their faces in St. Petersburg again. They probably would not be horsewhipped or jailed, but at the very least they'd be branded as liars and the shame of it would follow them for years.

Sweating profusely from muggy heat and nervousness, they gained the hole in the wooded hillside the boys used as a cave entrance. They slid into the cool darkness without being seen, and Tom struck a Lucifer to fire up one of the oil-soaked rag torches they stored inside.

Zane took a deep breath of the cool, fifty-two degree air. What a relief!

Tom led the way along the winding passageway, black smoke from the burning coal oil torch disappearing into the darkness far above. A hundred paces in, Tom stopped, backed up a few yards, and held the torch down.

"Hmmm . . . this likely ain't the best place to hide the sack. Somebody might come nosing around looking for more of the treasure we found here and see where there's been a lot of dirt disturbed."

Counting aloud, he stepped off exactly a dozen paces and

stopped where eons of water had grooved a small alcove out of the rock wall of the main passage. It was completely dry. Fine red soil covered the bottom.

Tom handed the torch to Zane and then dropped to his hands and knees and began ripping at the soft dirt with his Barlow knife. In about two minutes he had a hole eighteen inches deep. He paused for breath. "Jest a bit more, I'm thinking." He went at it like a burrowing badger once more. Then he took the wooden blocks from the sack and snugged them into the bottom of the hole, carved sides down.

He and Zane filled the hole and Tom stamped down the dirt with the toughened soles of his bare feet. Taking the gunnysack, he dragged it lightly and carefully over the soft red soil until all his prints and evidence of digging had been erased.

"There. That should do it," he said, stepping back to admire his handiwork.

"Why don't you chop them up with an axe and burn them?" Zane asked. "That way you'd be sure nobody would find them. Or sink them in the mud of a swamp across the river?"

"You're starting to sound like Huck Finn—dull as a temperance tract," Tom said. "Where's your sense of adventure? This here is akin to burying pirate treasure. It's evidence that could send us to the gallows. Besides, who knows when we might need these blocks again?"

"Again?"

"Sure. If rain has washed out those tracks on Westport Island, we might have to get Jim to make some more prints. And, as you know, carving these was a mighty tough job."

Zane knew the chances of persuading Jim to duplicate the footprints were slim to none. But he kept silent.

In order not to waste any more of the torch, they retreated to the hillside hole where they'd entered. Tom snuffed and stowed the torch. Then they sank down on the soft dirt a few yards from the entrance where they could have some light and talked for a bit, discussing the success of the conspiracy.

Within minutes, relaxed by the delicious coolness and the pervasive quiet, they drifted off to sleep.

CHAPTER 14

Bit Barjee was tired of paddling. Even slipping along in the slack water near the shore, paddling a loaded canoe upstream for ten hours a day in the heat was a wearing task. And his dog was no help with this work.

He gripped a small tree root projecting from the side of a cutbank and held his canoe in place while watching an up-bound steamer hug the distant Illinois shore, churning slowly out of sight around the next bend.

"What about it, boy?" he said, rubbing the dog's head as it turned to look back at him as if to ask why they'd stopped. "I know you're not tired, but I am."

He'd been working his way north from St. Louis for several days now. During that time, he and the unnamed dog had gotten used to each other and become friends as they island-hopped or camped on thick towheads. Barjee had not known how much he missed companionship. Except for his lucky strike among prospectors, followed by the disastrous end of his sojourn in the goldfields and his really disastrous time at Fort Kearny, he'd been alone for months. Heavy saddlebags of gold coins, however reassuring, did not provide good company—especially when a man was hiding out and couldn't move freely in society.

Unable to travel this dangerous river at night, he'd been very careful not to be seen by any fishermen or crewmen of scows, rafts, ferries, or steamboats. He even had to buck the current in mid-stream and cross the river to avoid occasional woodyards. The riverside hamlets were the most troublesome because there were often fishermen out from these places during daylight hours.

Even after the steamboat had been out of sight for five minutes, Barjee lingered in the shade. There was no breeze here and irritating black gnats buzzed around his nose and ears. He had to decide where he was going. He had given it much thought in the past few days, and his long-term goal was Canada. He'd decided to follow the river to its source in Minnesota, and then sell the canoe and go the rest of the way by coach. He was gambling the law would not be looking for him in this northern country.

But he was tired of traveling by river, paddling all those extra miles to follow its twists and turns. Why not make the greater part of his journey overland? It would be dangerous because he'd meet more people that he couldn't avoid—unlike this wild river where thousands of hiding places were easily accessible. But perhaps he could travel by road easier at night. Now might be a good time to sell the canoe, buy a buckboard and horse, and continue along the river road the rest of the way. He could make much better time. But with his dog he couldn't travel by horseback.

He hated to let go of this canoe. It had become a lifeline for him in the few days he'd had it. To keep from burning his bridges behind him, he decided to stop at the next town to see about buying a rig. He would hide his canoe somewhere so it would be handy if he decided to come back for it.

With a new resolve, he let go of the projecting root and stroked away toward a chute a half-mile ahead. He would be on the lookout for the next town.

Afternoon shadows were beginning to stretch across the green water when he turned the bow into a boat landing of rough logs and looked up at a town on a low bluff a few yards above him. He didn't know where he'd landed, but it was a village on the Missouri side.

Without an invitation, the dog hopped out, lifted his leg on a nearby bush, then stood waiting. Barjee had no leash, but he and the dog had bonded in a few short days in each other's company, and the animal seemed to obey his voice commands. "Wish I knew your name," he muttered. "Guess I'll have to give you a new one to get used to."

He heaved the bow of the canoe up high out of the water into some weeds and pulled a piece of canvas over the load. He saw nobody around, but it was a big chance leaving his gold here unattended, along with the fancy Grimsley saddle. He had killed a man to retain possession of that gold he'd dug and panned from the California soil. He didn't want some sneak thief to make off with it now. The canvas sacks of gold coins were small, but heavy. He didn't want to carry the saddlebags with him, and he didn't want to leave them in the canoe. Then he noticed a pile of partially burned brush and limbs fifteen yards away where someone had attempted to dispose of a huge jam of driftwood. He hid the saddlebags under the tangle of blackened branches, covering the bags with damp ashes. Safe enough there for the short time he'd be in the village.

He rinsed his hands in the river while the dog got a drink.

"Ready?" Barjee said aloud.

They started up the crooked, rocky path to the village.

Barjee hadn't shaved in several days, and he knew his dark whiskers must be looking pretty scruffy. It would be difficult to keep from attracting attention in a tiny place like this, but he wanted to remain clean-shaven so he wouldn't resemble the picture on his wanted poster.

The dirt street paralleling the river was mostly deserted— lined with several whitewashed stores, a billiard parlor, a barbershop, a saloon, a general store, a small post office, and a couple of more substantial-looking red brick buildings, one of them a bank. Sun and floods over time had done their worst and the rickety boardwalk that fronted most of these buildings wavered up and down and was missing a board here and there where someone had apparently used the boards to bridge mud-holes in the street. But from lack of recent rain, the street was nothing but dry ruts. Most of the covered boardwalk was also missing its roof.

Barjee, his dog following at his heels, stepped up to the barbershop. "Stay here!" he ordered softly, pointing his finger at the dog.

He opened the door and went inside. The place smelled of bay rum and cigars. The barber, hearing the bell chime over the door, removed a newspaper from his face and stepped out of the single barber chair.

"Howdy, stranger. Shave, or haircut—or both?" He raked his ten-strand comb-over across his bare scalp with his fingers.

Barjee grinned, as he rubbed his bristly chin and glanced at himself in the back mirror. Sunburned and shaggy. "Shave, and maybe a little information."

"Yessir."

Barjee sat down and the barber got right to work, draping him with a sheet and tucking it in around his collar.

He lifted a pan of steaming water off a tiny stove and poured it into a shaving cup and began to whip it into a lather with a brush. Then he soaked a small towel and wrapped Barjee's face.

"You're new here."

"Just passing through."

"By horse or wagon?"

"Boat."

"Well, if you've a mind to stay awhile, Bitterville is a nice town."

"Does Bitterville have a livery stable?" Barjee asked. "Or a stage stop?" he added as an afterthought.

"Neither one."

"Hmmm . . . then I guess I'll have to continue on by boat."

"This ain't a regular steamboat landing, but any o'the twice-a-day boats will stop for a hail." The barber stropped his razor with rapid strokes on a wide strip of leather attached to the chair. Then he unwound the hot towel from Barjee's face and began dabbing thick lather on the dark whiskers.

"Anyone got a trap and horse to sell? I'm tired of paddling."

"Let me think. Well . . . Charlie Haskins down at the mercantile has an old buggy that belonged to his wife, and her horse he's having to feed, too."

"She doesn't want it?"

"Don't reckon so. She's been gone since last winter."

"Oh. Sorry to hear it."

"Charlie ain't. She run off with a dry goods drummer who peddled hosiery and galluses. I think Charlie would've kicked in a few double eagles to help her on her way if the salesman had asked."

Barjee grinned. "Not a marriage made in heaven, then?"

"You could say that. He's sure been a lot jollier the past few months."

"Thanks for the tip. I'll pay Charlie a visit. And I need to freshen up my wardrobe, too."

"Well, being the only general store around for miles, he's likely got nearly anything you could want." The barber tipped Barjee's head back a little and carefully applied the razor's edge to a sideburn.

"That old buggy out behind the store for sale?" Barjee asked an hour later as he shopped in the mercantile.

"Oh, you musta been talkin' to Bob Lattimore, the barber."

"Just came from there."

Haskins frowned "I wish Bob would be a bit more circumspect with his gossip." The rotund store owner laid out a soft white shirt on the counter and indicated a rack of shoes nearby. He cast an eye at the dog, who was sniffing the base of a counter that held beef jerky and horehound candy.

"He was only trying to be helpful."

"I've decided to keep that buggy and use it myself," Haskins said. "But I'll sell my old buckboard. Bearings in the left rear hub are shot, but a blacksmith can fix it. You can have the wagon for a good price."

"Does Bitterville have a blacksmith?"

"Sure. Second door from the end of this street."

"Got a horse for the buckboard?"

"Yeah. That was my wife's. It needs some exercise. You can have both for a bargain price—and I'll throw in the harness for free. I need to get rid of all that and clean up my back lot."

"Let me finish up here and I'll take a look."

There was still more than an hour of daylight left when Barjee paid the blacksmith with a quarter eagle, climbed to the wooden seat of the wagon, and took up the reins. He was satisfied he'd made an excellent deal all around by trading the Grimsley saddle and a half eagle for a new set of clothing and shoes, ammunition for his Colt, and some cornmeal, bacon, and a few dried food items, including apricots and several dried biscuits.

Before hauling the saddle upslope to Haskins, Barjee had used his knife to carefully cut out a tiny circle of leather that bore the stamped CS initials. Nothing else on the saddle could possibly connect it to its late owner, Senator Cyrus Shirten. The expensive saddle was in prime condition and Haskins proudly put it on a wooden saddle rack for display. Barjee paid in gold for the wagon and horse.

While the blacksmith was working on the wheel bearings, Barjee hauled up his bedroll wrapped around the dried food and personal items and dumped it on the ground.

Then he hoisted the canoe, balanced it over his head, and portaged it to the blacksmith shop. He wasn't about to part with it. Life was uncertain, especially for a man on the run. He might need it if he had to take to the river again. The canoe was nearly eighteen feet long, and he turned it upside down lengthwise across the buckboard, lashing the bow across the wooden seat in front, and the stern across the tailgate where it protruded out a couple of feet. It looked a bit awkward, but the arrangement would suffice.

The dog hopped up beside him and he drove the wagon as close as he could to the path to the river. He paused when he saw a local fisherman hauling the bow of a skiff out of the water. They nodded to each other as the man took a string of fish and started up to the village.

As soon as he was out of sight, Barjee dug the saddlebags from the deep ashes and shoved them under the tarp he'd purchased to cover his small load on the buckboard. He slapped the reins over the dun's back and they were off, heading north out of Bitterville along the river road, the dog lying in back on a corner of the canvas cover.

The river road at the supper hour appeared deserted, but Barjee knew he would likely encounter travelers sooner or later because this was the main route, paralleling the river for many miles. He also realized he'd left traces of himself that any detective could pick up. But there was no telegraph, so if the law was actively looking for him, word that he'd been at Bitterville would travel slowly along the river, and any pursuit would be equally slow in coming.

The river road along here had been indifferently maintained, and the heat of a dry summer had allowed time for low spots to completely dry, and new detours to become packed and passable with many hooves and wagon wheels. The road, winding mostly through heavily wooded areas, dipped and rose and at places curved away from the river far enough to lose sight of the mighty waterway.

But they were making good time. He was dry, comfortable, and shaved, and best of all, he did not have to paddle. He had to believe the dog was comfortable as well. But apparently the animal was hungry, because Barjee noticed him shoving his nose under the tarp, sniffing at the sack that held the side of bacon.

Barjee's own appetite, depressed by the heat, was also returning as the day began to cool in the shade of the forest. Neither of them had eaten since early morning. As dusk came on, he began to watch for a good place to pull off and camp.

It was nearly a half-hour later that he came out of a copse of trees into a clearing several acres in size and was surprised to see a two-story clapboard house. While they moved steadily closer, he studied the place. The road curved inland here, but he got a full view. It was larger than he thought. In fact, it also appeared deserted. A few of the windows were missing glass, and appeared to stare with empty eyes at the broad river.

"Whoa, gal!" He reined up forty yards away and studied the layout. A tumbledown rotting rail fence encircled a yard that was rank with tall grass and weeds. Saplings had sprouted in the yard as the forest was beginning to reclaim the open space. No horses, farm animals, harrows, or hay rakes were in evidence. Five outbuildings occupied the back lot. One was a privy. Another was a small barn, leaning drunkenly. From their size and shape two others might have been a woodshed and smokehouse. The last was about the size of a slave cabin.

He looped the reins around the brake handle and stepped down. The dog jumped out and followed at his heels. He had time to take a closer look. The lonely effect of the place gave off the miasma of a living presence, yet it was obvious no one was actually living here. Or were they? He had a crawly feeling the place had been very recently occupied—that somebody might yet be here and was watching him. But he shrugged off the presentiment. He was a practical man. Unless there was a skunk or pack rat inside or possibly a snake, this might do for a night's shelter.

Why had this nice house been deserted? As Barjee waded through the deep grass, the dog stopped and the hair rose on his back. He emitted a low growl.

Barjee paused and pulled his Colt. The dog had sensed something. But what? Surely the place wasn't still occupied, unless by some animal, or a transient, like himself.

When he came around to the front porch that faced the river, he saw the reason for abandonment: The river was undercutting the dirt bank only a few yards from the sagging porch. Somebody's nice home would shortly become another victim of the hungry current. This house could have been built as much as a mile from the river, but the unpredictable swings of the current had eaten away the shoreline over time. The thousands of cubic yards of soil that had originally separated this house from the Mississippi were probably loam on somebody's fields far downstream by now, or were silting in some chute.

The house was unlike most he'd seen in this region. This was no crude, double log cabin with a dogtrot in the middle. This was a two-story house that would not have been out of place in some of the better neighborhoods of Cincinnati or St. Louis.

"C'mon, boy," he said softly to the dog and continued walking. The dog crept forward reluctantly, tail between his legs. He stepped up onto the front porch and a rotten board collapsed under his weight. Startled, he pulled his foot out of the hole, then moved slowly forward and carefully shoved aside the sagging door. The whole house was a bit cockeyed as if it were already settling toward its final doom.

From the looks of the front parlor, this house had been abandoned in haste and all the furniture left. The room smelled of mold. Dust and rodent droppings were everywhere. There was no rug or carpet on the wide floor planks. But what caught his attention was a long streak where the dust had been disturbed, along with several partial footprints of a shoe or boot. Someone had been here recently.

He thumbed back the hammer on his Colt and walked softly to the stairs at the left side of the room. Someone had trod these steps within the past week. He quietly ascended the steps while the dog stayed below, watching him. In spite of his efforts at stealth, the stairs creaked and groaned under his weight.

Senses alert, he examined the hallway. The doors to three bedrooms stood open and evidence in the dust showed some human had gone in and out. The bed in the room at the top of the stairs contained a feather tick that bore the indent of a human form from top to bottom where a person had recently slept.

After a cursory examination of the rest of the floor, he uncocked his pistol and holstered it. The house may have sheltered tramp or traveler, but it seemed empty now, and it would suffice to keep off the weather for him and his dog for one night.

He went back outside and glanced at the white thunderheads towering high overhead, the vanished sun tinting them a gorgeous rose color. Somewhere beyond the treeline to the west came a grumble of thunder from the darkened cloud base.

"How about something to eat?" Barjee said to the dog, who was sniffing around the front porch. "We got a dry place to settle in for the night."

The dog cocked his head and gave him a quizzical look.

Barjee drove the rig up close to one side of the house near

the cellar door where it was not obvious from the road. Then he unhitched the horse and led it to a stall in the barn on the back lot. The hay he pulled down from the loft was still dry and not moldy.

He expected the leather collar on the pump to be so dry as to be unusable. But, after a bit of priming, it began to take hold, creating suction, and he pumped two buckets of water. Whoever had been here had used this pump.

An unusual stroke of luck provided a small country ham hanging by a wire in the smokehouse. "Somebody must've been in a big hurry if they overlooked this," he muttered to the dog. It looked to be thoroughly cured and resembled a dried-out hunk of deteriorating leather. But he knew better. He sniffed it and the smoky aroma made his mouth water. It had been carefully hung out of reach of any animals.

His luck continued when he found that even the lamps in the house still contained coal oil, and the fruit cellar had jars of canned goods. This house must not have been abandoned until the last minute when the residents felt they were in imminent danger of falling into the river. Besides the fruit in the cool cellar, he found several bottles of red wine that appeared homemade. Again, signs in the disturbed dust showed some visitor had helped himself to the canned goods and to the wine. But there was still plenty left.

Barjee had no illusions whatever that a benevolent Providence had provided all this for him—a murderer. In fact, he didn't believe in Providence of any kind—good or bad. To him, this was just dumb luck. Good luck, bad luck. He'd had his share of both. The ups and downs evened out over time. Beyond that, he neither knew nor cared if something beyond his control was nudging events that controlled his destiny.

The wine was of more immediate interest. The dust had been wiped from several of the hand-inscribed labels. Every bottle of the red wine looked the same and bore a bottling date from three years earlier, perhaps when grapevines on the property had been producing. He knew he had a fondness for alcohol that had led him into trouble, and would again, if he allowed it to master him.

As he struck a Lucifer to one of the lamps and set about building a fire in the kitchen cookstove, he couldn't keep from eyeing the stoppered bottle he'd selected to complement this feast. The house was more modern in that the kitchen was part of the main house instead of being detached, as were earlier kitchens for fire safety and to avoid excessive heat buildup in summer.

Ashes in the stove were cold, but didn't look old. Whoever had been here was gone. Barjee felt a slight chill. Had this unknown resident slipped out when he saw Barjee and the dog approaching? The dog had now settled down, and was lying on the floor nearby, watching him provide food. Barjee was satisfied this dog, he'd begun to call "Louis" after the city where they'd joined forces, would prove valuable as a watchdog, in addition to being a friend and companion.

Thunder in the west again. A satisfying meal, wine, and restful sleep, he thought—even a dog to share his fortune. It was all undeserved, but he'd take it.

CHAPTER 15

Tom, Huck, Becky, Jim, and Zane were heroes of the village. They were interviewed, written up in the newspaper, talked about, and pointed out on the street.

They were even praised from the pulpit the following Sunday, resulting in a standing ovation from the congregation. With the exception of Jim, the objects of all this adulation and envy were present in the pews of the white clapboard church—attendance for at least two of them being under duress.

But when the damp, sweltering crowd was dismissed after the final blessing more than an hour later, even Tom and Huck had to admit this was one of the proudest moments of their lives, rivaling even the stunning resurrection at their own funeral two years earlier.

Becky, starch wilting in the collar of her Sunday frock, even looked pleased as she shook hands with the preacher and greeted many of the ladies of St. Petersburg. The Widow Douglas, face screened by a sunbonnet, came up and offered her hand. "That must have been a dreadful experience for you, Becky," she said.

"Yes'am," she nodded, self-consciously wiping her palms on a lace-trimmed handkerchief. "My hands are perspiring so, I should have worn my gloves," she said to change the subject.

"Yes, my dear, we're certainly having a spell of hem-puckering weather," the widow agreed.

They exchanged a few more pleasantries, then went their

separate ways to seek some shade.

As far as most people knew, the youngsters and Jim had eliminated the immediate threat to the village, and the people were heaving a huge sigh of relief.

Those thoughtful souls who gave the problem closer scrutiny had only a couple of niggling doubts—how did the youngsters know to carry several pistols on a fishing trip? Was it only as a precaution because of the posted warning? How did Tom happen to have all that tallow with him? And what would Gus Weir say if he came out of his coma? His attacker—whoever or whatever it was—had escaped and was still at large. And there remained the unanswered question—who had posted the newspaper article and the handwritten note on the post office bulletin board?

But for now, the village rejoiced and gave thanks to Providence that St. Petersburg was blessed with young folks and a freed slave who were courageous and resourceful. Only Becky seemed rather subdued, but most thought that was the normal reaction to the trauma she had suffered. But Zane, watching her closely, decided it was from a guilty conscience. Unlike Tom and Huck, she had never lied on such a monumental scale before.

When Zane mentioned this privately to the other boys, Tom's rejoinder was, "It's her own dern fault for being so pushy and sticking her nose into our business. I reckon this conspiracy was jest way too big for her."

Huck, he thought the same.

Jim had been staying out of the glare of publicity, humbly acknowledging a compliment when he received one, and only going into detail with other blacks who sought him out for the gory details of his monster-slaying. In the evenings behind the widow's house, they gathered to hear his tale. They were awed, shivering, and wide-eyed at his recitation. "Ooooohhh!!" they moaned low in unison when he reached the part of his story where he swung the oar with all his might and whacked the hairy giant across the throat, putting him down for good.

Zane had passed nearby one evening on his way to see Huck when he overheard part of Jim's story. It brought to mind another tale about the slaying of a mythical giant. He pictured a mead hall a thousand years earlier, full of Danish warriors cheering Beowulf for killing the giant, Grendel, who'd devastated their ranks.

Zane privately thought Jim, being the upright God-fearing man he was, also had regrets about his part in the deception. But that didn't stop him from having fun with the retelling and embellishment of the scary adventure. He didn't even bring witches into the story, taking the credit for himself and the youngsters.

Late on Sunday afternoon, Jim, Huck, Tom, and Zane met in the woods on Cardiff Hill behind the widow's small farm. Jim seemed to have other concerns besides the deception of their conspiracy.

"De sheriff, he seen tracks dat ah sho didn't make," Jim said with a worried look. "De word spread 'round about dat. But when ah tells *my* story ah don't lets on to know nuffin 'bout no mo monsters. And dat's de truth."

"None of us do, Jim, and it's mighty worrisome," Tom said.

"Mebbe we's waded into into sumpin' dat make our conspiracy look like a game o'scotch-hoppers."

"Any idea what coulda made them tracks?" Huck directed his question to the group.

They looked blankly at each other.

"Maybe it really *is* a bear," Zane ventured. "That's what Sheriff Stiles guessed."

"I been 'round this village and this river all my life, and I ain't never seen or heard of a black bear in these parts," Tom said.

"Me, neither," Huck agreed. "Onliest place I heard tell of them is in the mountains up east somers, a long way from here." He paused. "I reckon they could be a few living in them miles o'thick woods away back from the river, where nobody ever goes."

"We's commenced t'foolin' wid spirits and creturs from de dark side," Jim said. "You 'spose we's done rousted up Satan, de king o'witches and demons?"

"Naw," Huck said. "Miss Watson told me oncet that Satan can disguise hisself in all kinds o'ways, but he can't hide his cloven hooves."

"What's dis 'cloven'?" Jim asked.

"A two-toed double hoof, like a sheep has," Huck said.

"Why do Satan have dat?"

"I dunno. Guess God made him thataway. Anyhow, the sheriff said the tracks he saw weren't cloven. They was more like bear paw prints with four or five toes."

"Dat still don't mean witches ain't somehow mixed up in dis," Jim insisted.

"Jim, maybe folks believe that kinda trash in far-off Africa or somers, but everybody around here knows better," Tom said.

"There's places closer than Africa where a lot o'that goes on," Zane said. "I've heard about voodoo being practiced in New Orleans and the Caribbean islands where lots of slaves live."

"What's voodoo?" Huck asked.

"Not real sure, but I think it's kind of a mixture of Christian and pagan beliefs with lots of superstition thrown in—black magic, casting spells, witchcraft—stuff like that," Zane said. "Weird and scary."

"Blacks making magic?" Huck said.

152

"Black magic ain't referring to black people," Tom said. "It's jest a certain kind o'magic that conjures up the devil."

"But witchcraft mean dat witches *do* cast dere spells," Jim said.

"I guess so. I don't know. Look, I didn't mean to get off on this subject," Zane said, somewhat exasperated. "Voodoo probably doesn't have anything at all to do with this giant we're talking about."

"Then what're we gonna do about this other giant story?" Huck asked.

"*Do* about it?" Tom said. "Why, we won't do *nuthin'* about it. We'll hunker down and stick to our story and let things play out as they may. That tale the sheriff told jest makes our conspiracy stronger and shows us as heroes a thousand times over—because we was able to kill *our* giant hairy monster, but Gus Weir, who's a strong, mean kidnapper and slaver, was nearly killed by his'n."

"Never thought of it that way," Huck said. "Tom, you got a head on your shoulders. I shouldn't wonder if you ain't a justice o'the peace someday."

By Tuesday morning, Sheriff Rueben Stiles decided it was about time to catch a steamboat south to Hamburg and check on Gus Weir's condition. He'd received no word from the doctor in six days and assumed Weir was either still hanging on, or possibly had died.

Stiles let Judge Thatcher and others know his intent and bought a ticket on the morning boat down from Keokuk, promising to be back the next day with news.

Zane, Tom, and Huck were on edge the rest of the day. Trying to put their minds on something else, they went swimming in Bear Creek. But that diversion tired them out by noon. Then Tom suggested they take the yawl over to Jackson's Island and do some fishing, and maybe sail upriver a few miles, since the weather was glorious with a cool breeze and high mare's tails streaking the blue sky.

Becky Thatcher hadn't been seen around town for three or four days and Tom said he hoped she was remembering her oath to keep mum about their conspiracy. Zane said she probably was or she'd be in as much trouble as the rest of them.

The widow had Jim working cleaning out the implement shed so he was unavailable.

But while the three boys were on Jackson's Island, Tom confided that the main reason he wanted to get away from his house and village was that Sid had returned a few days before and was snooping around, asking questions of villagers and other young people. Tom didn't want his half-brother grilling him about anything to do with the conspiracy. "Sid is sneaky and would try to trip me up with lots of questions, acting like he was jest curious about our adventure," Tom said. "Cousin Mary is no problem. She's sweet and nice and believes whatever I tell her. Or, at least she don't call me a liar to my face."

"I reckon Sid is also probably jealous because you're a hero again," Zane said.

About one o'clock next afternoon, a northbound stern-wheeler docked at the St. Petersburg levee, discharged and took on passengers and freight, and was off within twenty minutes. Shortly thereafter the brass bell on the ferryboat began to clang, announcing to one and all that some newsworthy event was taking place.

Tom, Huck, and Zane had just finished eating congealed and sliced white bean sandwiches and fresh tomatoes for lunch provided by Aunt Polly. Sid and Mary were also there, and all five trooped outside to see what the commotion was about, although Tom, Huck, and Zane had already figured it was a town meeting in Judge Thatcher's courtroom to hear whatever news Sheriff Stiles had obtained about Gus Weir.

Zane's heart was beating faster than normal but he tried to appear calm. No matter what happened, he told himself, he was watching this drama from afar as an outsider so, if things got too dicey, he could always escape back into his 21st century world. The only problem with thinking like that was the worrisome fact that he didn't have the foggiest notion *how* to return to his former life.

The courtroom filled as it had several days earlier. But this time, there were no prolonged recitations.

"Now we'll hear from Sheriff Stiles," Judge Thatcher announced, backing away to his swivel chair behind the desk.

The sheriff got right to the point. "Gus Weir is still alive and the doctor says he has a better than even chance of survival," Stiles said, standing on the dais so the whole crowd could see and hear him. "His gashes have not mortified, and the doc has set his broken bones as best he can," the sheriff announced. "But, more to the point, he's awake and able to take nourishment much of the time and, despite being hit in the head, seems fairly lucid. I asked him what had attacked him, and you won't believe what he said." He paused.

"Tell us!" somebody yelled.

"He said it was something that looked like a big gorilla about nine feet tall. It had the features of a huge, hairy *man*—not an ape."

The crowd erupted, and somebody shouted, "Then it warn't a bear?"

"I pressed that question, and Weir stated flatly it was *not* a bear. He said there was a full moon and he had seen black bears before, and this creature walked and ran on its hind legs. He said the thing stunk to high heavens, and let out a roar that was more like the high-pitched screech of a mountain lion." He paused to lick his lips and shifted from one foot to another.

The crowd was leaning forward, and several in the back rows were standing.

"As you probably now, Weir catches runaway slaves for the rewards—when he ain't kidnapping kids for ransom," he added in a disgusted tone. "I was able to talk to him for only a minute or so because he was in severe pain and his doctor had to give him a dose of laudanum, which made him doze off. But here's what he told me—he said he was after a runaway Negro name of Bull Brady, the big brawler from Louisiana some o'you mighta heard tell of. This black buck is a huge man by all accounts and a professional fighter who earns piles of money for his owner taking on all comers in rough and tumble matches. He escaped from his master offen a steamboat two or three weeks ago somewhere in that area. Anyways, Weir thought he'd spotted him on Osprey Island and tried to run him down. He couldn't catch up to him in the woods and fired a couple warning shots to make him stop. Weir thinks maybe one of his shots in the dark mighta hit this giant and that's what got him enraged enough to attack."

"Then it warn't Bull Brady?" a voice yelled.

"It was not."

The newspaper editor stood up. "Maybe Weir was scared out of his wits and it was dark and he *mistook* Bull Brady for some giant prehistoric man. I reckon *I* would have."

There was a ripple of laughter that broke the tension.

Sheriff Stiles smiled, then grew serious again.

"That might very well be what happened. But it can't be explained away that easily. My brains weren't rattled by any blows to the head. And it was daylight when I found Weir. I saw the tracks with my own eyes. They were far apart and deep like something big and heavy had pounded its feet deep into the damp sand while running onto that bar. If they were human tracks, they were from the largest feet I ever knew existed.

Whatever it was appeared to stomp around Weir a bit. Then the tracks—not as far apart—led back toward the thick woods as if the thing was walking upright. That's all I had time to see because Weir needed attention badly."

The hum of conversation took over. The judge didn't try to gavel it down.

Zane was sitting near the front of the room with the other boys and Jim. The Widow Douglas was behind them as were Aunt Polly, Sid, and Mary. Zane was able to locate Becky sitting with two girlfriends on the other side of the room. Zane nudged Tom and pointed her out. She looked pale.

The old soldier, Colonel Elder, raised his hand and stood up.

"Yes, Colonel," the judge said.

"I propose we raise a company of armed volunteers, including the patrollers, and go down there and make a sweep of those islands and get rid of whatever creatures are there, once and for all. We need to confront those prehistoric men—or beasts. That's the only way to put our minds at ease. I don't think anyone here will sleep well until we do."

There was a cheer of approval at this suggestion.

Zane glanced at the boys and at Jim, wondering if the colonel meant for them to be part of this force. Maybe the former Army man felt it was time for professionals to take over.

"We'll put it to a vote," Judge Thatcher said. "A show of hands. All in favor?"

A forest of hands shot up with a shouted *"Yes!"*

"All opposed?"

Three or four hands hesitatingly went up in back, but were withdrawn.

"The proposal passes!" the judge declared, banging the gavel. "The colonel, as the man with the most experience at this, will be in charge of organizing the raiding force. This meeting is adjourned!" He rapped the gavel again and the crowd began to break up.

As everyone was shuffling out the back door, Becky Thatcher left her girlfriends and pushed her way to the boys. "I need to talk to you," she said quietly to Tom.

She got him aside in the street and Zane saw them talking earnestly, Tom doing more listening than talking.

Then Becky left and went to catch up with her father, the judge, who was waiting for her in the shade and talking to the colonel.

"She wants to come with us if we're part of this force Colonel Elder is getting up," Tom told Zane, Huck, and Jim as they sidled away down the street. "But she said her father would almost certainly forbid it this time."

"We might not be able to go, either," Zane said. "It might be for adults only."

"Ah ain't sure ah wants to be part o'dis," Jim said.

"Wal, the colonel says he's gettin' up a *volunteer* force, so I reckon we kin volunteer if we ain't asked," Huck said. "Anyways, we need to show'em where the tracks are on Westport Island."

"A bunch o'men can find'em easy enough," Zane said, not too eager. "Maybe it's best we not be along so they can't ask us any questions."

"You reckon I'm gonna jest retire from the field, lie low, and not be part o'this hunt for a *real* giant, after all we been through to set up the make-believe one?" Tom said scornfully. "Why, Providence has dropped this chance in our laps like a gift from heaven. It couldn't be no better if we'd ordered it up like a plate o'ham and hominy."

They all paused and silently considered this.

"We been heroes again for a fortnight," Tom said. "Mebbe we won't be heroes this time, but you never know what kin happen.

Could be we'll save the whole village again."

"We didn't save nobody the *fust* time," Jim said.

Tom ignored this comment. "Could be this adventure will turn out to be even more dangersome than going amongst them Sioux Injuns."

"Okay," Zane reluctantly agreed.

"We hafta get the guns and ammunition and our traps outa Aunt Polly's woodshed," Huck said. "I reckon the colonel and them patrollers has guns and skiffs enough to take'em downriver. We kin take our own yawl."

"Jim, you been in on this from the start," Tom said. "You gotta come with us and see it through. And the colonel will want you along for sure."

"Ah reckon de Missus be agreeable," Jim said without much enthusiasm. "But we keep foolin' wid fire, we sho nuff gonna get burnt, by-n-by."

The village was astir the rest of that day preparing for the expedition that was to leave early next morning. Young men in their late teens and twenties, who made up the patrollers, arranged to be absent from their jobs. Wives prepared food and jugs of coffee and lemonade to take along.

Colonel Elder appointed a young man to make up a roster of volunteers and he set up a recruiting station at a table inside the mercantile. Everyone was to bring his own weapon, if he had one. If not, he would be supplied a musket. Extra powder and shot and caps would be carried for a variety of calibers for everything from smoothbore, single-shot antique pistols to the latest Colts.

Zane looked at the variety of long arms leaning against the inside wall of the mercantile. He saw a .52 caliber Jenks breech-loading carbine; a Musketoon, of .54 caliber; another musket of Eli Whitney manufacture from New Haven, Connecticut; and a strange-looking Cochrane revolving rifle in .36 caliber. But oddest of all was a blunderbuss from the very early 1800s with its flared barrel, almost bell-shaped at the muzzle.

"Look at this thing," he said to Tom. "I've seen these in Yosemite Sam cartoons. I didn't know they really existed."

"Who's Yosemite Sam?" Tom asked.

"Never mind. Just someone from my other life."

"Yeah," Tom said. "A blunderbuss will shoot 'most anything— gravel, screws, washers, glass beads. Don't have to have no lead bullets, or even percussion caps. See? It's a flintlock."

Zane left the store thinking that the U.S. Mounted Dragoons probably weren't equipped with any more firepower than was being handed out to these farmers and merchants to gun down whatever threat was out there.

When the boys went to sign up, young Josh Bagwell, who was functioning as the clerk, accepted them without batting an eye. Jim signed with an *X* and his mark was witnessed by Tom and Huck. They told Bagwell they had their own weapons, food, and boat.

While the boys were at the yawl, stowing beef jerky, corn pone, fresh tomatoes and onions, fishing lines and a can of worms, blankets, utensils, and tarp, Tom handed Huck the pepperbox pistol he'd used before.

"Reckon I'll make me a club from a hick'ry stick." Huck said, declining the gun. "Onliest time I shot that thing, it chainfired all six cylinders at oncet and like to'uv took my hand off. The widow's lye soap couldn't even scrub the burnt powder offen my skin and out from under my fingernails. Good thing I warn't shooting at sumpin' real, 'cause I got the worst o'that."

Shortly after supper, in the long twilight, Tom, Huck, and Zane retired to the top of the levee with large slices of ripe watermelon and a salt shaker. Aunt Polly had urged this special treat on them as if they were going over the ocean to battle and needed a last meal. Sid and Mary chose not to join them.

The ripe, red melon was delicious, Zane had to admit, although watermelon was something he seldom ate in his other world. Their faces and hands were covered with sticky juice as they munched the pulp and spat seeds right and left. Juice ran down their arms and dripped off their elbows. In the gathering dusk, mosquitoes found them and joined the feast, driving the boys crazy with bites.

As they were finishing and washing up in the edge of the river, Becky Thatcher came down the darkening street and up the grassy bank to join them.

She sat down dejectedly. "Daddy won't let me come on this adventure," she said.

"You kept mum about the conspiracy, didn't you?" Tom asked.

"Oh, yes. In fact, that's one reason he won't let me come. He thinks he's straining Divine Providence by putting me in danger too often."

"Well, Becky, we ain't got no idea what we could be getting into this time," Tom said somewhat condescendingly. "This might be dangersome for sure, and not jest fun like before."

"Well, I guess I'll have to miss the most exciting thing that's happened in this village since I been alive," she lamented, getting up without another word and walking off down the slope toward home.

"You gonna just let her go like that?" Zane asked.

Tom looked grieved as he distractedly scratched a bite on his arm. "She was able to talk him into it last time. But I ain't her father, so I reckon there ain't nuthin' I can do about it. Even if I was to give away the conspiracy to show that she warn't in no danger last time, it wouldn't convince him to let her go this time when they's likely to be real danger. And giving away the conspiracy would only cause trouble for all of us."

CHAPTER 16

As it turned out, the expedition didn't set off next morning as planned. Conrad Tuttle, the thirty-year-old captain of the patrollers, had gone to Keokuk, Iowa, on business, and Colonel Elder decided to wait for him to return the next afternoon.

When all the excitement and loud talk and rushing around was over, it turned out that only Colonel Elder and six other men had actually volunteered and put their names on the line, besides Tom, Huck, Zane, and Jim. Colonel Elder—a little embarrassed, Zane thought—voiced the opinion that perhaps Tuttle, as the leader of the patrollers, might be able to influence a few more able-bodied adults to join the search force.

The boys and Jim decided to take off on schedule. "This yawl's a lot faster than a skiff and we'll be down there in a jiffy today," Tom said. "It's best we get a jump on the rest so's we'll have a chance to look around and scout out the lay of things in case we have to change our story."

"Mebbe we'll need those carved blocks to make more tracks," Huck said.

"No, we don't want to chance it," Tom said. "Too dangersome with those other men coming along tomorrow. Besides, Jim made enough the first time and it ain't rained to wash'em out. And I give the judge those molds, so they're safe."

"Mebbe best we wait for the men afore we take in after sumpin' in the deep woods," Huck suggested.

"Good thinking," Zane agreed with a slight shiver.

Once Becky turned her back on the expedition, and all hope of joining it, she launched a campaign of her own—to persuade her father to allow her to ride her pony, unattended, nearly thirty miles down the river road to Marsville to visit her cousins. Just as she had done earlier when she wanted to join Tom and Huck and the others to Westport Island, she again argued that since she and her father's visit there had been interrupted earlier in the summer, she should be allowed to go now. When the judge demurred, she followed up by saying that she'd proven herself worthy of being given a little independence by withstanding severe hazards, yet winning through by grit and determination with only a scare and a few scratches. She ended by arguing she had to grow up *sometime*.

Unbeknownst to her, the judge had been harboring ambitions of his own to join Colonel Elder's expedition. He'd already ordered his law clerk to cancel the next ten days of his summer court schedule. Until all this giant business was settled, he couldn't picture himself sitting bored for hours every day in a hot courtroom thinking of more exciting events. He was nearly as old as Colonel Elder, but felt his sedentary lifestyle needed to be jarred out of a comfortable rut. Even if Colonel Elder refused to let him join the force, and he didn't go downriver, Judge Thatcher felt it was an appropriate time for a summer break. But the judge was hopeful his services would be needed since the volunteers were few in number.

Without knowing she'd caught him in a moment of distracted indecision, Becky congratulated herself on her feminine powers of persuasion. But those powers weren't quite enough.

"Becky, you know what happened last time we were on that river road," her father said. "I was with you and it was broad daylight, but the kidnappers still jumped us."

She looked forlorn and turned away, thinking of the smothering blanket of boredom that would descend on her for the next week or two.

"Well, maybe we can work out some arrangement," he added in a more conciliatory tone. "Less than an hour ago, I ran into Orville Henson at the mercantile. He mentioned that he and his boy were hauling a wagonload of produce to Marsville tomorrow. Orville always carries a shotgun when he goes out of town—not so much for protection but more in hopes of bagging a duck or a pheasant. If he's agreeable, would you mind riding along with him? There's safety in numbers."

Becky nodded, but then said, "Which one of his sons is going?"

"Seth, I reckon. He's the oldest."

Becky grimaced.

"What's the matter?"

"I knew him from school last year before he was expelled by the headmaster. He's about seventeen years old and had a head on him like a woodchuck. Couldn't learn anything and was always talking out loud without being called on. All the younger kids laughed at him."

"That's no reason to make fun . . ."

"It ain't that. He was nearly grown and he kept making eyes at the younger girls in that one-room schoolhouse. He was forever disrupting things and was really rude, until the headmaster couldn't put up with it and sent him home to the farm."

"Hmm . . . Probably best I guess. But for this trip his father, Orville, will be along, and will keep the boy on a tight rein. He won't bother you. You'll just be riding along on your pony."

"Do I *have* to?" she groaned.

"I don't know of anyone else who could escort you. It's either that or you'll have to stay home."

"Okay, I'll go with them."

"The Henson farm is only a couple miles from town. I'll ride over there and make arrangements."

When he returned, he told her Orville had agreed, and the judge had tipped the old farmer two silver dollars for his trouble.

Judge Thatcher also gave Becky money and aided with her preparations, instructing her on what to do if she should have an accident, or her horse threw a shoe, or she should run into any kind of trouble. "Of course, I don't know how much help Orville and his son would be in an emergency, but he'll be armed."

Much to her surprise, the judge took a dark blue, shiny pocket pistol from his desk drawer and instructed her on its operation if she should encounter some dangerous crisis where she had to use it to protect herself.

The judge had high hopes of joining the expedition, and felt she'd be better off with relatives than home alone with only the part-time cook in the house.

Becky kissed her father and mounted her pinto pony, Jasmine, while everything was still wet with dew and the sun was barely peeking over the treeline on the Illinois shore. She was excited to be getting away even if she did have to be protected like a child. Her pony, not having been ridden or exercised for a time, was fiddle-footing as if eager to be off as well.

"Mister Henson said he'd meet you at the town pump at sunup," the judge said, waving to her. "Don't keep him waiting."

She waved her hat at him, and gave the mare her head. The animal broke into an easy trot down the street toward the center of the village. She gave only a fleeting thought to the boys and Jim leaving at this very hour for the downriver islands. But then she put all that from her mind and thought of what lay ahead.

She was especially looking forward to seeing Pamela, her fifteen-year-old cousin who was only a year or so older than herself. Pamela was a risk-taker, bright and bubbly and eager for any exciting adventure. She was nearly the female equivalent of Tom Sawyer. Maybe that's why Becky and Pam got along so well. Becky wished they lived nearer each other so they could do things together every day. She and her cousin had been best friends all their lives.

But Pamela was forced by circumstances to work hard on her family's sixty-acre farm, and rarely had time for fun and frivolity. Pam had once told Becky that she almost looked forward to her country school starting in the autumn because time in the classroom gave her a slight break from slopping hogs, harrowing the fields, chopping firewood, drawing well water, washing clothes on a scrub board, helping her mother cook, and dozens of other chores she had to perform during the summer. Her parents worked just as hard to make a go of their acreage, but Pam had told Becky she could foresee the time when her father, who was a skilled carpenter, would have to take a job in town to supplement their income.

Becky's musings were interrupted as she reined up near the town pump. Her stomach contracted when she recognized the hulking lout, Seth Henson, seated on the farm wagon, hat pulled down until the tops of his ears stuck out. He hadn't shaved in several days. He was leering at her with a half-grin. She forced a smile at the father and called out, "Ready to go!"

Orville nodded and slapped the reins over his span of mules and the heavy wagon rumbled away toward the river road.

Becky had to hold Jasmine back. Even if they'd been traveling alone, she didn't want the pony to wear herself out before they were a third of the way.

The sun rose and the day grew warmer. She allowed the plodding mules to get a hundred yards or more ahead, put her pony to a trot to catch up, then pulled her to a walk again. It was boring and would take the entire day to reach Marsville at this pace. The wagon was loaded to the tops of the sideboards with fresh corn, tomatoes, green beans, squash, and onions so Farmer Henson was not trying to push the mules too hard.

Although eager to finish her journey, Becky was careful to hold Jasmine back from overexertion as the sun rose and the day grew warmer. She trotted for a short distance and then walked her mount for a while.

There were stretches where the trees grew close to the single-track dirt road, arching their huge limbs overhead until they intertwined and formed a green tree-tunnel. At one of these stretches, she had let the wagon run on at least a quarter mile ahead. She was suddenly nervous and thought of fairy tales she'd read as a child where children were lost in a deep, dark forest and encountering a terrible witch or goblin. Common sense told her there was no such thing in these Missouri woods, but nevertheless, her heart began to beat faster. And what was this woodland creature that had attacked Gus Weir? Could it be lurking out there, picking off lone travelers? In the deep shade of these tree tunnels, if the road was not too badly rutted, she urged Jasmine into an easy lope for a few hundred yards until they broke out into the partial sunshine again and the wagon was no more than twenty yards away.

Becky had been to her aunt and uncle's farm often enough to know the way. The farm lay about seven miles this side of Marsville, a village that held semimonthly markets during the growing season. There was also a livestock auction. The town was considerably larger than St. Petersburg, but just as dull, unless it was market weekend. She and her father had traveled this way before, but most trips had been by steamboat. It was an easier journey, though the loops and bends of the river stretched the distance to about fifty miles.

When she judged by the sun and her stomach that it was lunchtime, she wanted to rein up and get down to stretch her legs while she ate the lunch the cook had packed for her. But the wagon showed no signs of stopping, and she let it continue as she saw Seth munching on a tomato.

She reined up in a grassy area between the road and the river, loosened the cinch, and removed the bit so Jasmine could graze and drink. She placed hobbles on the pony's front feet. She sat under a tree and ate a small sandwich of bacon, cheese, and sliced cucumber, prepared by her father's cook, Elsa, who treated Becky like her own daughter. Washed down with canteen water, the lunch was satisfying and filling.

After resting for another ten minutes, she started again. Before they caught up with the Hensons, she met a farm wagon traveling in the opposite direction. The young Negro driver touched his hat to her as he passed. She noted the wagon was piled high with ripe watermelons—the kind Tom and Huck referred to as "rattlesnakes" because of their jagged, dark green stripes. She urged Jasmine to a lope and caught up with the Hensons' wagon in a little over a mile.

Seth gave her a gap-toothed grin. "Whar ya been, missy? Takin' a pee?"

"Hush up, Seth! That ain't no way to talk." The father jabbed his son with an elbow.

"Mister Henson," Becky said, guiding her pony up to the right side of the wagon. "I reckon it's only a few more miles to my cousin's farm. Thank you kindly for the escort, but it's getting on toward suppertime and I'm going to push ahead."

"Whatever you think best," the old man said.

Becky set her pony to a gallop, relieved to be rid of this encumbrance.

The afternoon shadows were elongated when she rode into the lane that led up to the clapboard farmhouse. Chickens scattered in front of her pony, and two hounds set up deep-throated barking as she reined up in front of the porch.

"My lands! Pamela, it's your cousin, Becky!" Pamela's mother, Adelaide Palmer, came rushing out the front door, wiping her hands on her apron.

Becky dismounted a bit stiffly, and hugged her aunt.

"Let me look at you!" The older woman thrust Becky back at arm's length. "You're growing—healthy and brown as a nut!" she exclaimed. "You don't look any the worse for your encounter with that . . . that . . . thing."

"How'd you hear about that?"

"Oh, we get mail riders up and down this road a lot. And I think the news of that even beat the mail rider this time."

Pamela came out the door, flour whitening her forearms. Apparently, Becky had caught them in the midst of preparing dinner.

"Where are the little ones?" Becky asked, looking around.

"Oh, they're out playing in the corncrib or somers, probably trying to catch mice or snakes I shouldn't wonder," Mrs. Palmer said. "Come in, come in."

"Have any trouble on the road?" Pam asked as they went into the kitchen.

"No. Nice ride."

"It's hot in here," her aunt said. "We put a roast in the oven for supper."

"I need to see about my pony," Becky said.

"Yes, yes. And bring in your things and put them in Pamela's room. Would you like a cold drink of water? Pamela, help her with her pony and give it some grain and water." The woman was running on, apparently very glad to have company.

That evening, after supper, the two cousins walked out toward the cornfield behind the farmyard of bare ground enclosed by a rail fence. As the sun was setting, they climbed over the stile and wandered down to the edge of a cornfield.

"I don't know how you manage this place without a slave or two or extra help," Becky said.

"Well, as you know, we're from Iowa and don't believe in slavery. And Papa can't afford to hire anyone right now. Even if we did own slaves, it's not cheap. We'd have to feed and house them, and take care of them if they got sick, not to mention what the initial cost would be to buy them."

"We have a boy named Zane visiting our village this summer who says there's a war coming a few years from now—a war between slave and free states."

"How does he know that?"

"I'm not sure," Becky said, not wanting to risk her cousin's ridicule by telling her Zane was from the 21st century. "He's a strange boy in lots of ways, but very nice and very smart. Kind of skinny, although he's growing and has put on some weight since he's been here. His mother's people are from China."

"Well, he sounds a lot more interesting than anything around here," Pam said, brushing back her dark hair. "Actually, Becky, I've been bored to death with this place. I know lots of kids in my school who'd give anything to live on a farm. They think it's all fun and they could have a horse to ride, and play hide and seek in the cornfields and all that. But the work here never ends. And my two little brothers are too young to help much."

Pamela was a pretty brunette about two inches taller than Becky, her natural complexion made even darker by exposure to the sun. Becky noticed that Pam's hands were roughened and calloused by work, and guessed her cousin was probably as strong as any of the boys she knew.

"But let's not talk about work and chores and all that stuff. Leave that to the grownups to worry about," Pam said. "How long can you stay?"

"I guess as long as I like," Becky said, realizing her father had not put a time limit on her visit.

"Great! I have some things lined up for us to do while you're here. We'll have fun. It ain't harvest time yet, so my chores're a bit lighter now." She led Becky over to a sawed-off tree stump where the field had been cleared years before. "Here, come sit down. While we're alone, you *got* to tell me all about that creature that attacked you and the boys. I don't think we heard the straight of it. Tell me all the details. I'll bet you were fit to be tied."

"I can't."

"Why?"

"I took an oath I wouldn't say nothing about that."

"An oath? My lands, who to? The giant? He's dead. He won't care." She laughed.

"Tom Sawyer."

"*Tom Sawyer?* Oh, please tell me it's more than that. Tom's a nice boy, but kinda bossy. I know you like him, but you ain't his slave. How's he ever gonna know you told me? I'm your cousin. I'm family. I'm your best friend. You can trust me to keep a secret."

"Pam, I ain't been very truthful lately. Now, if I go and break this oath besides, I'll feel even worse than I already do."

"Maybe by letting go and telling me, you'll feel better."

Becky considered this. Maybe her cousin was right. Suppressing a secret of that magnitude was like trying to compress a giant spring. Pam wasn't likely to be in St. Petersburg anytime soon, so there was no danger she might leak the story to anyone there.

"Promise you'll not say a word to a *soul?*" she asked.

"Cross my heart and hope to die."

"Okay, then, I take you at your word. Here's what happened . . ." Becky said, and proceeded to relate the whole conspiracy.

"Land o'Goshen!" Pam exclaimed when she'd finished. "So it was all a big hoax—a giant joke on the village. I can see why you didn't want to say nothing. Grownups don't take kindly to that sort of thing."

"Yeah. Tom Sawyer loves adventure more than pie. He lives for it, and I reckon that will always be so, even if he has to create it himself. If I hadn't butted in on what he, Huck, Zane, and Jim were doing, I wouldn't have been part of this and not known anything about it. My nosiness just made trouble for me 'cause I couldn't stand to be left out of anything," Becky confessed. "Now I know a secret I can never tell in our village." She turned to her cousin. "And don't you say anything, or I'm *dead*. If this gets back to my father, he'll never trust me again. I wish I'd never gotten mixed up in this whole mess."

"You can count on me," Pamela said, swatting a mosquito on her bare arm. "But what about this other big hairy creature?"

"Oh, that thing that supposedly attacked Gus Weir?"

"Yeah. Is that real?"

Becky shrugged. "Seems so. At least the sheriff believes it's real. *Something* almost killed that kidnapper while he was hunting a runaway slave. And it was something that made some mighty big footprints, the sheriff said."

"Lordy!" Pamela breathed softly.

"We might find out in a few days because there's a few men with guns going down to search those islands. The boys and Jim are going back there, too, and they left today. They're probably there by now with that nice new boat. My father absolutely refused to let me go with them."

"What did you say the name of that island was?"

"Westport. And Osprey Island just alongside and below it."

Pamela thought for a moment. "You know, those two islands ain't too far from here."

"Really? When I went with the boys and Jim, it seemed like a long ways to Westport. Took us most of the day, with both the current and sails. Tom said it was about fifty miles or more from St. Petersburg."

"It likely is—by water. But the river road cuts off all those bends and oxbows," Pamela said, "so it ain't but about thirty to your town overland from here."

The girls were silent for a few moments.

"Wish my father had let me go with them," Becky sighed. "But after we lied about fighting off that great hairy creature, he wasn't about to let me travel to that island a second time."

"That's all right," Pam said, cheerfully. "We'll hear all about it later. Meanwhile, there's something pretty scary I want to show you between here and Marsville."

"What's that?"

"An old haunted house."

"Haunted?"

"Yeah. Big old mansion on the river. The family that lived there've been gone more than a year."

"Why'd they leave?"

"Current is gnawing away the low bluff it sets on. When it seemed the river would likely eat off their front porch by and by, they just up and left, hauling away whatever they could carry in a couple wagons. Last time I was down that way, it 'pears t'me the big old house likely won't last out the year if that power o'water gets to whippin' and snarlin' out of its banks again like it generally does every few months."

"What makes you think the house is haunted?"

"There've been reports travelers along the river road have seen lights and heard strange noises in there after dark."

"Nobody's gone to investigate?"

"After a power o'folks kept on reporting about it, the sheriff went up there in daylight, but said the place was empty. All cluttered up with stuff the family left behind. But nothin' scarier than evidence of pack rats and such. He speculated there was probably a tramp sheltering in there at some time or other."

Becky's eyes gleamed. "Then we could likely be the first ones to explore it after dark."

"Right."

Then Becky had a deflating thought. "Your folks might be like my father and not let us go there at night—especially if they've heard all the rumors and powwow about the giant beast."

Pam thought for a moment. "I got it! I'll pretend we're going down that way to take a quick look at the place in daylight, and say we're really just on our way to spend the night with Betsy Clark."

"Who?"

"She's a classmate of mine. Always trying to get me to come and visit. Her folks have a little acreage this side of Marsville."

"You think she'd care if I come along, too?"

"No matter. She'd be glad of the company. Betsy's a nice girl, but she's too much of a homebody for me—more interested in sewing and cooking and such, so I been kinda stalling off visiting. She doesn't cotton to anything that smacks of excitement and danger. Haven't seen her since school let out for the summer."

"Seeing that old house sounds good to me," Becky said, now enthused at the idea of at least something adventurous.

"I can't promise you a ghost or a hairy monster," Pam said, grinning, "but who knows what we might run into?"

"My very thought," Becky replied, reaching into the deep pocket of her skirt and drawing out the revolver her father had given her. It gleamed a sinister blue-black in the afterglow of the setting sun.

"Oh, lordy, where'd you get that?" Pam gasped.

"Daddy gave it to me in case I ran into trouble." She grinned. "He didn't tell me the trouble might be *you.*"

They bent over with laughter.

"Cousin, I envy you. That kidnapping you went through would have scared the very devil out of me. Nobody knew if you'd be found alive. Then this conspiracy, and now maybe a real monster . . . Well, you've had more adventures this one summer than I've had in my whole life."

"And there's more to come."

"Keep that gun out of sight."

"I will," Becky said, shoving it back into her pocket. "You know the boys and Jim are probably at Westport Island already. And those other men should be arriving in two or three skiffs by this time tomorrow. But you and I will be busy with our own adventure. When can you get away?"

"Tomorrow is good."

"Yeah. That'll work out because my pony, Jasmine, needs a good night of rest after the trip down here today."

"Yeah. But to be safe, since you've got a pistol, I'll tote a weapon, too. My dad has a short shotgun in the barn he keeps handy for rattlesnakes and to shoot a duck for Sunday dinner now and then. It's all cleaned up and in good shape. I'll bring it along."

"You know how to use a shotgun?"

"I learned to shoot that twelve-gauge when I was so little it used to knock me flat unless I braced myself against a tree," Pam said. "You know, both of us being armed night raiders, we could become famous as the only pair of women outlaw cousins on the river."

"Now you're beginning to sound like Tom Sawyer when he's letting on to be a pirate—'The Terror of the Seas'—he calls himself."

The girls burst into uncontrollable laughter.

"Oh my gosh, I'm so glad I came to visit!" Becky gasped when she was able to get her breath again.

"I wouldn't have any excitement at all if you didn't show up now and then," Pam said.

Becky brushed away a mosquito buzzing near her ear.

"Let's go inside before these skeeters eat me alive," Pam said as she rose and led the way toward the farmhouse. "We'll talk some more tonight after everybody's in bed."

CHAPTER 17

After much gossip and late-night planning, the girls worked out the details of their overnight stay at Betsy Clark's place, following the main object of their trip—an exploration of the haunted mansion.

Following breakfast next morning, when Mister Palmer and his two young sons had gone off to do their chores, Pam proposed the plan to her mother.

"But Betsy won't be expecting you," Mrs. Palmer said.

"No matter," Pam replied. "She'll be home, since she never goes anywhere except to church. We'll be welcome. She's been begging me to come down and spend some time with her this summer."

"I just wish you had a way to let me know when you've arrived there safely."

"Don't worry, mother. I'm nearly grown. I can take care of myself. We have Becky's pony who can carry us double if need be. And I'm taking the old shotgun, just for good measure." She glanced at Becky across the table. "And my cousin has shown she can take care of herself as well."

Mrs. Palmer looked at the two girls, worry creases forming a V between her eyebrows. At length, she sighed and set the coffee pot back on the stove. "Well, life's a gamble, I reckon, and it wouldn't do for me to coddle you the rest of your life. You haven't done anything to vex your father and me, so may your guardian angels protect both of you from harm."

"Amen," Pam finished.

While the girls gathered a few extra clothes into a leather saddlebag, Mrs. Palmer packed them some food, including sandwiches, home-canned pickles, and two large canteens of spring water.

"That was a bit easier than I expected," Becky remarked an hour later when they were on their way, headed south. She rode Jasmine while Pam walked along the river road, leading the pony.

"I'm not sure my father would have allowed it. But I knew Mom would. I think she wishes she'd been more adventurous as a girl, so she gives me a bit more leeway."

Becky nodded.

"They've always encouraged me to be independent," Pam went on. "I'm the oldest, and I think my dad wanted a boy. But since he got me, he's treated me pretty much like a boy, teaching me to swim and fish and hunt and make campfires and such. Besides, I'm older and bigger than you are and I was raised up on a farm. That makes a difference."

"Yeah, I guess I've had it pretty easy in town," Becky said. "I've learned to cook some, but I ain't too good at that other stuff. I've even taken a few piano lessons from Tom's cousin, Mary. My father wants me to learn a lot of ladylike things." She paused. "But I wish I was more like you, and could do some practical stuff. I do want to learn how to sew. I've seen some beautiful quilts the ladies in the village made."

"You ain't so delicate," Pam said. "From what happened to you earlier this summer, I'd say you're tougher than I am. I don't think I could have gone through all that. Trouble with being a girl out here is that I'm expected to do a lot of cooking and washing and cleaning like my mom does, as well as work like a boy. My younger brothers won't have to do *all* of that as they get older."

"Here, carry this," Becky said, unhooking the lantern from the saddle horn. "The coal oil is sloshing out."

Pam took the lantern. "That shotgun rubbing your leg?"

"No. It's tucked up under this flap of leather. It ain't very long."

"Yeah. That's called a coach gun 'cause stagecoach drivers and guards use them. My dad traded for it in town years ago. Got it cheap 'cause the stock was cracked. But he put a couple screws in it and it's as good as new."

After a half-hour, the girls switched places and Pam rode and Becky led the pinto.

The road wound back and forth, sometimes near enough to the river where the broad, majestic sweep of water could be seen through the trees, and at other times, almost a mile back from the water where sight of it was completely shut off.

Shortly after they judged it was past noon, they paused in a grassy spot, in the shade of some giant oaks, to rest and eat lunch. They hobbled Jasmine to graze and poured some water from one of the canteens into the hollow at the base of a tree for the animal to drink.

They lingered longer than they intended, but were having so much fun talking and enjoying the pleasant day, it didn't matter. Pam said they didn't want to arrive at the haunted house too early in the afternoon.

When they resumed their slow trip, Pam was in the saddle while Becky led the pony.

The sun was beating down fiercely now in the open stretches of the river road during the hottest part of the day. Conversation dragged while they continued their slow walk.

A short time later, the sun went under a cloud, much to their relief. A breeze sprang up and Becky pushed up her sleeves and loosened the collar of her blouse to let the wind cool her sweaty skin.

The sky continued to darken and a grumble of thunder drew her eyes to the western sky above the treeline. "Well, it looks like Mother Nature is going to make our exploration a little scarier," Becky said.

"I'd almost welcome a cooling shower," Pam said. "And a good rain would help our pastures and crops," she added. "Our cistern's nearly dry, too."

Twenty minutes later, the trees thinned and in the dimmer light of the gathering storm, the girls spotted a two-story house standing in a weedy yard.

"There 'tis," Pam said. "We'll tie the pony here in the trees, then go take a look around inside before the rain hits."

With its vacant windows and peeling paint, the place looked sad and forlorn, Becky thought. If houses could have feelings, this place would certainly be suffering from melancholia.

They walked Jasmine thirty yards back into the woods near a patch of grass and hobbled her to graze.

Becky's heart was beginning to beat faster as the girls crept quietly toward the back of the house.

"We'll light the lantern when we get inside," Pam whispered.

They detoured around the rail fence rather than climbing over and came to a side door that was slightly askew. The house had settled enough to pop the door out of its frame, and Pam gripped the handle and pulled. With a complaining screech, the door came open and shards of the remaining glass tinkled down.

The girls cringed at the noise, which seemed loud in the breathless hush of the charged atmosphere. Lightning flickered in the distance.

Pam drew a Lucifer from her pocket and struck it on the metal base of the lantern while Becky opened it enough so the flame could be applied to the wick.

Stepping inside, Pam held up the lantern. It gave off a soft, warm glow and illuminated three steps that led up to the main floor.

Becky gripped the small pistol in the pocket of her skirt. Pam was carrying the shotgun in her free hand as she led the way.

On the main level, they turned to the right and entered the kitchen. Pam stopped and put her mouth to Becky's ear. "Do you smell woodsmoke?"

Becky nodded. "Recent fire," she whispered. "Fried ham, too."

Pam made a face. "Is somebody in here now?"

Becky shook her head and then nodded toward the front parlor. The girls tiptoed down a short hallway and came to the dust-covered room. Recent scuff marks crisscrossed the dust on the bare floor. Becky sniffed damp mold and guessed the smell was leaking up from the cracks where the house had settled and wrenched the floorboards apart. Besides abandoned furniture and musty bookcases, there was nothing of interest to be seen in this room. Lighter spots on the stained wallpaper showed where pictures had been removed. A flicker of lightning lit up two curtainless window openings in the far wall.

Pam pointed with the shotgun toward a staircase along the wall that led to the upper floor.

Becky hesitated. If they were trapped upstairs by someone, they might have to shoot their way out. Her heart began to thump harder, and seemed to be shaking her whole body. But she couldn't back down now, and admit to her cousin that she had let her fear overwhelm her. Pam had called her courageous. She had to live up to that, and forced herself to nod in agreement.

Pam set the lantern down on a step. Double clicks sounded loud in the silence as she thumbed back both hammers of the shotgun. Then she picked up the lantern and started slowly up the darkened staircase, shafts of light bouncing off the wall and the steps.

Becky followed, pistol drawn. Even though she had a free hand, she didn't touch the rickety banister for fear it would collapse and create even more noise.

The steps creaked and groaned. Becky kept her gaze focused downward to be sure she placed her feet where Pam had trod to be sure they would take her weight.

Becky let out a long breath when they reached the upstairs hall. She saw nothing distinctive about the peeling, pale wallpaper. Two bedroom doors stood ajar, and Pam moved toward the first one, swinging the coach gun up level.

Both girls stepped inside. A long trench in the feather tick on the bed showed where someone had lain on it. There was nothing else but a nightstand with a porcelain bowl and pitcher. The room smelled musty in the dead air. Oppressive silence smothered them.

Whoof! Whoof! Whoof! The sharp barks below them ripped through the silence.

"Ahh!" Pam jerked the triggers and both barrels erupted with a sheet of yellow flame, blasting out the window and sash. She staggered back from the recoil and into Becky, who fell against the bed.

"Run!" Pam yelled.

In a rush, they shot out of the room, thundering down the stairs and toward the side door.

Halfway across the weedy field, Becky gasped her first breath.

Brilliant lightning lit up the whole scene for an instant, then flashed out, blinding them. Booming thunder rolled over them like a giant wave, shaking the ground and numbing their senses. Becky barely felt the stinging rain that swept across the clearing as she and her cousin dove into the shelter of the trees.

The sharp barking of the dog, Louis, two feet from his head, followed by the shotgun blast woke Bit Barjee from a drunken sleep in the root cellar.

What was that? He rolled over and sat up, somewhat befuddled. A flash of lightning showed through the open cellar door and then a crash of thunder. The wind came gusting, catching the canted cellar door and slamming it shut, leaving him in complete darkness.

Oh, nothing but the storm, he thought, his senses clearing. He sat still for several seconds while Louis kept up a strident barking. He knew it wasn't only the storm that had awakened him. He'd heard enough gunfire in his life to distinguish it from thunder.

Someone was in the house upstairs. He reached for his hat and felt to make sure his loaded Colt was holstered on his belt. He hefted the saddlebags with the sacks of gold coins he always kept by his side. It was time to make a fast retreat until he could find out who was after him. Maybe no one, he thought, as he quieted the dog, then put his shoulder to the wooden cellar door and heaved it upward, throwing it all the way back. Gusting wind and rain lashed at his face, bringing him more alert. His natural caution returned. Someone could have followed him easily enough from Bitterville, he thought. Or, whoever he'd startled from this house earlier might have returned.

The buckboard with his inverted canoe lashed on top was parked only a few yards from the cellar door. He'd left a rain slicker rolled up inside it. This would be the time to slide out in the storm and vacate the house until daylight when he could see if it was safe to return. He might be overcautious, but other outlaws had been caught by relaxing into the illusion of safety. The reward notices were out on him, and there were always bounty hunters to take up the challenge. He was still a bit tipsy, but his mind was clear.

He stood inside the cellar and listened intently for two full minutes, but the fury of the wind and thunder drowned any other sounds. He slid outside and got the slicker and slipped it over his head, more to keep his gun dry than himself. He slashed the lashing on the canoe rather than fumbling with the wet knots. Pulling the canoe off the wagon, he called softly to the dog, who was reluctant to come out into the storm. Trying to coax Louis outside, he went back down the cellar steps. Then he thought of the warming effects of the wine. On impulse, he snatched up two full, corked bottles and slid them into the side pockets of his slicker.

"C'mon, boy! Let's go." He shoved the dog outside

Making sure Louis was following, he waited for a flash of lightning to show him where the lowest part of the riverbank was, and then went for it, dragging the canoe by its painter in the wet grass.

Over the lip of the bank he went, slipping and sliding down the mud to the water's edge. He lifted the dog into the boat, then shoved off and jumped in, taking up his paddle. The rain pounded down and Louis attempted to protect his head by scrunching up under a thwart.

Barjee would use the lightning to guide him to one of these islands where he could shelter for the night. The sluggish current carried the canoe along, and he had to fend off in the narrow chute to keep from running aground. The frequent flashes showed there was only scrubby vegetation; he was looking for heavy timber to hide and shelter him. He and the dog could hunker down under the canoe until the storm passed. Even though he had matches in his pocket, it was probably too wet to kindle a fire. And a fire would signal his presence. He could stand the discomfort. The slashing drops were not too chilly.

Less than a half-hour later, he saw a spot of light. Surely there was no steamboat chancing the blackness of this night? He stopped paddling and watched it for a time, and realized the light was not moving. Another long, wavering flash of lightning showed this was a fire near the end of an island on his left about two hundred yards away.

Drifting along, he pondered an idea for a full minute. Then he dug in his paddle and drove the canoe toward the light.

CHAPTER 18

At Tom's direction, Zane shoved the tiller over and the yawl pivoted in toward the low shoreline near the foot of Westport Island.

Huck and Jim dropped the sails and they all pulled the bow of the boat up onto the beach.

"We best be gatherin' up some dry wood," Jim said as they piled their gear on a blanket.

"It ain't time for supper yet," Tom said.

"It gwine t'rain directly," Jim said.

"Looks clear to me," Huck said. "But I reckon you know the signs. I'll get the axe and collect some driftwood."

"If it's going to rain, I hope the men from the village get here before it starts," Zane said. He noted the afternoon sun had gone behind a bank of clouds. At least that cooled things off a bit.

They went about setting up camp, and Tom took the precaution of stringing their tarp between two trees and slanting it at an angle to shield them from a westwind; hopefully it would protect the fire as well.

Huck and Jim set a trotline, and then they all trooped off north through the woods to see if Jim's tracks were still there in case the raiding party wanted to see them.

Water had seeped into some of them and the edges weren't as distinct, but the fake footprints still held up.

They all retreated to camp and shortly Jim and Huck's

trotlines produced a decent-sized bass, two bluegills, and a cat-fish.

Zane missed Becky's help, but didn't say anything about her not being here. They just had to make do. Not only did he miss her help, but he also missed her company and her generally sunny disposition. She usually saved her sarcasm for Tom, often trying to let on that she didn't like him.

"Might as well go ahead and eat as long as we already caught some fish," Tom said. "Then we'll have that out of the way and will be ready to help the others when they show up."

"You reckon the colonel can find us?" Huck inquired.

"I told 'em we'd be right at the foot of Westport Island," Tom said.

They started a fire and let it burn down while cleaning the fish. Hot water hoecakes and boiled turnip greens completed the meal, all washed down with canteens of fresh water they'd fetched along.

Afterward, Huck and Jim lounged on the blanket and fired up their cob pipes. Tom and Zane were both watching the weather approach from the west, and were nervously pacing along the sand near the water's edge watching for the skiffs with the "raiding party," as it had come to be called.

A cooling breeze sprang up bringing the smell of rain. "Looks like Jim was right," Zane said. "Although I would have bet against it two hours ago."

"He watches the birds and kin gener'ly tell about things like that," Tom said. He kept turning to look upriver. "They shoulda been here by now. Mebbe we ought to've waited and come along with them, instead of sailing on ahead."

"Too late now," Zane said. Then he thought of something. "Lemme see that map of the river you got at the mercantile."

Tom pulled it from under his shirt and they unrolled it on the sand.

"Look here," Zane said, pointing. "They'll likely want all the help they can get from the current so I'd bet they come down the channel outside of Schwanigan Island that overlaps this island by almost a mile. We'll never see'em if they do."

"You're right," Tom said. "What a fool I am! Sure enough that's the way they'll go 'cause Weir was attacked on Osprey Island. That's where they'll land and start from."

Zane pointed at the map again. "See . . . Osprey Island is tucked right in the slot between the tail o'Westport where we are, and Schwanigan on the outside." He looked up at the dense woods across a narrow channel. "That's Osprey right over there, due east and south of us. Why don't we take the boat over? It's only a couple hundred feet across."

Tom bit his lip and thought for minute and then looked back at their camp and at the threatening sky.

"We still got daylight," Zane urged.

"Naw," Tom shook his head. "Osprey is nearly a mile long and they'll be landing on the south end of it on the sandbar where Weir was attacked. That's where the sheriff seen the footprints. They ain't gonna plunge right into the heavy woods on this end with night coming on and not knowing what they might run into. They'll likely spread out and sweep the island from south to north come daylight." He rolled up his map and tucked it back inside his shirt. "We're already settled in here. We kin wait 'til morning and catch up with them come sunup. Then we kin help'em search Westport here, which is a lot bigger. We'll show'em how brave we are." He grinned. "But we both know there ain't nuthin' on *this* island to be afeered of, 'less it be a snake or quicksand or sumpin'. The rain will likely be past by then, too."

The two walked back toward the campfire.

"Do you think there *is* some wild critter living over there on Osprey Island?" Zane asked.

"There's all manner o'stuff in this world we don't know nuthin' about," Tom said soberly. "Lots o'grownups who been to college and traveled around a good deal think they know everything there is to know. They act uppity and look down on other folks. They figure if they don't know about sumpin', then it don't exist."

"You're right about that," Zane said. "In my time I've heard my father call it 'intellectual arrogance.' He said a person should always keep an open mind to learn new things."

Even though an hour or two of daylight remained, the approaching thunderstorm darkened the sky to twilight. Thunder and lightning heralded its approach. They threw plenty of dry wood on the fire until they had a roaring blaze going that might survive the drenching that was sure to come. Then the four of them huddled up under the tarp shelter as the thunder boomed and the lightning flashed.

"Dis gwine to be a ripper!" Jim said.

The boys began to guess how close it was by counting the seconds between each flash and the following crash of thunder.

Minutes later, a blast of cool wind gusted across the camp, whirling up dust and leaves and scattering sparks from the campfire as the storm bore down from behind the sheltering tarp where they crouched. One brilliant flash of lightning was followed immediately by a numbing crash of thunder and then a veil of rain swept across them.

Hunkering down, Zane held onto his straw hat and ducked his head.

It seemed like a long time, but was probably less than a half-hour, Zane thought, when he sensed the rain letting up a bit. Or maybe it was just the slackening of the wind. He raised his head. The fire was steaming, but still burning underneath the big logs while a steady rain poured straight down. He was wet, in spite of their partial shelter cloth.

"Whew!" Jim shook the water off his shapeless flop hat and replaced it. "If dat be all she kin do, I reckon we's safe," he said, standing up and stretching.

In another fifteen minutes, the rain was only a drizzle but a fog was forming rapidly. The cooler rain was creating a thick mist over the islands and river, which had been baked in the sun for many hours.

"Dis be like dashin' a cup o'water on a hot stove lid," Jim said. "We's gonna be steamed like mussels fo' a while."

Huck and Zane built the fire back up, kicking aside the soaked logs and replacing them on the bed of coals with dry wood they'd gathered and protected earlier.

They scraped away the top layer of wet sand and unrolled the dry blankets.

"Look there . . ." Tom said, pointing to the west at a definite line that marked the back edge of the clouds. Apparently, they would not be cheated out of the last hour of daylight. The sun was already behind the treeline on the low bluffs, but the pale sky was lighter and their spirits brightened as the fire blazed up and the drizzle began to slacken.

"Let's have some coffee," Tom suggested.

Everyone was in favor. The coffee pot was dug out and filled with clean water, two handfuls of grounds thrown into it, and the pot set on the iron spider over the flames to boil.

Zane thought he heard a noise and glanced up. He flinched and a chill swept over him under his wet shirt. A man and dog appeared at the edge of the firelight, moving out of the thickening fog. "Ahh . . . !" He cried aloud. "Who are you?"

The other three jumped back, Tom reaching for his pistol under his belt.

The double click of a hammer being cocked sounded loud in the stillness. "Keep your hand off that gun, kid," a deep voice commanded.

Zane could hardly believe this was real. The big blob of black looked like a demon straight from hell—tall, black hat, and a wide, shiny black slicker shielding his body. A black and white dog with stringy wet fur stood by his side.

"Ah figured we's gonna roust up Satan by messin' wid dat hairy beast," Jim gasped, the whites of his eyes showing in the firelight.

Tom seemed to be the first to recover from the shock of this apparition out of the fog. He slowly removed his hand from his gun butt. "It ain't Satan 'cause the evil one don't have no need of guns," he said.

Zane's eyes were again drawn to the black muzzle of the revolver trained on them.

"I ain't gonna hurt any of you," Barjee said. "Just sit back down and relax."

Nobody moved.

"Are you a ghost?" Huck ventured.

"Not yet."

A limb blazed up brighter in the fire and the light under his hat brim showed a hard-angled face with several hours' worth of black stubble. The man's eyes looked a bit bleary.

"What do you want?" Zane managed to ask without his voice quivering.

"Just a fire and some company for a few hours. And I might take a cup o'that java and a little food for my dog," he added, moving a few steps closer. "Any guns you got, you pull 'em out easy and toss'em on the blanket there," he said.

His words and his movements were not sharp or steady, Zane noted.

Barjee staggered slightly and unsteadily sat down on the sand as if to keep from falling. The big Colt sagged in his fist. The dog lay down beside him.

Tom slid the pistol from his belt and laid it down. Jim pulled the widow's pocket pistol out and placed it on a blanket. Huck did the same with the Smith & Wesson and the pepperbox.

"That all of 'em?" Barjee asked.

"Yes," Tom said.

"Lemme check on the coffee," Zane said, not daring to make any abrupt moves. He used a small stick to lift the lid on the coffee pot. It was beginning to boil. "Not done yet," he said.

Becky and her cousin, Pamela, reached Becky's pony, Jasmine, and grabbed the animal by its halter as the pony was frantically hopping on its hobbled front feet. Pam held the halter while Becky managed to grab the legs without getting kicked, and she loosened the hobbles.

"Go for the barn!" Pam yelled above the uproar. Pam handed over her shotgun and started on a run through the trees, leading the panicked pony. Becky followed. The barn was far enough from the house that it seemed like a safe shelter. As they dashed for its protection, Becky squinted through the blinding rain trying to keep up.

Frequent flashes lit up the house a hundred yards away, the old place appearing to lean crazily away from the gusting wind. She caught a glimpse of several wooden shakes being ripped off the roof and go flying. Then the lightning blinked out into total blackness. At the last second, she saw the corner of a fence and veered around it. She half expected the next flash of lightning to show the wreck of a house collapsing over the bluff into the river.

"Whoa, girl!" Pam pulled the pony to a halt inside the open barn door. A flash of lightning lit up the empty stalls. A horse whinnied and hooves thudded against a wooden barrier.

"There's another horse in here!" Becky cried.

"Then there *is* someone . . . in the house," Pam said, stroking

Jasmine's neck, trying to calm the animal.

Both girls were panting heavily. "I heard . . . a dog . . . really close," Becky gasped. She pulled out her pistol.

"Shotgun's empty," Pam said.

"Pistol should be . . . all right if the powder . . . didn't get wet," Becky panted.

"Stay quiet 'til this storm passes," Pam said, tying the pony's reins to a post. "We could spend the night here if there warn't nobody around."

They stood, soaked and shivering, in the darkness. During the frequent flashes, Becky found an old feed sack and began to wipe her pony's flanks and neck, and blotting water off the leather saddle.

"Where's the lantern?"

"Don't know," Pam said. "Guess I dropped it. That dog sounded like it was right under my feet, nearly. Scared the liver outa me."

"Yeah, I know. Me, too."

"Who do you reckon is in there?" Becky said, her breathing and heart rate beginning to slow.

"Well, it ain't no ghost, that's for sure," Pam said, "unless they've taken to riding horses and owning dogs."

Becky chuckled in spite of herself. She was wet, somewhat chilled, panicked, and trembling. She hung the dry feed sack over a stall and leaned against a post, drawing a deep breath and trying to calm herself. She took a few looks at the pistol in the lightning flashes. She had shoved it into her skirt pocket when they dashed out the side door. It seemed to be dry enough to fire since the powder was packed inside the chambers. She blew on the back edge of the cylinder to be sure there was no moisture near the caps. "Did you bring any more ammunition for that shotgun?"

"No. That was it. Didn't expect to have to use it," Pam said.

"Well, I'd test my gun, but I don't want to make any noise by firing a shot," Becky said, rational thought returning.

"We'll be all right," Pam said, stroking the pony's neck. "It's likely only some traveler on the river road who took shelter there for the night. We don't get many tramps along this road."

The storm raged on for another fifteen minutes while the girls cooled down from their run, but then had to shiver themselves warm again in their damp clothes.

"I haven't heard anything from the house," Becky said.

"If that dog is still there, he can't hear us over all this thunder. Besides, we're a good ways off from the house," Pam said. "If it weren't for this horse in here, I'd think maybe that dog was a stray and just took shelter under the porch or something."

The rain slacked off to a drizzle and the sky began to lighten. Becky rolled up her sleeves and was rubbing her chilled arms as she looked out the open barn door. "The storm is passing on, and we still got an hour or more before dark. See how bright the sky is back behind that black cloud?"

"Yeah."

They stood watching the rain move rapidly to the east.

"We came all this way to see a haunted house," Becky said. "But we didn't even get to explore half of it before that dog scared the daylights out of us."

"That's likely a good thing," Pam said, "or we might've run into whatever human is in there—maybe some crazy man or murderer."

"Probably saved by Providence or our guardian angels," Becky agreed.

"Sorry it didn't work out like I planned," Pam said. "Now all we have to look forward to is an evening with boring Betsy Clark. Oh . . . I guess that was an unkind thing to say. She's a really nice girl."

The cousins stared out at the lightening sky. Becky was

contemplating their prospects for the rest of the night. After a time, she said, "Did you say Westport Island was close by here someplace?"

"Yep. Fact is, in good daylight, you can see it from the bluff in front of this house."

"I wonder if Tom and Huck and Jim are over there right now?" Becky mused.

"If they are, I'd guess they're soaked," Pam grinned. "Whew! This blouse is really clammy." She peeled off the clinging cotton shirtwaist. "The rain is passed. Dig out our spare clothes from those saddlebags. I'm all for getting into something dry and comfortable."

A few minutes later while Becky was wringing out and draping their wet clothing over a stall partition, Pam took a few paces deeper into the barn, examining it by daylight that filtered through the open door and the wide cracks in the walls. Nothing but musty straw. A worn-out harness, a cracked leather saddle, and an old horse collar hung on the walls.

"Well, would you lookee here!"

"What?" Becky moved past the strange horse that was munching hay in a stall.

"A canoe. Here, help me lift it off these hooks." Pam took hold of one end.

When they'd set the dusty canoe on the ground, Becky could see why the owners had not bothered to haul it away. The thin strips of wood had dried out and shrunk and it looked as if it probably leaked in a half-dozen places. At least the boards still seemed firmly fastened to the frames.

"Look around for a paddle," Pam said.

"Why?"

"I think Providence has just furnished us a plan for the evening. You up for it?"

"What?" Becky had an uneasy feeling

195

"We still got plenty of daylight. What say we take this canoe over to Westport Island and see if we can hook up with the boys?"

Becky's stomach contracted at this daring proposal. "I'm not so sure about that. What about Betsy Clark?"

"If we get over there and can't find Tom and Huck, we'll come back and go on to Betsy's. She ain't expecting us, so it don't matter if we even get there at all."

"Well, if our only other choices are spending the night in this barn or going on to Betsy's, I reckon I'm for trying for Westport Island. I just hope whoever's in the house don't come out here and find Jasmine while we're gone."

"Ain't likely. C'mon, it'll be fun to surprise the boys. I thought you were adventurous," Pam chided her. "You still have your loaded pistol."

Becky couldn't show the white feather now, although she quailed inwardly at the thought of the treacherous river.

Becky put Jasmine in a stall with some hay and, outside the door, she found an old tin pan that had a few inches of rainwater in it.

"In case that dog's still there or somebody's watching from the house, bend around toward the road and we'll approach the river through the trees," Pam said as the girls lugged the fourteen-foot canoe out the back side of the barn. "We're a good way off from the house and there's some outbuildings between us."

Several minutes later they set the canoe down among the trees.

"Rip off a few handfuls of that tree moss to use for caulking," Pam said.

As they worked, Becky thought her cousin must consider her completely fearless, just because she'd been a captive of kidnappers for a week and had been all the way to Indian Territory, and come back unhurt.

They stuffed moss into all the cracks until the craft seemed reasonably watertight. Then they dragged it to the edge of the bluff, staying under cover of the trees. After pausing to look cautiously around, they slipped and slid down the muddy bank to the water's edge.

"You see that long skinny island in the chute between here and Westport?" Pam said, pointing. "That's called Kickapoo Island. And just beyond in what's left of the chute that's begun to silt up are a couple of long sandbars."

"So, what's that mean?"

"It means we can take this in easy stages. Paddle a few yards over to Kickapoo, then drag the canoe eighty yards or so across it, then paddle over to the sandbars. From there it's only a short hop to Westport."

"I don't know . . . That sounds mighty chancy." Becky saw an ominous enemy in the pewter-colored water sliding past in front of them.

"Easy as pie. Probably ain't no open water more'an a hundred feet across," Pam said. "We'll start a good ways upstream and just paddle along and drift down," she added. "Since early June we've had a dry summer and the river is low. Narrower strips of water. More and bigger sandbars sticking up. We won't have any trouble."

In spite of her cousin's confidence, Becky was still uneasy. "You ever done this before?"

"A time or two. A boy I know from Marsville was with me."

"And you didn't have any trouble?"

"Nary a bit. Lookee here, the current in the chute is slow— not like the current in the channel, which runs swifter. And even the channel current don't run over three mile an hour when the water's really low."

"We don't have any paddles."

"No matter, I got this shotgun. We'll paddle with the stock."

Becky said no more as they carried the canoe upstream fifty yards and carefully launched it, then stepped through the mud and seated themselves on the two thwarts. Pam shoved off with the shotgun stock and took the first turn at paddling, stroking them along in the sluggish current of the narrow chute, which was only twenty yards wide.

"It's roughly a quarter mile to the foot of Kickapoo Island, and maybe a bit farther to the foot of Westport," she said, settling into a rhythm with the shotgun, and forcing the skiff along at a steady clip. Every few strokes, she had to switch from starboard to larboard to keep a straight course.

"Here, I'll take it for a while," Becky said, beginning to lose her fear of this wild river. It was still light enough to see the foot of Kickapoo slide past. The chute widened.

The skiff was leaking and water sloshed around their ankles.

"Okay, head left and make straight for that line of woods," Pam said. "That's the lower end of Westport. We'll coast along the shore to the foot. That's about the best place to camp. The rest of that island is mostly woods and swamp."

"Yeah, I know," Becky said. "It's starting to look familiar now. That's where we went when I was with the boys and Jim the first time."

A few minutes later, Pam said, "It's getting foggy."

"Yeah," Becky said. "We don't need that. If we really get fogged in, we might have to spend the night over here. You got any matches?"

"Right here in an inside pocket. All nice and dry." Pam patted the coarse cotton skirt.

Twenty minutes later, through the thickening mist, Becky spotted a dim glow flickering in and out of sight between the trees. "There's a campfire. That must be it."

"Gimme that shotgun paddle," Pam said. "Make sure you

got your pistol handy. That could be anybody. We don't want to be caught unawares."

CHAPTER 19

"This stuff is terrible," Bit Barjee said, grimacing at the cup of coffee he held.

"Sorry. Guess I let it boil too long," Tom Sawyer said.

"You got any sugar or honey?"

"We didn't bring none."

Barjee tossed the coffee to one side and set the cup down.

Zane saw a bottle of wine appear from a deep side pocket of the man's slicker. He pulled the cork with his teeth and poured the cup full. Replacing the cork, he took a long swig from the tin cup.

"Ah . . . that's more like it. Warms a man's innards." He took another swallow and stared across the fire at them.

Zane got the impression the man was drunk when he'd showed up and was now pushing his condition further along.

"We got some leftover fish," Huck said. "You want it?"

"Naw, but my dog's hungry, ain't you, Louis?"

Huck took two hunks of fried, greasy fish and tossed it down on the blanket in front of the dog. The animal made short work of it, licking the blanket and looking around for more.

"Tom and Huck! Hey, boys, it's me!" A shout came from the edge of the firelight and Becky and Pam walked into view.

Zane and Tom jumped to their feet to yell a warning for them to stay back. But it was too late. Barjee had snapped out of his relaxed lethargy and was training his big Colt on them.

The boys' guns lay on the edge of the blanket out of reach

and Barjee crouched to one side, swinging the gun barrel between the intruders and the boys.

"This seems to be a popular place," he said, slightly slurring his words. "Come on in and join the party, girls," he said, motioning with the pistol. "Take a seat over there. And drop that shotgun with those other guns. Who might you be?"

"Becky."

"Pam."

"Well, it's a pleasure to meet you. I reckon you must be friends of these boys and this black man."

The girls said nothing as they hesitantly moved around the fire near the boys and knelt down on the sand.

"We don't know who he is," Tom said. "He ain't said his name."

"Out here names don't matter," Barjee said. "But you can call me 'Your Highness' if you want." He barked a laugh. "How many more of you out there in the dark?"

Huck cleared his throat. "Ain't tryin' to tell you what to do, Your Highness," he said, "But it might be time for you to move on afore a passel o'men with guns shows up."

"Is that a fact, now?" Barjee smiled and poured himself another cup of wine.

"That's right," Zane jumped in. "There's five or six boatloads of men coming down from upriver to search these islands." He exaggerated the numbers. "And they all got guns."

"Searching for what?" The tone was derisive as he took a drink.

"Escaped prisoners and slaves," Tom said swiftly without mentioning the real reason for the raiding party.

"And I reckon that's one of 'em sitting right there." He pointed at Jim.

"No. He's a free man."

"Why is he with you?"

Nobody answered.

"Well, I reckon everyone has his own secrets," Barjee said, without pressing the matter. His face went somber as if his thoughts were turning inward.

Zane looked at Becky and Pam. How had they shown up here? Where had they come from? "Who is this?" Zane asked, pointing to Pam. He wanted to keep the conversation away from what this gunman was thinking or plotting.

"This is my cousin, Pamela," Becky said, glancing toward Barjee as if to see his reaction. But the fugitive continued to stare into his cup. His Colt was lying in his lap on the spread slicker.

"That's a nice-looking dog you got, mister," Zane ventured when the conversation lagged.

"Yeah, I wouldn't take anything for him." He reached over and petted the dog's head. "You startin' to dry off by this fire, Louis?" He felt of the dog's longish black and white coat. Louis wagged his tail at the attention. "I ain't had him long, but he's the best friend I got," he added. "Don't give me no sass; always there when I need him."

"Dogs're great," Huck ventured. "I wisht I had one. But I hain't been around none o'em much, 'cepten hounds." He paused. "What kind is he?"

"Oh, a mix, I suppose. Not too sure. But he's better'an any human company I ever saw."

Zane was beginning to lose his fear of this man, who was becoming more and more intoxicated. He decided to probe a bit. "Where you headed?"

"I reckon lots o'folks would like to know that," he snorted. "I'm going as far as necessary to avoid humans who mean me harm."

Zane assumed the man was some kind of outlaw on the run.

"You travelin' by river?" Tom asked.

"You think I'm gonna tell you that? I'm travelin' by balloon mostly," he remarked with a laugh, "unless it's stormin', like tonight."

It was obvious this man was not going to give them any information they could pass onto the law.

The dog, Louis, got up and wandered over to the two girls and began sniffing them. Becky and Pam both looked alarmed.

"He ain't gonna hurt ya," Barjee said. "He thinks maybe you got something to eat in your pockets, like licorice or something. Take everything out of your pockets and show him."

A sudden look of panic came over Becky's face.

Barjee snapped to a more alert position, raising his pistol. "I said, empty your pockets!"

Becky slowly pulled the pistol she carried.

"Well, now, ain't that lovely? Thinkin' to catch me when I wasn't paying attention, and shoot me?"

"No, sir . . . er, Your Highness," Becky stammered. "I forgot I had it."

"I'll bet you did. Drop it on the blanket."

She complied.

"Either of you got anything else I should know about?"

The girls both shook their heads.

Becky petted the dog, who'd continued to sniff near them. "I think he likes me."

"You always been good with animals," Pam said.

The dog raised his head and bristled. A low growl issued from his throat and he walked stiff-legged away from her toward the woods.

"C'mere, Louis!" Barjee called.

The dog halted but continued to stare into the dark forest. Then he started walking away from them again.

"Here, Louis!"

The dog ignored him.

"He's got something spotted out there," Barjee said. "Likely a possum or a 'coon." He gestured at Becky. "You got a way with animals. Go get him and bring him back. I don't want him lost in those woods."

Becky moved away toward the dog past the circle of firelight. A nearly full moon was beaming down on them from a sky clear of storm clouds. While they'd been talking, the surface fog had lifted, blown away on a light breeze.

Whoof! Whoof! Whoof!

"Here, boy!" Becky called. "Here, Louis!"

She reached the dog. "C'mon, boy," she said, gently, taking a handful of fur at the base of his neck and starting back. The dog followed her.

"What was he after?" Barjee asked.

"Dunno. Somethng really stunk bad. Maybe a dead animal."

"He don't act that way over something dead."

"Didn't see nothing," Becky said, but she looked pale, and glanced at Pam.

Pop! Bang! Pop! Pop!

Barjee jumped up, Colt in hand, and looked east toward Osprey Island across the narrow channel.

Nothing visible but a mass of dark trees in the moonlight.

The firing continued, and Zane thought it must be the raiding party.

"They've treed something," Huck said.

"What'd you say?" Barjee jerked his head around.

"The armed men we told you about," Tom said.

Bullets began to zip over their heads and into the brush.

"Ah!" Barjee gasped and fell, dropping his weapon.

The others were on the ground trying to take cover, but the lead was now plowing up the sand nearby.

Yelling could be heard from the woods across the narrow strip of water.

Barjee rolled over, grabbing at his thigh.

More shooting, and Zane hugged the ground and the others did the same.

A bullet smashed their coffee pot and brown liquid spewed, hissing, over hot coals.

The firing slowed, but occasional yells could still be heard in the woods.

Barjee, groaning, struggled to his feet. "I have to git outa here," he gritted between his teeth. But he took two steps and collapsed onto the sand.

Nobody moved. Only the dog trotted over to him.

"I'm shot." He swore bitterly. "I can't believe the bad luck. Not now!" He threw back the slicker and Zane could see blood between the man's fingers as he gripped his thigh.

The firing had stopped for the moment.

"Even if he ain't much account, we gotta help him," Huck said.

"He was holding us at gunpoint," Tom reminded him. "Leave him be."

Huck pounced on Barjee's Colt before the wounded man could reach for it. "He ain't gonna hurt nobody now." He handed the gun to Zane. "Keep an eye on him."

"Lemme see your leg," Huck said, crouching by Barjee.

The slicker was flung to one side, and Barjee moved his hands away.

Huck opened his Barlow knife and slit the pants leg several inches and exposed the bullet hole in the muscular thigh. "Fetch me a firebrand so's we can see sumpin' here," he said.

Jim brought a blazing stick from the fire and held it close.

"It isn't pumping blood, so it didn't hit an artery," Zane said. "That's good."

Pam and Becky crept a bit closer trying to see.

"Turn over, so we kin see if the bullet went through," Tom said.

Huck slit the pants leg down the back of Barjee's leg.

The shooting had stopped, but shouts could still be heard in the woods on nearby Osprey Island.

"It didn't go through," Huck said.

"Almost did," Tom said. "Lookee here." He put his finger on a lump under the skin. "I kin cut that out."

"You ain't no doctor," Huck said.

"You see any physicians around here?" Tom said. "It's us or nobody." He opened his own Barlow knife.

"Wait," Zane said, taking Tom's knife and holding the blade in the fire of Jim's blazing stick. "There, that'll sterilize it, and maybe cauterize it at the same time." They might not know the meaning of these terms, but he didn't stop to explain.

"Hang on, Your Highness," Huck said, with no trace of sarcasm.

Tom slit the skin and the lead ball popped out. Then he laid the flat of the hot knife blade against the cut.

"Ahh!" Barjee winced in pain, drawing up his leg.

"Hold still."

"Anybody got a clean cloth for a bandage?" Zane asked.

Nobody did.

Zane retrieved the bottle of wine from the sand. It still had a few swallows in it.

"Here, this might keep it from mortifying," he said, sloshing some onto the entry wound. This increased the bleeding.

Jim came up with something in his hand, and slapped it down on the wound, holding it in place.

"What's that?"

"It's a poultice of damp tobacco and tree moss," Huck answered. "I seen him use it before."

"No telling how many bugs in that," Zane said, cringing.

"The tobacco is probably okay if it stops the bleeding."

"Let's do it this way," Tom said. "Rip off a strip o'that blanket and bind it right over the wound and the poultice. That'll help stop the bleeding."

"Yeah," Zane said. "His pants leg is soaked with blood and won't serve as a bandage. But that poultice and the pressure might work until he can find a doctor."

"I have to get away from here," Barjee said.

"We'll put you in our boat and take you upriver four miles to Hamburg," Tom said. "They's a doctor there."

"No . . . you don't understand. I can't go with you. I have to get away right now. I'll be all right. Just help me into my canoe."

Tom was ripping a strip off the blanket with his knife.

Jim took the blanket strip and tied it around the leg to hold the poultice in place.

"Not too tight so it doesn't cut off circulation," Zane said, "or that would even be worse."

Barjee struggled to his hands and knees and tried to stand. Jim assisted him.

"C'mon, Louis." Barjee gave a low whistle. He took a step and went down again. Jim helped him up. "We's got to help you," he said.

"Just help me into my canoe and give me a shove off. I can make it from there," Barjee gritted. He felt for the other wine bottle in his slicker pocket.

The dog was whining, sensing something wrong.

Zane still had the man's pistol.

Jim, Tom, Huck, and Zane almost lifted the heavy man into the canoe that was drawn up on the beach.

"Here, Louis!" The dog jumped in and licked his face.

Jim brought another blazing stick that would burn longer. Zane saw Barjee's face was pale. He looked almost sober.

"You might be going into shock," Zane said. "Bring him some coffee."

"Ain't none. A bullet hit our coffee pot," Huck said. He tossed Barjee's hat into the canoe.

Barjee fumbled in his saddlebags in the semidarkness. "Here!" He thrust something into Huck's hand.

"What's this?"

"Just take it!" Barjee said impatiently. "No time to argue. Where's my gun?" he asked.

Zane looked at Huck and Tom. Should he keep the weapon? The man might need it for defense or to kill some food.

Instinctively, Zane knew this man was no longer a threat to them. He handed over the Colt, butt first. "Likely got some grit in it," he said.

Barjee slipped the gun into his holster without looking at it. Then he squirmed to a sitting position and eased his injured leg out straight in front of him. "Ohhh!" he groaned softly, bowing his head.

Becky came up and set something in the canoe beside him. "Some leftover hoecakes," she said. "You'll need something to keep up your strength."

Zane saw she had torn off the tail of her blouse to wrap up the food for the stranger.

"You kids . . . don't say *nothing* about seeing me. You hear? *Nothing.* I'm a ghost that came out of the fog." He looked at Jim. "I was conjured up by witches and now they're taking me away."

Without another word, Barjee dug the paddle into the sand and shoved the canoe backward into the river. Two more backstrokes and the bow swung around to the sluggish current.

Within seconds the canoe, with man and dog, was only a black silhouette in the moonlight.

Jim's firebrand had gone out and he dropped the stick on the ground.

All of them stood mute, watching the receding figure until it melted into the darkness.

Then they walked back to the fire and Jim threw on an arm-load of half-dry brush. The flames flared up. "Dis oughter keep de rest o'de witches away," he said.

"Mebbe them gun-happy fools over yonder kin see us now," Tom said.

Huck glanced across the narrow channel to the other island where a few voices of the raiding party could still be heard, calling to one another in the cover of the thick forest. "Blamed if I don't think they could've shot us all and never knowed it."

"They were after something pretty hot and heavy," Zane said. "Thought I recognized the colonel's voice."

"Wonder what it was?" Becky said.

"Reckon we'll find out in the morning," Tom said. "I ain't for rushing over there in the dark and risk getting shot or attacked by some hairy giant."

"I saw something moving back in the woods," Becky ventured hesitantly, looking from one to the other. "That's what the dog was bristling at."

"*Whaaat?*" A chill went over Zane as he stared hard at the black woods.

"Did you get a good look at it?" Tom asked, sounding shaky.

"Not really. Too dark. Only a patch or two of moonlight. But it was something big," she added.

"Like a bear?" Tom urged.

"Not unless it was standing up," Becky said with a slight shiver, moving closer to the fire.

"Dey be sumpin' close by," Jim said, solemnly, eyes wide in the firelight as he looked toward the forest. "Maybe you youngsters oughts t'hunker down in de boat, shove offshore a ways and anchor. Dat be safer den sleepin' on dis islan'. Ah'll stay heah wid a gun and keep de fire blazin' up. Witches 'n hairy giants don't much cotton to de light."

"That's a good idea, Jim," Tom said, glancing around uneasily. Then he turned his attention to Huck. "But first off, show us what that outlaw give you." Tom indicated the small rawhide bag Huck still held in his hand.

"Uh . . . I dunno. Lemme see." Huck worked the drawstring loose and poured the contents out into his hand. Firelight gleamed on a small pile of gold coins.

"Oohhh!" They crowded around to see.

"Here, lemme spread it out," Huck said.

The boys and girls sat down on the blanket and Huck counted it out. Jim stood looking over their shoulders. Several eagles and half eagles. It amounted to $480. They looked at it, dumbfounded.

"What're you gonna do with it?" Tom asked.

"Me?" Huck said. "It ain't mine. He shoved it in my hand 'cause I happened to be standing close by. I reckon we'll split it up. Somebody cipher out how much that is."

"That's $80 each, split six ways," Zane said.

"You reckon he was some kinda river pirate or stagecoach robber?" Tom wondered.

"Them saddlebags in the canoe musta been full o'loot," Huck said. "He didn't even count it—jest shoved his hand in there and pulled out this little bag. I guess he give us this for helping him."

"We don't even know his name."

"That's right," Tom said. "If we was to tell the colonel or the judge a man and a dog jest appeared out of the fog, and the man, who went by the title of 'Your Highness,' give us a bunch o'gold, they'd think our brains was scattered like fluffy dandelions."

"But we got the proof right here," Huck said.

"We'd best keep mum about all this," Tom said. "We'll jest keep the gold outa sight. That all right with you, Pam and Becky?"

The girls nodded.

"I'll figure some way of putting most of mine where my parents can find it without knowing where it come from," Pam said. "Maybe leave it on the chopping block in the kitchen or on my folks' bedroom table. I'll be all wonderment when they find it and maybe blame it on Providence or generous Irish fairies, or something."

"You could say we came over to the island to meet the boys and discovered a hunter who'd accidentally shot himself in the leg, so we took care of his wound," Becky suggested. "And he gave us this gold as a reward before he left."

"Probably closer to the truth," Pam said, "but I daresay my parents wouldn't believe that any more than the Irish fairies story. They'd want to know the name of this rich hunter who was walking around carrying that much heavy gold."

"Well, you've got a little time yet to come up with a good story," Tom said.

"Maybe I could get someone they don't know in Marsville to deposit the gold in their bank account there . . ." Pam mused, her voice trailing off.

"Jim, I have more gold than I kin ever spend, like enough," Huck said. "And here and now I'm givin' you my $80 share to help toward buying your family out of bondage."

"Me, too," Tom said, not to be outdone. "That's a hundred and sixty right there. Who'd a thunk that doing good deeds could pay off so handsomely?"

"Well, Miss Watson used to believe it," Huck recalled, "but she always said our reward would come in the hereafter, amongst the angels. Wouldn't she be surprised at this!"

"Jim, you can have half o'mine," Zane said. "You could have it all, except I owe my landlady at the boarding house about $14 right now and the rent's due for August." He turned to stare thoughtfully out at the moonlit surface of the river. "Who do you suppose that man is?"

"Once we're back home, I'll start watching the papers," Tom said. "Maybe there's been some big robbery somers."

"If he warn't an outlaw, he woulda let us take him to the doctor," Huck said.

"Boys, ah wants to thank you for making me a rich man," Jim said, obviously moved by their generosity. "Ah's got a hairy breas, and I tole Huck last year dat's one o'de signs I's gwine to be rich someday. And I reckon dat day is now."

"Two hundred dollars don't make a man rich, Jim."

"It would take ole Jim a mighty long time workin' fo' wages to earn dat much, Mars Tom. Even if I didn't spend none of it."

"Is it right to accept stolen money?" Becky asked.

"We don't know it's stolen," Tom said. "Mebbe he inherited it."

"Not likely," she said.

"By the way, Becky, how did the two of you come to be here? You ain't told us your story yet," Tom said. "Let's hear it."

So Becky and Pam related their tale, to the delight of the boys.

"So we left my pony in the barn, and have to rescue her in the morning," Becky concluded. "You can take us to shore in your yawl. Pam's parents are expecting us home tomorrow."

"What about that other horse we found?" Pam said. "Whose is that?"

"If nobody claims the animal and that house is empty, I reckon we'll have to care for it—maybe see if we can trace the brand on it," Becky said. "By the way, Jim, I'm adding half of my $80 to your $200. That'll give you $240 even. Pam can have the other half to give her folks who need help on the farm. I don't need it, and I sure don't want to try explaining the source of it to my father should he discover I have that much gold."

Two miles downstream from Osprey Island, a driftwood log nudged up against the muddy bank on the Illinois side of the river. The figure of a man pushed away from the log and clawed his way up onto the grassy slope and lay still, breathing heavily.

Ten minutes later the moon slid out from behind a cloud and the man stood up. Bull Brady, all six feet, eight of him, paused for a moment, dripping water from his ragged clothing, and looked out across the shining surface of the great river. He was not of a philosophical turn of mind and saw no irony in the fact that he'd gone from living in an abandoned house with a feather bed and plenty to eat to being hunted like an animal in the foggy woods. He dealt with events as they arose, whether good or bad, without speculating about their meaning.

Sagging from fatigue, hunger, and thirst, oozing blood from a wound in his left arm, with trackless sloughs and unknown miles of forest and prairie ahead of him, he nevertheless squared his shoulders, took a deep breath, and stepped off into a free state.

CHAPTER 20

When dawn crept up, streaking the eastern sky with enough light to see, Huck heaved up the yawl's anchor from eight feet of water thirty yards off Westport Island. As the boat began to drift, he and Tom broke out the oars and Zane took his place at the tiller. Becky scooped a bucketful of water from the river so she and Pam could freshen up. They both looked pale and hollow-eyed.

It had been a long, mostly sleepless, night for all of them, dozing fitfully in itchy, damp clothes on the boat's hard wood, mosquitoes buzzing and biting, bright moonlight in their eyes further retarding sleep.

There was little talking as Tom and Huck rowed north a half-mile in slack water along the edge of Westport. Then, with Pam directing them, they cut west to the narrow chute that separated Kickapoo Island from the Missouri shore. Thirty minutes later, when the sun was peeking over the Illinois treeline, they put the girls ashore below the derelict house on a low bluff.

"I'll be home in less than a fortnight," Becky said, climbing out of the boat. "If you see my father, don't mention any of this."

"I wouldn't breathe a word if I was being tortured with hot coals," Tom replied.

She smiled at his hyperbole.

"We'll see you in a few days, then," Zane said, with a wave. "Nice to meet you, Pam."

Pam saluted him with the empty shotgun, and the girls turned away to climb the bank.

With a few easy strokes and the aid of the current, the boys drifted the yawl back down to their camp at the foot of the island where Jim was keeping watch.

But Jim was sitting on the ground, back against a big log, head down between his knees, asleep.

The boys rousted him up.

"Oh my!" he said, starting awake and glancing around with bleary eyes. "Ah musta dozed off fo' a catnap," he said, stretching mightily.

"Some guard you are," Tom said, looking around at the dead ashes of their campfire. "That hairy giant could've had you for supper, Jim."

"It was pooty quiet," Jim said.

"Well he didn't make enough noise to wake you, anyways," Tom allowed. "We best be packing up and pulling for home."

When they were putting the last of their utensils in a sack, three skiffs with the raiding party hove into view, and beached their boats nearby.

"We heard all that shooting last night," Huck said.

"Yeah," Tom added. "Don't know what you was shooting at but you like to got us, too. Bullets was buzzing through here like bumblebees."

"Sorry about that, boys," Colonel Elder said, stepping out of the boat. "We had one of them spotted in the trees when that fog lifted after moonrise. Thought we'd better go for him while we had the chance instead of waiting for daylight. One of my men is almost sure he winged him with a shot. But he somehow gave us the slip. Come daylight, we took another look and couldn't locate him anywhere. Not only that, but I reckon the hard rainstorm that hit last night before we got here must have washed out all those tracks that Sheriff Stiles said he saw around Gus Weir."

"There was no trace of them?" Zane was stunned.

"Nary a print." The colonel coughed and spat to one side. "That sand was washed smooth as a baby's butt."

Zane thought the leader looked very tired and out of sorts.

"You fixing t'search Westport here?" Tom asked.

"Yeah." The colonel turned to the others in his party. "C'mon, boys, shake a leg. Look lively. You ain't *that* tired. Get you a bite o'cold rations and check your weapons. I want to be combing those woods in ten minutes."

That elicited some grumblings, but nobody spoke outright.

The colonel sat down on a log and began to clean his musket. "You boys see or hear anything last night?"

"Only lots o'shooting and hollering from over there," Huck said.

The colonel picked up an empty wine bottle lying near the cold campfire. "Looks like you was having a little snort or three," he said, tossing the bottle to one side.

"I brought that along," Tom said. "Thought a little sip o'homemade wine would kinda calm our nerves whilst we was waiting to be attacked again. But all them bullets made us forget about the giants around here."

"You fellas can help us search," the colonel said.

The three boys looked at each other.

"I reckon we could stay for an hour or so," Tom said. "We'll show you where we saw them tracks on our first trip here before that beast come down on us. But we can't stay too long. The widow wants Jim back on the job as soon as we can get him home. He's been gone a lot lately."

Jim and the three boys guided the raiding party and their leader to the marshy ground where the remnants of the fake footprints, full of rainwater, still showed in the soft mud.

While the men were following up on Jim's old prints, Tom said, "We'll be off now."

The colonel didn't look happy at their departure.

"When can I tell the judge and the sheriff you'll be along?" Tom inquired innocently.

"Whenever we get one of these giant hairy men, dead or alive," Colonel Elder snapped, turning away.

The rainstorm had brought with it somewhat cooler, drier air with a fresh westerly breeze. As a result, the yawl was able to sail back, tacking much of the way. On the upriver trip, the boys and Jim had several hours to discuss all the details of what had happened.

"Best we keep mum about all this," Huck said. "O'course that includes Becky, 'cause she knows all about it, too."

"Yeah, I reckon she has enough sense not to say nothing without she talks to us first," Tom said.

They speculated about the identity of their armed and wealthy visitor of the night before. For lack of a better name than "Your Highness," Tom referred to him as the "river pirate." "He might be one o' Murrell's gang," Tom speculated.

" 'Tain't likely," Huck said. "I hear tell Murrell died years back after he was let outa prison. This fella warn't that old."

"Wal, I'll keep a sharp eye on the St. Louis papers for a few weeks to see if they's any news about a big robbery somers, or even if this man is caught by the law," Tom said.

"How do you even know he's an outlaw?" Zane asked.

"He didn't want no doctor," Jim said.

"And he held his gun on us," Tom added.

"When he heard all that shooting from the raiding party, he jest naturally figured somebody was after *him*. He wouldn't tell his name or where he was headed. That's a man running from the law for sure," Huck concluded.

"And most folks don't go around lugging that much gold unless they's looking for a place to hide it 'cause it's stole," Tom said.

"I guess you have him pegged all right," Zane agreed. "But that was a serious wound. If he lives, he'll be stove up for a while and maybe have a permanent limp if there is nerve damage. If it mortifies, he could die." Zane was falling easily into the habit of talking more like his 19th century friends. He found it easier to communicate that way. "But we did all we could for him."

"And he paid us a lot more than it was worth," Tom said.

"A man's life be worth mo' den all de gold in creation," Jim observed.

"Right you are," Zane said, shoving the tiller away from him. The mainsail flapped heavily and then steadied on the starboard tack as they came around a bend in the river and moved away from the wind-smothering trees.

By suppertime the yawl was gliding into the levee at St. Petersburg.

They reported to one and all, including Aunt Polly, Sid and Mary, and the Widow Douglas that it had been a quiet trip and they had nothing new to add to the hunt for the giant man.

They told everyone the raiding party was still searching and had had a run-in with one of the creatures, but it had escaped. Colonel Elder and his men were still searching the islands and would be back directly.

It turned out Judge Thatcher had not joined the search as he'd been tempted to do. He privately admitted to the boys that his own bed, come nightfall, had proved too strong a lure for his middle-aged bones.

Jim went back to work, and the boys hunkered down into their old routine, staying out of the public eye as if nothing had happened. But, secretly, when they met together on Jackson's Island or in the cave, they released pent-up tensions, bursting to discuss their secrets with one another, speculating what the raiding party might find. They had taken their share of the gold the river pirate had given them and buried it in the cave. Jim said he didn't want the care and worry of hiding it anywhere near the widow's.

While awaiting the return of the men from downriver, Sheriff Stiles decided it was time to go check on Gus Weir at Hamburg.

He returned by steamboat two days later to report that Gus Weir had died. The doctor said he'd been slowly recovering, but had a relapse and died within a few minutes. The physician speculated that a blood clot had traveled to Weir's lungs and killed him.

This was shocking news, especially to the sheriff. Now that Weir was gone, and the boys had reported the tracks of his attacker on Osprey Island were washed away, Stiles had no hard proof that a giant hairy man had even existed. He had only his own testimony about the tracks, and the doctor's description of the types of wounds Weir had suffered. And, of course, the youngsters and a freed slave claimed they had killed one of the giants, and the judge had the tallow molds of its prints. But the sheriff said little after he applied in writing to the state of Missouri for the reward that was offered for Gus Weir. He'd wait until the raiding party returned to see what they'd found.

The village newspaper reported events as they unfolded, and the citizens of the town were abuzz with speculation of every kind as to what all this meant.

Becky cut her visit short and rode her pony home five days later from her aunt and uncle's farm near Marsville. She arrived late in the afternoon and reported to her father.

"Daddy, I'll take care of Jasmine in a few minutes," she said. "There's something I have to do before supper. I might be a few minutes late."

She hurried off on foot to Tom's house and found his Aunt Polly fixing supper.

"Becky, would you like to stay and eat with us?" the old lady asked, red-faced from the cookstove heat as she came out of the kitchen. "Huck and Zane are joining us—me and Mary and Sid, that is. I made sweet potato pie for dessert."

"No'am. Thank you anyway. My father is expecting me. Where are the boys?"

"Down by the town pump, I believe."

She hurried away and found them a few minutes later.

"Becky! You're back early." Tom's face lit up.

"C'mere!" She motioned to him. "I need to talk to all three of you."

She huddled with the boys on a deserted street corner.

"Listen to this. You know that horse me and Pam found at the haunted house? Well, Pam's father took that horse to Marsville and on down to Bitterville and asked around to see if he could find out who it belonged to. The owner of the mercantile in Bitterville said he'd sold it last week to a stranger passing through. And he also sold him a buckboard, which my uncle later found parked at the haunted house."

"Who was it?" Tom asked.

"The stranger had given his name as Smith or Jones or something common like that. I forget. The mercantile man said he figured it was a false name but he didn't care 'cause the man paid in gold."

"So, what of it?" Zane asked.

"The man he described fits exactly with our river pirate who was shot in our camp."

"Really?"

"Yeah. So he was the one who was in the house when me and Pam was creeping around inside that night, exploring. And that was his dog that scared us off."

"Sounds like you two mighta scared him off, too, and he come out to the island in that canoe."

"That's another thing. The blacksmith in Bitterville who fixed the buckboard wheel described this Smith or Jones. And the man had a canoe that he loaded on the wagon. Also a black and white dog was with him. It was our man for sure."

"Wow!" Zane said. "Wonder where he was headed?"

"Dunno, but he was agoin' back downriver last we seen him," Tom said.

"Wonder how far he'll get?"

"Likely 'til he kin find some help for that shot leg."

"Or dies of blood poisoning, all alone with his dog," Zane said, beginning to feel sorry for the stranger.

"You reckon we should tell Sheriff Stiles and see if there is a wanted poster on this man?" Zane asked. "Maybe there's a reward."

"No," Huck said. "We was to do that, he'd know we'd likely seen this fella somers before."

"And there'd be all kinds of questions and they'd know we lied about it. Then they might suspicion we lied about the giant we said we killed, too."

"This river pirate might be a criminal, but he didn't hurt us none," Tom said. "And he sure enough give us a reward already. I figure some o'that was for keeping mum about him."

"I vote we forget we ever saw him," Zane said. "What about you, Becky?"

"We sure ain't his judge," she nodded. "I'm beginning to look at people a lot different than I used to."

They nodded their understanding.

"We're all in this together," Tom said. "And Jim, he'll say the same."

Two days after Becky's return, the bedraggled raiding party

under Colonel Elder pulled their three skiffs to the levee at St. Petersburg.

Word spread through the village they were back and a crowd gravitated to the river landing, including a reporter from the newspaper. This time there was no gathering in the judge's courtroom for an announcement. Colonel Elder told them they'd spotted one of the hairy giants in the woods, and thought they'd wounded it. But, due to the dark and the dense forest they'd failed to capture or kill the creature. The party had later swept several of the small islands in the vicinity, but had run out of provisions after a few days. Now they had returned with nothing to show for their trip except one man who'd been bitten by a copperhead and had a swollen and feverish leg. Another man had a case of poison ivy.

The boys and Becky were there when the raiding party debarked and began to collect their traps. Zane thought Colonel Elder was visibly disgusted with the whole matter and stalked off down the street toward his house without saying much else.

The party reported finding two clues that made Zane's ears perk up. One was a pile of scat from a large, unidentified animal and the other was a tuft of coarse hair caught on the rough bark of a cottonwood tree nearly seven feet above the ground.

"Where'd you find those two things?" Tom asked as one of the patrollers was picking up his wet boots.

"On Schwanigan Island," the man replied.

"Can we see them?" Zane asked.

"We didn't scoop up that pile of dung," the man said. "We was looking for the beast that dropped it."

"What about the hair?" Becky asked.

"I gave it to the colonel. You'll have to ask him what he did with it."

"He's gone home," Zane said.

The man shrugged indifferently and started away from the

skiff toward town. Then he paused and looked back. "Oh, yeah, we did find the carcass of a deer. But there warn't much left and it smelt to high heavens. Don't know if sumpin' killed it, or it just died, and coyotes and foxes came along and ate it."

"You think the hairy giant might've killed it?"

"Could have, I reckon. But we couldn't tell 'cause it was pretty gnawed up and the bones busted for the marrow."

CHAPTER 21

The dog days of August settled over the Mississippi Valley. The villagers of St. Petersburg sweltered through steamy days, staying up far into the night to enjoy the relative coolness of the damp, dark hours.

Bear Creek and the river itself became havens for swimming. Stores shut down during the hottest parts of the afternoons. Children were not rolling hoops or flying kites, and were shooting marbles or playing dolls only in shady spots under the trees. All activities not absolutely necessary slowed to a crawl. Families rowed skiffs over to picnic on the long sandbar at the head of Jackson's Island. The always-cool cave south of town was thronged with people, many sitting for hours on rock ledges inside in comfort. Blocks of ice from the icehouse and lemonade were selling like never before.

Even the pastor of the church suspended services the third Sunday of the month. The newspaper editor, who had access to records going back years, reported that this was the hottest August since the town was settled.

Although Tom and Zane scanned as many St. Louis papers as they could get their hands on for three weeks, they saw nothing about the wounded man with the dog, their strange visitor Tom called "that river pirate with slathers of gold."

"After all that's happened, do you believe there really *is* a giant hairy man in those woods on the islands?" Zane asked as the boys and Jim lounged under the trees on Jackson's Island one Saturday afternoon, drying off after a cool swim.

"Seems thataway," Huck said.

"As a detective looking at the clues, I'd say there *is* a monster or three out there," Tom said, "but we'd best let sleeping giants alone. The more we keep things stirred up, the more somebody might sniff out our conspiracy."

"Dat be a good notion," Jim agreed. "We's done been rescued from dis whole mess, but like enough Providence be mighty tired o'foolin' wid us."

The boys nodded their agreement.

"Is you gwine back home, Mars Zane?" Jim asked, chewing on a stem of grass.

"Jim, I know how I got here, but I don't dare try to reverse the process, or I could likely die."

"How's dat?"

"I ate a bar of chocolate candy with peanuts," he replied, "two things I'm violently allergic to and got really sick and passed out. Woke up here. But who knows if that would work to take me back?"

"What's dis 'allergic'?"

"Doctors have discovered that different people react to food and other stuff differently. I guess we're not all made alike."

"Dat's so."

"Some folks get sick if they eat catfish or honey or drink milk. Some get rashes on their skin if they touch poison ivy or oak."

"Yeah," Tom said. "I could jest waller in poison ivy and eat it for breakfast and it don't turn my skin to scum. But cabbage makes me feel sick and I burp it all day."

"See? That's what I mean by 'allergic,' " Zane said.

"I knew a boy who was an apprentice at a printing office," Tom said. "But ink made him bust out in hives all over. He had to get another job."

"So, I don't know if I'll try to go home. I miss my family, but I don't want to do something crazy trying to return and wind up killing myself."

"I'll wager the man at the drugstore has some powders that might work," Huck said. "And an Argonaut back from the goldfields last week brought some stuff the Injuns give him. He called it pie . . . pay-o-tee. Strange name. Says the Injuns travel to other places when they eat it. Maybe that would take you home."

"No," Zane said. "I've read about peyote. That's a drug that just makes you have strange dreams and visions. You really don't go nowhere, except inside your head."

They were silent for a minute.

"Dat mean you's gwine to stay wif us?" Jim asked.

"I reckon so. I don't think I'll be starting school with you boys, though. I might get some books and study on my own."

"This might be my last year anyhow," Tom said. "I'm sick of school. I want to get out and do something useful—maybe learn a trade."

"Take it from one who's lived in the future," Zane said. "Stay in school as long as you can. Learn as much as you can. You won't regret it. I know it seems like a drag right now but, believe me, it pays off later. Just ask the judge or the schoolmaster." He paused for a moment. "Maybe you can be the one who discovers if the giant hairy man is real. You might become a biologist, or some kind of scientist."

"That's so." Tom nodded.

"Besides, you have enough gold so your Aunt Polly—and Sid and Mary, too—won't go hungry or not be able to pay the rent while you're in school. And the Widow Douglas doesn't need your earnings from a job, Huck."

"Talking about gold," Tom said, "we got that $240 in gold for you, Jim, and it's buried in the cave in a secret place. I asked Becky the other day to see if her father kin find out the price of what it would take to buy your wife and children outa bondage. The judge has a mighty smooth way of talking to folks so's he kin get a good deal."

"I don't reckon $240 is gonna do the job, though," Huck said. "But me and Tom is agreeable to kick in the rest, whatever it takes."

Tears welled up in Jim's eyes at this.

"We likely ain't doing you no gigantic favor, Jim," Tom cautioned. " 'Cause you're gonna hafta ask the widow for a raise or get a second job to support a family."

"Ah don't reckon I'll ever have no friends better'an you," Jim said, wiping a tear from his cheek.

"Why was I even thinking of going home now?" Zane said. "I want to stick around and see how all this turns out."

AUTHOR'S NOTE:
REAL AND IMAGINED

How would it feel, I wondered, to actually believe giant, hairy creatures were stalking the nearby woods, and no help was near?

I know that feeling, and attempted to re-create my own terror in the minds of Mark Twain's characters.

One May night in a remote part of the Great Smoky Mountains, two friends and I were camping in a big umbrella tent. After a supper of grilled burgers we sat around the campfire telling stories. The woods were thick, cutting off all view of the sky. A mountain stream was tumbling over boulders a few yards away.

While walking through the woods to the car, my friend saw two black bears on the trail. Hoping they'd stay away, we let the fire burn down, then retired early.

A thick carpet of pine needles and the noise of the rushing stream muffled all sound—until a sudden crashing of pots and pans startled us. Nothing but blackness was visible through the small window.

We cowered inside the zippered tent, helpless, hearts racing. Seconds later, the tent wall bulged inward as a bulky form brushed against it. The nearest humans were miles away; only feet away were hairy wild animals, bigger, stronger, and faster than any of us.

Not long out of hibernation, these hungry bears wanted our food. Luckily, only a loaf of bread was inside the tent. By daylight we found our cooler bashed, clawed, and empty. Only the wrapper was left from a pound of bacon. A carton of eggs was missing. A plastic gallon jug of beer was empty and flattened. Piles of dung were scattered about.

The gut-wrenching fear of that night I shifted to the protagonists in my story, while adding in their own dread of the unknown.

Other parts of the novel came easier—transposing personal adventures from my own Missouri boyhood, circa 1950. Three later excursions on the Mississippi River in a small sailboat provided material to describe their use of the yawl.

Often, the fun of writing is capturing real-life adventures and running them through the filter of imagination.

ABOUT THE AUTHOR

Tim Champlin was born in Fargo, North Dakota, the son of a large-animal veterinarian and a schoolteacher. He grew up in Nebraska, Missouri, and Arizona where he was graduated from St. Mary's High School, Phoenix, before moving to Tennessee.

After earning a BS degree from Middle Tennessee State College, he declined an offer to become a Border Patrol agent in order to finish work on a Master of Arts in English at Peabody College (now part of Vanderbilt University).

After thirty-nine rejection slips, he sold his first piece of writing in 1971 to *Boating* magazine. The photo article, "Sailing the Mississippi," is a dramatic account of a three-day, seventy-five-mile solo adventure on the big river from Memphis, Tennessee, to Helena, Arkansas, in a sixteen-foot fiberglass sailboat built from a kit in his basement. His only means of propulsion were river current, sails, and a canoe paddle.

Since then, thirty-eight of his historical novels have been published. Most are set in the Frontier West. A handful of them touch on the Civil War. Others deal with juvenile time travel, a clash between Jack the Ripper and Annie Oakley, the lost Templar treasure, and Mark Twain's hidden recordings.

Besides novels, he's written several dozen short stories and articles, plus two children's books. One of his recent books is an illustrated nonfiction survey of world-famous author Louis L'Amour and the Wild West.

He has twice been runner-up for a Spur Award from Western

Writers of America—once for his novel *The Secret of Lodestar* and once for his short story, "Color at Forty-Mile."

Tim is still creating enthralling new tales. Most of his books are available online as ebooks.

In 1994 he retired after working thirty years in the U.S. Civil Service. He and his wife, Ellen, have three grown children and ten grandchildren.

Active in sports all his life, he continues biking, shooting, sailing, and playing tennis.

The employees of Five Star Publishing hope you have enjoyed this book.

Our Five Star novels explore little-known chapters from America's history, stories told from unique perspectives that will entertain a broad range of readers.

Other Five Star books are available at your local library, bookstore, all major book distributors, and directly from Five Star/Gale.

Connect with Five Star Publishing

Visit us on Facebook:
  https://www.facebook.com/FiveStarCengage

Email:
  FiveStar@cengage.com

For information about titles and placing orders:
  (800) 223-1244
  gale.orders@cengage.com

To share your comments, write to us:
  Five Star Publishing
  Attn: Publisher
  10 Water St., Suite 310
  Waterville, ME 04901